Cherry
A Willow Hills Novel

Bretta Elaine

Content Warning

Cherry features strong language, explicit sexual
situations, and mature situations that
may be triggering for some.
Reader discretion is advised.

To everyone faking it till they make it.

Chapter One

I'm not sure how I got here—sitting on my childhood bedroom closet floor, hiding. My only company is the half-empty bottle of wine resting between my legs and my old, out-of-date winter coats from high school.

Tucked away between my old prom dresses and the wall, I sip on my bottle of Cupcake Moscato. I always end up in this exact spot every time my family gets together. The floor of my dark closet is my only solace during these "cheerful" times. It's the best hiding place in the entire house. Not that anyone but me would know. As the youngest of three kids, I was always left out.

My brother and sister are twins and four years older than me, so I was always the odd man out. Their type of sibling bond is impenetrable. I never stood a chance. Growing up, Bailey and Rian never made room for me in their lives. Even as adults, I'm still an outsider.

I balance the wine on my knee with one hand while scrolling through my Instagram feed with the other. Pictures of smiling families enjoying the holidays fill me with a mixture of happiness and envy. I want that. I crave the picture-perfect family. Scratch that. I have the picture-perfect family, and they're sitting downstairs without me, with their new families.

Picture after picture, I double tap on every photo I see, leaving a little red heart while taking more and more sips of my wine as I go. With a slight buzz, I find my favorite person's number and press call.

It only takes two rings before Sutton's bubbly voice slurs through my phone.

"Vivvvvvvvvvv!"

"Suttttton," I drag out, trying to match her enthusiasm without letting on how drunk I might be.

"Viv, what are you doing?"

"Nothing," I spit out a little too fast.

"Vivian," she scolds, "It isn't even seven o'clock. Are you in your closet already?"

Damn, she knows me so well. Okay, this may be my holiday tradition with her. She always gets a lonely call from my closet floor, but it tends to happen much later in the evening than this.

"Maybe." It's all I can say before her laughter rings in my ears through the phone.

"What is so funny?"

"Nothing. It's just...you couldn't even make it two full hours with your family this year before you ran to hide from them." Her drunk laughter pierces my ears as she grows louder and louder.

"What's your point?"

"You hate it. Every holiday, you end up calling me from behind your coats, drunk and wanting to be anywhere but with the beautiful bitch Bensons," Sutton says, stating the facts to me as if I don't already know.

"So, as I said before, what's your point?" I reach above me, tugging on an old puffer coat from Abercrombie as I try to deduce where she's going with all this.

"You need to stop spending time with them."

"I wish I could. You know that is not an actual option for me. I think it would be even worse if I spent the season alone."

"Yeah, I know. That's why you need to come out with me on New Year's Eve."

"Ugh, New Year's Eve," I groan. "I hate New Year's. It's nothing but an excuse for people to get shit-faced and make horrible life choices."

"Unlike what you're doing?"

I scoff into the phone as loud as I can, placing the bottle on the floor. I fan my hand over my chest as if she could see it. Using my best Southern belle impression, I joke, "Well, I never. I am not drunk."

Also talking in her favorite fake-Southern accent, she says, "Why, you wouldn't lie to me now, would you? Respectable ladies never lie."

With a grin, I revert to my regular voice. "This is why you're my best friend. You get me."

"And you get me. Now agree to spend New Year's with me, and I'll support your closet-wine-drinking habit whenever you're with your douchey family." Amusement drips from Sutton's voice, and it forces a smile to my face.

"Awe, you support my self-isolation. Now I have no choice but to spend my New Year's with you."

"Yay," she shouts. "Okay, finish up your bottle of wine and hour of solitude. Then get your ass downstairs and pretend to enjoy your family's company for the sake of presents. Love you! Byes."

She hangs up before I can talk her into wallowing with me in self-pity. I put my phone on the floor, bring the wine bottle back to my lips, and gulp down the delicious crisp liquid until the bottle is empty.

As I wait for the alcohol's usual warm and fuzzy feeling to take effect, my fingers pluck at the pink marshmallow coat I had put on moments before. It's the coat I wore every day of fall and winter during my junior year of high school. With the collar at my nose, I inhale the familiar scent of Love Spell, another junior-year staple. Okay, it was my signature scent during the last two years of high school. Yeah, I was pretty basic back then.

Who am I kidding? I'm still basic as hell. But honestly, I don't think there is anything wrong with that. It simply means a ton of other women have the same excellent taste as me.

"Vivian?" A distant shout sounds from somewhere in the house, rendering me frozen. *Shit*. I must have been here longer than I planned if they've noticed my absence. "Vivian! It's time for presents, so get your ass in here."

I jump up, tiptoeing to the closet door and opening it a sliver, enough to peek through the crack. Verifying that the coast is clear, I walk out into my bedroom. Once down the hall, I run my fingers through my long copper hair to tame the mess, catching on the tangles at the base of my neck. My hair is a constant tangle that can't be prevented. It could—and *would*—turn into a ratted mess if someone breathed on me.

I force myself down the dark mahogany stairs, doing my best to hide the fact I'm, at best, a tad tipsy. As I stroll in, they are all gathered, laughing in the living room. It doesn't take me long to notice there isn't a seat left for me, leaving the floor as the only spot to sit. Ugh, it's so classic that I am always pushed to the floor. Meanwhile, Rian and Bailey sit up on the couch and accent chairs, along with their spouses.

Okay, I understand that Rian and Amy, Bailey's wife, shouldn't be on the floor. They are both pregnant with their first babies and need the support and comfort. But their damn husbands could sit their asses on the floor for once.

I brought this up with Sally and Hank, my mother and father, at Thanksgiving. I can't even remember the last time I called them Mom and Dad—though Sally seems to prefer I give her the first-name treatment, anyway. Neither has ever been the warm and caring parent you see in movies. Well, they have, just not with me; it's been that way since I could read and write. Sally has always been kind and caring—maternal—with my older siblings. And Hank, well. Hank has always been the same quiet, distant man.

They seemed put off by me saying something so "selfish"; Sally's words, not mine. So today, I won't bother. I'll squat on the floor like the forgotten child I am.

From my spot beside the coffee table, I see nothing but smiles on their faces. Rian and her husband, Ian Shepard—otherwise known as Shep—are like a polished young Hollywood couple sitting together in one of the oversized armchairs. With her red lips, tan skin, and long, flowing brown hair, Rian is a classic beauty. Shep somehow accents Rian. With his dark-brown skin and million-dollar smile, he is every bit as pretty as she is. They look like they were born to be together.

"Vivian, go pass out the presents," Bailey commands me. I can tell by the expression on his dumb face that he didn't mean to sound like such an asshole. He just doesn't want to move from where he's sitting on the couch, rubbing Amy's feet while she lies with her head on the armrest, her silky black hair falling over the couch as she smiles.

I must admit, my big brother is a great husband. The two have been together for over ten years. When they started dating in college, I thought they would never last because Bailey was a dumb prick back then. But that all changed when he met her.

"Yeah, sure. What else am I here for?" I mutter as I reach for the mountain of presents under the tree. I sort and pass them out. Once I'm finished, I notice a slight—no, slight isn't the right word. *Enormous.* There's an enormous difference in the number of presents between me and everyone else. I pass out multiple gifts to my siblings, their spouses, and my parents. Large, small, and everything in between. While I sit with two presents—one of which is a card.

Struggling not to let the number of gifts get me down, I plaster on a smile. I'm not a child. I won't let a thing like someone getting more gifts upset me. And I won't let anyone see it get under my skin. Besides, sometimes the best things can come in small packages.

Chaos ensues as everyone tears into their gifts, smiling as they rip through the wrapping paper. I put hours and hours of research into each of them this year. I wanted to get them something so thoughtful that they'd never forget.

"This is amazing, Vivian," Amy says, cradling the expensive luxury blanket to her face. "I love it."

Noticing my unopened presents, my brother asks, "Aren't you going to open those?"

"Oh yeah, my turn." I smile down at the gifts. Starting with the box, I tear into the exquisite wrapping, which I know is from Rian by the appearance alone. She has always been neurotic about making the paper perfect. Opening the box, I stare as I lift out a self-tanning kit. "Thank you, Rian."

Her face lights up. "I saw it and instantly thought of you. Now you don't have to have that washed-out, pale skin tone anymore." There's excitement in her voice, so at least she is trying to be nice. My skin's lack of color and tanning ability has always been a sore spot for me, and she knows it. But over the years, I've learned to embrace my pale skin. To *respect* my skin.

I say nothing, though, keeping the smile plastered on my face because I can tell she tried.

With the tanning kit set aside, I open the envelope. Inside is a beautiful green-and-gold Christmas card. It's the same card Sally sent out to everyone this year. I know because she made me help her mail them all three weeks ago. I open it to find nothing changed from what she sent out to her acquaintances. The only thing different is the gift card stuck inside.

Relief rushes through me. Yes, a gift card. You can't go wrong with a gift card. I turn it over in my hands, my smile fading.

I was wrong. You *can* go wrong with a gift card.

My eyes find Sally. "It's a gift card...For the restaurant Sushi-Sushi."

Sally takes in my fallen expression as she blinks at me. "Yes, it is. What's the problem? I figured you would love it."

"You know I don't eat sushi. Or go there. You know that." Anger stirs in my lower belly.

"What? Of course you do, don't be ridiculous. Who doesn't eat sushi?" Her cheeks flush—not from her mistake but from my outburst.

Tears fill my eyes as I spring to my feet, moving a little too quickly for my wine-induced buzz. "You can't be serious. You cannot be this thoughtless, can you?" I gather my tanning kit but leave the gift card on the floor. "Senior year, my boyfriend Andy. Ringing any bells?"

When she doesn't answer, I continue, "I had an allergic reaction to something at Sushi-Sushi. When I came out of the bathroom, I found Andy making out with Allison, one of my best friends."

Her brow furrows as she looks to the others for help.

When no one says anything to help her, I start in on her again. "How can you not remember that I cried for a month? All my college plans had to change because of it. Are you this shitty of a mother?"

I stare, waiting to see if my words will affect her. When her facial expression doesn't change, I storm over to the bench by the front door, pick up my coat and purse, and walk out, slamming the door behind me.

Chapter Two

"Wait, she got you what?" Sutton screams across from me, jumping out of her seat at the coffee shop. My eyes grow wide looking at her. Dumbfounded, she looks back at me before turning her head to the elderly woman sitting across from us and the mom with her baby strapped to her chest, all staring in our direction. Then it hits her how loud she was. "Oh shit, sorry. Sorry, everyone."

"Sut," I chide her. "Language."

She tosses her hands up, rolling her dark-brown eyes. "Sorry again. My bad." Focusing her attention back on me, she adds, "You didn't answer my question. Did she or did she not get you a gift card to the place where you had the worst night of your life?"

"Oh, she sure as shit did. And she had the nerve to pretend she didn't know. As if it wasn't something that she should remember." With my coffee raised to my lips, I blow the steam away before taking a sip.

"If you don't say it, I will. Sally is a bitch. And so is Rian. They are both bitches, and there is no way in the fiery depths of hell you're related to any of those heartless assholes." Again, her voice carries across the room.

I chuckle. "You are beyond right. There must have been a mix-up in the hospital when I was born."

"It's the only plausible explanation. Like you are a goddess, and they are the product of Satan's taint."

A shiver dances across my skin as she talks. "Ew, Sut, don't say taint. That word is skeevy."

"Whatever," she scoffs, pouring enough sugar into her coffee to bake multiple cakes. "You are too good for them. All they ever do is tear you down."

"Yeah, but they're my family. What am I supposed to do?" I drop my face into my hands.

"Don't go over there anymore. It's that simple."

I raise my body off the table to glare into her eyes—something that makes her very uncomfortable. As she knows, the thought of not having them in my life makes me queasy, even if they are horrible. "You think I could do it? Cut them out of my life?"

She doesn't even try to break eye contact, trying to prove a point. If she can do this, I can break free of my family. "Yes. I know you can."

I grab my now-warm coffee, bringing it to my lips and consuming every drop. "I'll do it. It will be a fresh start for the new year."

Sutton bounces out of her chair to give me a hug. "Honestly, I'm so happy for you. I just know you'll be so much happier without them bringing you down or making you feel unloved." She draws back to look into my eyes again, setting her palms on my shoulders. "New Year, No Family."

"Well, that sounds depressing." I pout.

She lets go of me and sits back on her stool across from me. "Okay, how about 'New Year, New Family'?"

I lean on my elbows, and my eyebrows pull together. "That one doesn't even make sense. Who is this new family you speak of?"

"Ugh, you are exhausting sometimes." Sut tosses her long blond locks behind her shoulders. "You are your family, for one. Second, I am your family. And third, this is your chance to surround yourself with people you love, to make your own."

Her words bring a big, uncontrollable smile to my face. "You are the best friend I could ever ask for."

"Damn straight, I am." She stands, grabbing her purse. "Now we need to get our happy asses back before anybody notices how long we've been gone."

Refreshed and recharged, I walk back to my desk. With my head held high, I pretend like I didn't just take an hour-long coffee break instead of the fifteen minutes I'm allowed. Fake it till you make it. Right? Everyone will be none the wiser if I don't appear suspicious.

Normally, I wouldn't take such a long break away from my desk. As the assistant to one of Freeman, Tillan, and Will Architectural Firm's—or FTW for short—best architects and partners, Mr. John Tillan, my job is endless. Unless it is the holiday season. Mr. Tillan is a massive fan of taking a month off for the holidays. He makes sure all his accounts are completed, or he places everything and anything else on hold. So my job around this time of year is pretty much nothing. I schedule some prospective clients for the new year and respond to calls regarding upcoming projects. But this week, I'm just filing documents and organizing.

Having already parted ways with Sutton since her office is on a different floor, I glance around to see if anyone will notice me.

The coast is clear.

I walk as fast as I can, and with a smile, I thank whatever interior designer thought carpet was a good idea. Without it, the audible clicking of my heels would've given me away. I sag into my chair the moment I make it to my desk. But before I can set my purse down, my name echoes around the room.

"Vivian, how nice of you to remember that you work here. I wish all of us could be as unimportant as you," Hadlee, the front-desk secretary, says. Her snide voice reminds me of nails on a chalkboard.

I ignore her, picking up my desk phone and pressing the button to listen to my messages. I have two. One is from an established client wanting to open a new project with Mr. Tillan. The other was from Sutton, asking me to call the salon and see if we can add manicures to our hair appointments tomorrow.

Hadlee stands in front of my desk with her arms crossed. "Ahem."

Still not acknowledging her previous comments, I act surprised when I turn toward her. "Oh, Hadlee, I didn't see you there. Do you need something, or...?"

She places her hands on my desk as she leans in. "Whatever. Sure you didn't...I know you heard me. You know, someday Mr. Tillan will wake up and realize he needs someone who actually works, and when he does, I'll be here."

"Okay. Is that all?" I stare at her blankly until she huffs, sauntering away. The sway of her hips is exaggerated, and Jim from accounting turns to check out her ass as she strolls past him. How can he be charmed by her? So what if she has long, flowing blond hair? And sure, her breasts are constantly peeking out of her blouse.

Okay, I don't have anything negative to say about her appearance. The girl is stunning, and she is more than aware of it. But knowing her and how she acts, how can Jim or any other man want to be with her? They can't be that shallow, can they? It still shocks me that someone can be so picturesque yet so awful.

With my job on hold until the boss returns from his holiday, the lucky bastard, I take it upon myself to refresh some of our examples of project timelines and costs.

As a commercial architectural firm, we mainly deal with major businesses that only want digital copies of their paperwork. But oddly enough, we get quite a few that want a physical copy in their hands, and as the Girl Scout motto goes, always "be prepared." So I make hard copies. Not that I was ever a Girl Scout. Sally never would've allowed me to have wilderness skills. That would have been downright inconceivable. But Sutton was, and she used to repeat that damn motto every time she had something I didn't—ChapStick, a tampon, that weird beanie baby for cuddling when I'm stressed. The girl really is always on it.

I make my way to the copier, which sits in a room behind Hadlee and the reception desk. She ignores me, which is a blessing. Whenever I need to make copies, I curse Mr. T for not giving me that little LaserJet printer I've been eyeing for my desk.

Hadlee spins the long, coiled cord in her fingers as she giggles into the phone like a preteen girl talking to her first crush. This is the woman who had the nerve to call me out on my professionalism. "Sounds perfect, can't wait. And honey, I promise it will be a night you'll never want to forget. I'll make it worth your while." She hangs up the phone, eyeing me with disdain as I wait on my copies.

"Was that him?" Shelby asks from the seat next to her.

Hadlee nods. "I know; it's about damn time. He's taking me out on New Year's Eve."

"Jealous."

She smirks. "You should be. I'm telling you, the man is a smokeshow." She glowers at me as I gather my papers and walk by. "The two of us together will be a walking envy fest for some."

A small huff of laughter escapes my lips at her over-the-top self-perception.

"Is something funny, Vivian?" Hadlee sneers.

I inwardly groan at my mistake of showing any sort of reaction in front of that viper. I shake my head. "No," I tell her, not missing a beat as I try to get out of her den before she attacks.

I don't miss the sound of their cackling as I scurry away. I hate to admit it, but that woman scares me. Everything about her has me shrinking inside myself.

Maybe it's the pure confidence she shows to anyone and everyone, or maybe it's her "I don't give a flying fuck" attitude. Or maybe it's her annoying voice. Either way, she isn't someone I like to be around.

I'm dreading New Year's Eve. I had promised Sutton in a closet wine haze that I would go out with her. Little did I know, we were going to three parties. *Three.*

Sutton Hale, my beautiful best friend, had duped me into a night of full-on peopling.

Of those three parties, the one I'm dreading the most is our company party. FTW's annual New Year's Eve party is known for either being dull or notorious for causing people to quit out of embarrassment.

I don't fancy being subjected to either of those fates.

But it's too late to back out now.

Sutton and I got our nails done before our hair appointment. I chose a muted pink, almost-nude shade. Sutton stated it was the dullest color she had ever seen, but to me, it felt right. I didn't want a flash of color like Sutton's dark-blue nails. I liked my nails understated. Hell, I loved it.

While my nails were drying, my favorite stylist, Martha, worked wonders on my copper locks, giving me a much-needed trim. Somehow, she always had a way of making an inch feel like the weight of the world was falling off my shoulders.

As she twists the flat iron around my hair, I soak up every moment, enjoying having my hair played with, just as I did when I was a little girl. I imagine what I'll wear tonight, visualizing every dress in my closet. I'm so caught up in my head that I almost don't hear Martha when she says, "Done."

She spins the chair around to face the mirror. Loose copper curls hang over my shoulders. It's simple but so perfect. "I love it." I smile at her. "Thank you. Thank you! You are a hair goddess."

"Oh, stop it." She blushes. "You are such an easy client. You already have incredible hair. I just give it that extra something-something."

"Well, I love it either way." My hands were already tangling up in the silkiness of her masterpiece.

"Sutton talked you into going out on NYE? Do you think you're going to make it?" she asks, giving me a questioning look. "Don't you go to bed by nine on weekdays and ten on the weekends?"

I'm offended by her lack of faith in me. "Hey, I can hang." I fish out my wallet to pay her, adding, "And it's eleven on the weekends, FYI." This makes us both laugh until a minute later when we're interrupted by Sutton skipping into the room.

"It's time to go, chica. We have one more stop before we need to get ready for the wild evening ahead of us." Grabbing me by the arm, she pulls me along with her.

I give Martha one last look that pleads with her to save me before Sutton drags me away. Laughing, she calls out, "You're on your own. Have fun, girls."

The "last stop" before going home to relax before the long, torturous evening ended up being five.

Five. Stops.

I swear I would strangle her if I didn't love her so much.

Sutton still needed to get new shoes, a dress, a quick smoothie—which I'm thrilled we stopped for because my stomach was about to eat itself—some new lashes, and one fresh pair of underwear. Why only *one* pair? Because New Year, New Underwear. And in Sutton's own words, "You should always start the year fresh." She didn't just mean emotionally or metaphorically. She means physically. "You should have a fresh pair of panties, too, and in turn, have a fresh vagina." Again, her words.

She drops me off at my place around 4:00 p.m., stating she'll be back around eight to Uber to our first destination.

Four hours. That's all that stands between me and what will, without fail, be one of the worst nights of my life.

Deciding what to do with myself until I need to get ready at seven, I sit down and turn on Netflix, scrolling until I find what I'm looking for. My tried and true, my happy place, my favorite show, *The Vampire Diaries*. I don't know why, but this show comforts me. I sit back on the couch, sinking into my favorite spot. After a while, my eyelids are heavy as I drift off into sleep.

The loud screeching of my alarms startles me awake.

Frantically, I reach for my phone. It's only 7:00 p.m.

Whew.

Thank God I know myself and my ability to lose track of time. I didn't plan to fall asleep when I set it. But I knew the possibility of getting swept up in something else and not paying attention to the time was high. So I took precautions.

I race to the shower, carefully gathering all my hair up to protect it from the warm stream while I clean my body and shave anywhere it needs.

After drying off, I wrap myself in my cozy robe and make my way to my closet, picking up dress after dress. Nothing feels right. Either too tight, too short, too long, or not the right color. It simply wasn't working until I gave up on the idea of a dress. Looking in the back of my closet, I spot a green full-body, tapered-leg jumpsuit I bought last year on sale but had never had the guts to wear. Pulling it up to my body, I stare into the mirror.

The emerald green with shiny flakes covering the material is perfect. It's also long-sleeved, so I won't have to worry about bringing a jacket.

That settles it. I'll hold my head high and be fearless. I'm going to be the girl in the green jumpsuit. Laying it on my bed, I head back into my closet to find the perfect shoes. I settle on a pair of black booties with a low heel, knowing those shoes are the easiest to walk in and won't have my feet soaking in a foot bath by the end of the night.

Confident with my outfit, I look at the clock. Seven forty-five. Just enough time left to put on makeup and re-curl my hair wherever needed.

Since I have limited time, I settle on a light bronzing of my cheekbones and a simple cat eye with my black liquid liner. I curl my lashes before covering them in coats of mascara. Then I take the clip out of my hair and gently brush out any tangles. Thankfully, my hair is still perfect. Martha's work is still intact and ready to go. With a step back, I admire myself in the mirror.

Pretty, I think. I look pretty.

With minutes to spare until Sut is here, I throw on a bra and the new panties she made me buy before stepping into the jumpsuit. Pulling on the long-sleeve ensemble is a breeze. It fits.

As I slip my feet into my booties, the doorbell rings.

"Come on in, Sut," I yell from my room.

With one last look in the mirror, I realize just how low-cut the V is. There is no way I can wear this. But there's also no way I have time to find something else. I'm pulling my arms out of the sleeves when the front door opens and closes. Sutton is saying something to me, but I can't hear her. I unclasp my bra, freeing my breasts before sliding my arms back into the jumpsuit.

I continue adjusting myself until I see my bestie smiling back at me. "Girl, you are looking fine," she says, elongating her words.

"Not too shabby yourself." I look at her as she spins in a circle, showing me her new blue spiked heels and black dress. She is the bold one in every way, shape, and form. And I love her for it.

Chapter Three

The first party was a total bust. Sutton and I arrived to find out the hosts had gotten sick and had forgotten to cancel.

The second party was quick and easy. Some people were familiar, which was comforting. We chatted a little and had a few glasses of champagne before making our way to our last destination of the night—FTW's NYE party.

I knew who would be there, and the people I don't like outnumber the people I do. Dillon, Sut's on-and-off "boyfriend," would be in the former, along with his just-as-sleazy friend Jake. As if having to deal with two of the most immature men in the world at a party wasn't enough, Hadlee would also be there with her new boyfriend.

Of course she would have a man. Because all men care about is blond hair and boobs. They pay no mind to how ugly she is inside. As long as her outside is pretty, they seem to flock to her.

God, I sound like a bitter hag. But at least I'm self-aware.

A nausea-induced sweat forms around my hairline when we pull up to the old, run-down bar that our firm insists on having the party at every year.

I want to tell the Uber to turn around and take me to my apartment. But instead of doing that, I put on a smile, letting Sutton pull me out of the car behind her.

Oxygen fills my lungs as I take a deep breath before we walk into Shots and Ladders. It isn't the swanky party I expected. It's more like a local haunt full of rich, swanky people instead of its usual blue-collar crowd. My gaze moves across the jam-packed bar, noting the various members of the who's who in the architectural world, as well as contractors, designers, and clients.

With an exhale, I squeeze Sutton's hand, letting her know I'm heading to the bar. After ordering us our favorite drinks, I wait, watching the bartender mix Sutton's lemon drop and my cherry vodka sour.

Over my left shoulder, a loud, sleazy voice calls out, "Those drinks aren't the only things that are sweet tonight."

Disgusted, I don't turn around. But then the owner of the voice sidles up beside me, so I have no choice but to acknowledge Jake as he continues to flirt with or disgust me. I'm not sure which he is going for. Does he truly believe he has a chance with me?

"Come on, Vivi, baby. I know you heard me."

Twisting, I turn to face him as I speak. "Yes, I did." The corner of his lips turns up in a lewd smirk as his gaze lowers to my plunging neckline. I snap my fingers in front of him. "You know the saying, 'if you don't have anything nice to say, don't say anything at all'?"

"Oh, so not-so-sweet tonight. Sour it is." As he leans closer, the suffocating scent of alcohol wafts off him. With the top two buttons on his festive shirt undone, he is the walking definition of a slimeball "Either way, I want a taste."

A visible shiver of repulsion runs through my body. Which, naturally, Jake mistakes as attraction.

He licks his lips and glances at someone behind me.

Even as he's hitting on me, his eyes are wandering.

Ugh, pig.

I glance over my shoulder to see the bitch queen herself, Hadlee, looking like sex on a stick with a black dress that hugs her every curve and heels that make her legs stretch on for days.

Shit. The she-devil is already here. As if this night wasn't shaping up to be horrible without her annoying presence. I had hoped we would manage to miss her by going to the other parties first, but the universe is cruel.

"I can tell you want it." He touches my hair, and it's the last straw for me, causing me to lash out, unable to take it anymore. I can handle a gross come-on or two, but the moment he tries to touch me is when I can no longer keep my mouth shut.

Slapping his hand away from me, I shove him back. "Don't touch me, Jake. Ever." I grab the freshly poured drinks from the counter and try to walk away without showing how much that encounter affected me. Searching for Sutton, I take two sweeps around the bar before I spot her blond hair shaking as she laughs at whatever joke the couple in front of her is saying. I force my way to her, pushing through the crowd of people that look either somewhat familiar or like complete strangers, all while trying not to spill either drink.

When I make it to her, Dillon has replaced the couple she was talking with moments before. His shaggy hair falls over her shoulder as he puts his face in the nape of her neck. My stomach churns at their PDA. I will never understand his appeal.

I cannot handle being around his manhandling of her tonight; especially not after my encounter with Jake. Handing her the lemon drop, I say, "Hey, I'm going to find a table. Okay?"

She takes the drink and murmurs an "Okay," distracted by the hands on her waist.

It isn't long before I'm sitting in a booth by myself, having found a secluded place to hide out. The ice clinks against my empty glass as I stir it with the tiny straw.

Why did I even come tonight?

I had hoped for the best, but I always knew I would end up sitting alone, nursing the same drink for hours. Even so, I trusted my best friend when she said it would be worth it.

"Mind if I hide with you?"

I glance up from my drink to find two gorgeous blue eyes across from me.

"I'm sorry, what?" is all I could say, unsure if he was even talking to me, but the way his eyes are driving into mine, he must be.

"Can I hide with you?" he asks, slumping lower in the seat across from me.

I look all around me. I don't know who this man is, but he has just invaded my sanctuary, my safe place.

"Listen, guy, I'm sure you are awfully nice, but I don't want any company. So if you would just move it along." I gesture in an off-you-go motion.

My breath hitches at his smile. I've never seen someone whose smile could take my breath away. His entire face lights up, showing me his perfectly straight white teeth. I try not to stare, glancing away for a moment, but that only makes his smile grow. He has not one dimple on his left cheek but two. Two deep dimples. One near his mouth and the other on his cheek. I never realized how much I liked dimples until this moment.

I muster up a stern voice, averting my eyes from his perfect smile. "Seriously, go."

His smile drops a little. "I'm sorry. I didn't mean to bother you. I just needed to get away from all that." His hands fly up, gesturing to the party surrounding the bar. "I'll find somewhere else. Again, I'm sorry for interrupting your...peace?"

Right as he slides out of the booth, I reach over and grab his hand before I can think it through. "Stop. Stay."

His head turns, and he looks down at our hands. Well, my hand that's still holding on to his. Fire creeps up my cheeks, and I snatch my hand away, tucking a strand of hair behind my ear as I clear my throat. "Stay. I'm sorry for being an asshole. I'm not a big party person. Or a social one."

I don't dare peer up from my hands that are now in my lap to see if he sat back down. His presence has me on edge. It's like a small electrical current running through my veins, making me excited and petrified.

I sit like that for what seems like forever. Silent but aware of everything around me. Aware of him. Of his body. Of his full attention on me. And when I glance up, his piercing blue eyes lock on mine.

He shakes his head. "You weren't being an asshole."

"I was. But thank you for not acknowledging it." I bite down on my cheeks to prevent a smile from forming on my lips.

He shrugs. "It was the gentlemanly thing to do."

Despite my best efforts, a smirk tugs at my lips.

"Can we start over?" He reaches out, offering me his hand. "Hi, I'm Nate. May I please hide in this fine booth with you?"

Not wanting to be the asshole I was thirty seconds ago, I place my hand in his, shaking it. His skin is hardened with callouses that coat the pads of his palms but is somehow still smooth. The warmth of his touch sends a shiver down my spine.

He clears his throat, bringing me out of my thoughts. I'm still holding his hand in a considerably long handshake. Flustered, I let go, wiping my palm on the seat of the booth. "Vivian."

A smile twitches his lips as he pulls his hand back, almost as if he can see the fluttering in my stomach. "Vivian. Nice to meet you." He pauses, taking a sip of his beer. "Does this mean I can hide out here?"

"I'll allow it." I still my face as I speak to him. "That is, as long as you tell me why you need a hiding spot?"

"Ah, there are always strings attached." His hand lifts to his temple in what appears to be an attempt to shield his face from any observers. "Let's just say I desperately need an escape from this awful night."

"Wow, could you give fewer details?" I laugh. "You know that you just piqued my curiosity from a level two to a high seven. Now I need all the details. What are you hiding from, Nate?"

"I could ask you the same thing. What are you hiding from, Vivian?"

Neither of us gives an answer. We both stare into each other as if our complete attention is going to break the other, hoping to make the other confess not only why we are in the booth but all our deepest, darkest secrets.

Nate's lips part, and my focus drifts to his mouth. The tip of his tongue swipes across his bottom lip, and I suppress the urge to do the same. With a deep inhale, I bring my gaze back to his. His mouth opens again, and I'm sure he is about to break—that I will have won this minor battle. The night will have one victory in my column at the end. But the words never come out because as he goes to speak, a woman's voice pipes up beside us.

It startles me out of whatever trance this man had me under. I turn to see a woman dressed in all black. Black slacks, black shirt, vest, and tie. She's carrying a tray full of empty bottles and glasses. I have zero idea what she said, but she appears to be waiting for an answer from me. "I'm sorry. What did you say?"

"Do you want another drink?" She doesn't smile as she stares down at me, eyes glinting like knives. I don't know what I could've done to this woman, but whatever it was, she hates me for it.

"We'll have two of whatever that is." He points at my half-empty glass. "Vivian, what are you drinking?"

My stomach drops under their combined gaze. "Cherry vodka sour." It comes out so rushed; how anyone can understand it is beyond me.

"Two cherry vodka sours it is," Nate says, not taking his attention off me. The waitress, whose name tag I can now see reads Kayla, gives Nate a questioning look, silently asking, *Are you sure*? Kayla waits for a moment, offering a gleaming smile to Nate before leaving. But not me. No, I get another scowl.

The both of us break our silence, bursting into laughter. Tears form at the corner of my eyes, which makes me laugh more, causing Nate to snort—which does not help the situation in the slightest.

Before I realize it, we are both lying down in the booth. Nate grasps his stomach as his face contorts. Tears continue to roll down our faces as we stare at each other from the underside of the table.

His eyes grow wide, looking from my face to my chest. I look down to find I'm a second away from flashing him. I slap my hands over my boobs, forcing him to laugh harder and louder than before.

"If you don't stop, I'll end up peeing myself," he says with another snort, and whatever control I was gathering disappears. The pain from my laughter is becoming unbearable, but I cannot stop. And it appears neither can he.

The only thing that brings us out of our laughing fit is Kayla returning with our drinks. She says nothing as she sets the glasses down and walks away.

Nate pulls himself together quicker than I do, and his back straightens as he sits up in his seat. I study him from under the table while he adjusts his posture and tugs at the hem of his shirt.

My gaze drops to his hands—hands that were on mine earlier—and I suppress a moan. They look strong, and from the roughness I felt earlier, I would guess he works with them daily. Maybe in construction, but he's surely not an accountant or computer person.

With a quick shake of my head, I try to stop thinking about his hands. About how warm they were on my mine. I try not to linger on how the mere thought of *those* hands gives me goose bumps running up my arms.

After taking one last glimpse, I push myself up, still covering my chest, before I adjust the deep plunge of my jumpsuit to ensure all my lady goods are concealed.

My gaze lifts to find him staring at me—at my hands—as I untangle my curls. "What?"

His head shakes back and forth as he lifts his drink to his lips. "Nothing." He swallows a small taste of the vodka concoction. "What's in this?"

"Well, vodka, a sour mix, some grenadine, and cherries for that little extra, extra." I sip mine. "Do you like it?"

He brings the drink back to his mouth, drinking it until nothing but ice and two cherries are left. "Does that answer your question?"

"Honestly, no," I say with a little laugh.

"Well, for the record, I fucking love it. In fact, next time the mean server comes over here, let's order more." He beams.

Chapter Four

At some point, Nate and I ordered six more cherry vodka sours. All with the special request of three cherries in each.

"One, two, three...Go," Nate says as he presses the stopwatch on his phone.

We both shove a cherry stem into our mouths. Nate closes his eyes, looking like he's concentrating. "You better not be cheating."

Laughing, I tell him, "Oh, please, I don't need to cheat to win. I got the skills."

Clamping his lips together, he suppresses a laugh. His jaw moves from side to side as he attempts to tie his stem with his tongue before I do. I try to tear my eyes off his jaw, but I can't. It's glorious and strong, with stubble that would light me on fire with its touch.

For this round, I focus on the ceiling. I count the tiles as my tongue twists and turns. I almost have the stem tied when I close my eyes, concentrating. I take a deep breath before opening them, only to become flustered when I catch him staring at me, holding his hand palm up to show me his tied stem.

A deep blush rises from my chest to my cheeks as he gives me the most genuine "happy drunk" smile I've ever seen. At this moment, I want to know him. Have to know him. No...I *need* to know this handsome, cherry-stem-tying, drunk man who invaded my space.

"What? When? How?" I demand of the man who claimed to have never tried before. "Impossible."

"Oh, Vivian. Do you doubt my tongue's prowess?"

My eyes widen as my lips part, speechless. Did he mean to say that? To suggest that he is gifted with his tongue in ways that make me squirm in my seat?

His smile grows wider with my eyes. I take that as a yes—that he did indeed mean it that way.

Fanning myself, I ask, "Is it hot in here? Someone must have turned the thermostat up."

"Sure, the thermostat is the culprit."

"I'm going to run to the restroom really quick." Hopping up, I scurry from my seat. "Will you watch my drink?"

He nods as I turn and walk away.

The moment I get into one of the dim stalls, I push my back to the door, breathing in and out. I can do this.

He's just an attractive man.

An insanely attractive man who is flirting with me—I think.

There is no other explanation. In my experience, a man does not allude to oral sex with a woman unless he is interested in doing said act with her.

But then again, my experience with men has been less than stellar. Out of the seven men I've slept with, only two attempted to go down on me. And each time left me wondering if I'm incapable of having an orgasm.

But I know that isn't it. My trusty best friend in the bottom drawer of my nightstand knows otherwise.

It's the men I've been with. No matter what they did, I couldn't get off, even with the two who attempted oral. I say attempted for a reason. Even though I haven't had it often, I know they were not doing it 100 percent correctly. Both times were rushed and unfocused.

That being said, there was something about the look in Nate's eyes when he alluded to it that had every inch of me heating. I had no choice but to leave the room. I couldn't handle him knowing he was turning me on with just words.

A few minutes later, I muster up the nerve to go back out there. But first, I have to pee and primp.

The old faucet squeaks as I turn the water off after washing my hands. I flip my head upside down and run my fingers through any tangles, then swing my head upright to admire my hair in the mirror. Satisfied, I touch up the rest of myself, including my lips and mascara, before opening the bathroom door.

On my way back to my sacred booth, I spot Nate sitting closer to where I had been earlier instead of across from me. That he moved closer to where I was sitting makes me smile.

Air fills my lungs as I take a deep breath to soothe my nerves, and when I sit back down, I slide in a fraction more than earlier. "You up for round two of who has the most amazing tongue, the cherry-stem edition?"

"Round two? I thought maybe I had scared you off with my abilities." His dimples appear again, causing me to stare at my hands while suppressing a smile.

"Seems someone has underestimated me. I'm not as skittish as I seem." Biting a cherry off its stem, I study his face. "Or maybe it's that you overestimated yourself."

"Clearly."

With a flirtatious smile, I change the subject. "So, round two, how about whoever ties the most stems wins, and the loser pays the bar tab?"

"Oh, I didn't realize you enjoyed paying for things. You could have just told me. You don't have to embarrass yourself further by competing against a champion like me."

"You will regret those words when I'm crowned the victor."

He tries to fight the smile tugging at his lips, dipping his head into his chest. I reach into the pile of cherries and grab two. With one cherry between my teeth, I turn to my left, offering the other to him. For a moment, we both pause, looking down at our hands as they touch. He drags his fingers down my wrist to where the cherry sits in my palm. It feels like the most intimate moment in my life. As if everything and everyone else in the bar has faded away. As if we are in our own little world.

He slides closer to me just as the last person I want to see tonight interrupts us.

"Babe, there you are," Hadlee shouts, sliding into the circular booth. "I've been looking everywhere for you."

Flinching, I retract my hand faster than I ever thought possible. My eyes flutter between them as disbelief fills me. No, he couldn't be with her...He spent the last hour with me. *Flirting*.

No.

No. No. No.

It can't be.

Realization hits me; the man Hadlee was on the phone with while giggling like a schoolgirl was Nate.

Fuck.

A mixture of emotions hit me as Hadlee's hand finds his arm, wrapping her claws around his left bicep. Of *fucking* course he is with her. I mean, look at her. She's every man's wet dream, especially in that dress she's wearing. With its short length, it hugs every part of her body like a second skin. While I, on the other hand, am every man's idea of a little sister. The one you have fun with, joke around with, but never have sex with. Never want. I can't figure out what I am feeling.

Anger?

Jealousy?

Are my feelings hurt?

Ding, ding, ding. The answer is all of the above.

An intense need to get away washes over me, but my body stays glued to the seat. I cannot move. I need to know if he is with her. If I could have read this situation wrong.

Hadlee wastes no time jumping on the opportunity to embarrass me further. "Natey, baby, you must have been so lonely without me to have ended up here." She doesn't add "with Vivian," but with how she looks me up and down, it's obvious what she's implying.

Nate's face drops as he hears Hadlee's words. He opens his mouth to speak, but Hadlee cuts him off, talking again. "You know, you could have stayed by me. I would have made it worth it," she purrs at him as she leans in closer.

I'm more uncomfortable with every passing second.

I stand and clear my throat. "Well, I am just going to go now."

He jumps a little out of his seat. "No, Vivian. Don't go." His eyes are apologetic, softening. But maybe that is the alcohol taking effect in both of us.

Hesitating, I glance between them again. I try to focus on Hadlee's smug face as she rubs her hands up his arm to his shoulder. Disgust colors my face. I want to pry her hands off him as if he belongs to me. Which is crazy, right? I've known him for a night, and he is with her. I need to leave before this situation somehow gets any worse.

A scoff leaves my throat as I turn on my heels, moving away. I keep my head held high and my shoulders back. It's something I've done since I was a kid. A coping mechanism of sorts. If anyone was paying attention, they might recognize it as my tell. A way to detect when I was upset or angry. Somehow, the posturing helps me control my emotions and hone them. It makes me feel like I am above that person who has gotten into my head. To rise to be the bigger person.

Once at the bar, I tell the bartender I am ready to tab out, then ask for Nate's as well. He was the better of the two of us at a childish game. I refuse to let him think I am a sore loser. I don't want that man to have anything to hold over me. But more than anything, I don't want Hadlee to have something to hold over me.

As I wait for my receipt, the big countdown for midnight starts. People around the bar get closer to the special someone they hope to ring in the new year with. I see Sutton wrapped up in Dillon's arms, counting down with everyone else. A twinge of sadness tugs at my heart at having no one to kiss in a few seconds. I'm busy observing everyone else when someone walks up and sits at the bar stool closest to me.

With three seconds to go till midnight, a hand settles on my waist, pulling me to turn around. I spin, not realizing what is happening until it's too late.

Jake.

Jake is pulling me into him.

I throw my hands up a second too late, and his lips are on mine. One hand slinks around me, holding me in place while the other roams my body. Touching me. Violating me. I put my hands on his chest, trying to push him off. He somehow interprets my struggle as encouragement, attempting to stick his tongue into my mouth. A squeal vibrates up my throat while I fight to keep my mouth closed. This seems to get his attention enough that he backs up, smiling at me as he does.

"Now, see? We could've been doing that all these months if you hadn't been playing hard to get." He attempts to pull at my waist again as I stumble back until I am out of his reach.

I wipe the back of my hand across my mouth and look up at him, ready to scream. How dare he touch me. I knew Jake was a pig, but I never thought he was deplorable enough to touch my body or put his mouth on me without consent.

A wave of nausea rolls through me at the thought. At the memory of his hands and lips on me.

My mouth fills with saliva as he grins down at me. How could anyone mistake my expression for anything other than sickness?

I try to get away from him as fast as I can; I move to walk around him when he grabs for me again.

"Stop pretending you don't like my attention on you, Vivian. You should be grateful. It's not like you were my first choice tonight," he whispers against my ear with a slimy smile spread across his lips.

This time, I can't fight what is happening. Vomit rises through my throat. Before I know it, I am hunched over, puking up cherries and vodka all over his stupid bright-white shoes.

"No. You. Didn't." It's all I can make out of what Sutton is saying between her hysterical laughing. She attempted to keep a straight face while I told her about Jake and the visceral reaction I had to his mouth and hands but quickly lost the battle. She doubles over, crying, and last night's mascara runs down her face. She is going to regret laughing at my misery once she realizes she looks like an ugly raccoon because of it.

"Stop. It's not funny," I say, giving her a death stare. "I'm *humiliated*. The entire night was a disaster."

She wipes away the remaining tears. "Okay, okay. I'll try to stop." We both sit in silence as she takes several deep breaths to regain her composure.

"Better?" she asks as she achieves a calm exterior. That's the thing about Sutton. The girl can mask her emotions like a pro. I once asked her how she bottles up her feelings on demand. The only answer she could give me was that it was natural for her. That it was an instinct and ability she has always had. It's her fight-or-flight response.

"Yes, thank you. I'm serious, though. The night was a disaster."

"It wasn't a complete disaster. You met that hottie, Nate, which I would count as a success."

"Did you forget the part where he is with the she-devil, and I ended the night with vomit in my hair?"

"Please, you were the hottest thing there, vomit and all."

I have to give it to her. Sutton has a way of making me feel better. She's been my biggest supporter since the day we met.

With every bite I take out of the hangover food Sutton ordered for us, I moan in delight. Never have I been so thankful for not only my best friend but for the breakfast diner around the block. Pancakes, eggs, bacon, and hash browns from Toasted always make me feel better after an awful night. Or a good night. Their food pretty much makes me happy at all times. Hell, everything about the place makes me smile, like the fact it's constantly being mistaken for a local marijuana shop, which has only helped their business.

When Sut stumbled into my apartment at nine this morning, I was ready to scream at her for last night. That was, until I got a good glimpse at her wearing Dillon's sweats, carrying last night's heels in one hand and our favorite food in the other. Once I saw how she looked, I let go of my anger. She looked as awful as I felt.

She and Dillon didn't stop drinking until well after midnight. By the time they made it back to his place, they were both too far gone to be around each other. One or both started a fight before they had gone to bed for the night, and she ended up sleeping alone in his bed. When she woke up, Dillon wasn't there. It wasn't until she went to go pee that she found him asleep in the bathtub, using a towel as a blanket.

The story of our New Year's Eve failures kept us laughing all morning. We spent the rest of the day napping and stuffing our faces with candy while we watched a Freddie Prinze Jr. rom-com marathon.

"Why can't we find men like him, Sut? Why?" I groan, wiping my cheeks with my sleeve. What is it about watching Freddie find happiness with all the women he loves that always has me shedding a tear or two?

Sutton wraps her warm arms around me. "Because he is an actor, and all of those sweet, romantic lines you love were most likely written by a woman."

"True." Though her words don't stop me from wondering if men like these characters are out there. If Nate finds his happiness with Hadlee.

I need to stop thinking about him. Yes, he was fucking attractive, with brown curls that looked so soft I wanted to run my fingers through every single one of them. And his eyes. I could get lost looking into those mesmerizing blues of his. Oh, and that jawline, covered with stubble.

Gah, snap out of it, Viv. He is with Hadlee. A girl who was on *The Bachelor* for, like, five weeks. She is well-versed in dating and the games that are played.

I am not.

It's time to forget about him and the few stolen moments we shared.

Chapter Five

When Monday rolls around, the office is buzzing from the postholiday return of the upper-level employees, including my boss, Mr. Tillan. Coworkers gather around each other's desks, catching up on what's happened since they last spoke. Whether it be about Christmas or New Year's, there's gossip in the air, and I hope it's not about me.

Wearing a mauve-pink long-sleeve chiffon top with a tie around the neck, black pixie pants that hit just above my ankle, and black flats that are heaven on my feet, I make my way across the room to my desk. Just as I sit down, Mr. Tillan makes his way across the lobby. He is the sort of man who demands attention and respect when he enters a room.

He's in his midfifties and is balding, but he's fit as can be and built like a Mack truck. He takes excellent care of himself, which has made me reevaluate my habits. To everyone else, he looks like he would be a tough man to work with, but honestly, the man is the best person

I know. He is a complete family man and treats me like one of his own.

"Get ready for a long one, Vivian," he says, making his way past me to his office and closing the large wooden double doors behind him.

I sweep my hair into a quick ponytail, getting ready for a day full of running around. Mr. Tillan and I have an established routine for days that are going to be full of clients and bullshit. It is a secret code between us. If he walks in and gives me the "long one" line, it means it is time to make a coffee run and grab us our usual in the largest size available.

When I return from gathering our drinks, the office floor is still a buzz, with coworkers whispering to each other and gossiping.

Please, God, let it be about someone other than me. Please.

I'm unsure if anyone witnessed me puking on Jake or running out of Shots and Ladders with vomit in my hair, and I'd rather not find out. I enter Mr. T's office, close the doors behind me, and hand him a coffee. He grins up at me as he takes it. "So, Viv, did anything riveting happen while I was away?"

My heart pounds as my nerves take over. He must know about New Year's Eve. I plaster on the most innocent face I can muster. "Not that I am aware of."

With a sip of his coffee, he leans back in his chair. "Hmm." He pauses. "I just assumed something must have happened based on how those idiots out there are whispering among themselves."

I exhale as relief flows through me. He doesn't know how I humiliated myself not once but twice the other night. "Oh, yeah. I was wondering the same thing. But alas, no one wants to whisper all the hot office gossip to me."

I stare at him as he frowns. Then, as if it suddenly hits him, he remarks, "Ah, your friendship with Ms. Hale."

"They all think I'm a little narc, waiting to snitch to my best friend to get them fired." Well, they aren't wrong. I would, without a doubt, tell Sut everything I hear up here. But she would never use that information against anyone unless it was something serious that could cause legal issues. Which has happened before.

This past year, I walked in on two coworkers going at it in the supply closet. Naturally, I told Sutton about it. Legally, she had to have them acknowledge their relationship in writing so nothing could come back and bite the company in the ass later.

Well, that was an issue, because both employees were married...to other people. Let's just say it caused a lot of drama, and now everyone avoids letting me in on anything remotely juicy out of fear.

"That's ridiculous. What happened with Mrs. Smith and Mrs. Reeves was not yours or Ms. Hale's fault." He adds emphasis to the Mrs. in both of their names, assuring me that everything that happened with their mess was indeed their fault, not mine.

I take a big swig of my coffee, savoring the mocha goodness before responding, "I know, but it sucks."

He props his elbows on his desk, his chin resting on his interlaced fingers. "Let's brainstorm ideas on how to find out."

Confusion must show on my face because he beams at me while he waits for me to respond. "When are we going to find time today? You said it was going to be a long one?"

"Yeah, a long one of us finding out juicy gossip." He all but says duh at me. We both laugh before getting to work on concocting a scheme to find out all the details of what is going on.

Our suggestions for finding out what was going around the office rumor mill were less than genius. Hell, if I'm being honest, they were downright idiotic.

We had ideas of sneaking into air vents and listening from above. We thought of going to a spy store and buying supplies to bug everyone's phones with listening devices. One of us even thought we could buy a disguise and stand close enough that we would hear as they spilled all the information.

Yes, I am very much ashamed to say that it was me who thought we could solve all our problems with wigs and mustaches. In my defense, I've always wanted to dress up in disguise and see what would happen.

Eventually, we both have the brilliant idea of planting Mr. Tillan's old iPhone for us to listen in with AirPods.

We decide it's best to do it while everyone is away at lunch so when they all get back, we will hear all the juicy tidbits they learned over their meals. I hid his old phone at the place we both agreed would be the epicenter of office gossip—behind a photograph on Hadlee's desk.

After lunch, we listen as she relays her NYE to another one of the head architect's assistants. "I'm telling you, Shelby, he couldn't keep his hands off me." Heat creeps up my neck and to my face as jealousy pangs through my chest. I have to keep listening, though. It's the only thing that will help me get over whatever crush I'm harboring for this man I met for a cool minute.

"Oh my God, you are the luckiest woman ever. He is gorgeous," Shelby says.

"So, at one point, I lose him while catching up with Elliot and Lauren about their new baby. Talking to them bored me out of my fucking mind, though. Can you imagine having a baby at our age? I mean, we are only twenty-six."

Mr. Tillan and I share a glance. "Anyway, it had been forever since he left to go to the restroom or whatever, but when I searched for him, I couldn't find him anywhere." She pauses, then gushes, "You'll never guess where, or I should say *who*, I found him with."

"Oh my God, who?" Shelby gasps.

I, of course, already know who...*Me*.

I want to shut it off, but I can't. I need to know more about this moment from another person's point of view.

"Vivian."

Mr. T's brows shoot up.

"Shut up! Vivian? Like, redhead Vivian? Like, Tillan's desk Vivian?"

"Mm-hmm, one and the same."

"What were they doing?"

"Okay, so I watch them for a minute, waiting to see what is going on. And then I see it. She is throwing herself at him while they talk." That pang of jealousy I had felt earlier vanishes as my body tenses. How dare she lie about me? I was not all over him. Yes, I might have been flirting, but so was he. And none of it was me throwing myself at him or anyone else.

My boss gives me a "don't worry about it, kid" look. As if he knows her story about me isn't true.

"No fucking way. That little slut."

Hadlee laughs. "She wishes. I swooped in to save him, and she scurried off with her tail between her legs." There is a pause, then..."But wait, it gets better. After she leaves our table, she goes to the bar and throws herself at another guy. This time, I see them make out for a second, only to stop because she throws up."

Their laughter fills our ears. I rip the AirPod out of my ear, slamming it on his desk. Pressing my palms into my eyes, I bend forward in the chair. "This cannot be happening. She is making things up. I mean, yes, some parts are true. But nothing that makes me look desperate."

"Hey, kid, don't worry about it. You know the truth, and that's all that matters. It wouldn't even matter if it were true. And I am not saying it is, because I know you. Everyone here knows you, and better than that, everyone knows Hadlee. She exaggerates. They all know it. Don't let her get in your head. Okay?"

I take a few deep breaths before willing my eyes to open when I know I won't cry. "Okay." I place the AirPod back in my ear.

"You still want to listen?" His eyebrows raise as he gives me a questioning glance.

My shoulders lift as I shrug. "How can I not?"

"Anyway, he took me home. I expected him to come in and fuck my brains out, but nope. He wouldn't even let me give him a blowie or anything." Hadlee's words pour out of her like a brag.

"What a freaking gentleman."

"I know, right? How did I get so lucky? The only problem was that I was and still am horny as hell for him."

Shelby chuckles. "How will you ever survive?"

"Masturbation, hun. Masturbation." It's the last thing Hadlee says before Tillan and I burst into laughter, pulling out our AirPods.

"I think we can agree we don't want to hear any more." His words come out between chuckles.

"Agreed."

Chapter Six

Seven weeks later

It took a week or two before the New Year's fiasco died down in my head and at work. Hadlee and the other rumor mills found bigger, better stories to spread. I was a thing of the past, thank God. After working for that same company for six years, I should be used to all the office drama. But no, I am still surprised every time a new rumor starts or, hell, is confirmed. I might not be the talk of the cubicles anymore, but today was shaping up to be just as horrible.

My anxiety kicks up the moment my half-asleep ass catches a glance of my clock. I was already an hour late for work. I had planned on showering this morning. In fact, I was counting on it. My hair is a greasy mess. I had gone one-too-many days without washing it. Any other time I forgot a hair-washing day, I would throw some tight French braids in my hair so not a soul could tell how disgusting it was.

But today, that isn't an option. I don't have an extra ten to twenty minutes to spend braiding. A messy bun and a shit ton of dry shampoo will have to do. And when I say messy, I mean it. I pick up yesterday's black slacks off the floor and grab a sweater from my closet, throwing them on as I run out the door.

Today is a shit day for me to be late. Mr. Tillan has a day full of back-to-back meetings, most of which are with new clients and companies to collaborate with on ongoing projects.

I love Mr. T, but the man couldn't identify who the hell he was meeting or why if it weren't for me. If I can't get there in time, he will flounder like a fucking fish out of water.

I just need to get there before 9:00 a.m., when his first meeting with a landscaping company is scheduled.

As I walk into the building, my anxiety doesn't calm down. No, it continues to build, and I anxiously bounce on my toes as I ride the elevator up to the sixth floor. "Come on, come on." Impatience swallows me whole. I shoot Mr. Tillan a text, letting him know I'm here and how sorry I am about being late.

The moment the doors open to the sixth floor, I bound out of the elevator, still staring at my phone as I turn the first corner.

That is, until I hit something hard.

Falling back, I shout, "Fuck" as I hit the floor.

"Shit," someone mutters.

Frantically, I gather up the spilled contents of my purse. I look up to see what or who I ran into.

A man. I hit a fucking man.

And from the backside of him, I gather he is a fit man at that. The broad shoulders filling out his dark-green sweater and his perfectly shaped ass make me forget all about being late.

Who is he? Surely, he doesn't work for this firm. He can't be new because Sutton always tells me when new eye candy is hired. I would know if someone with a Jon Snow ass worked for this company.

"I'm so, so sorry." I stand as he turns to face me. *That face.* I know that face. "I-I wasn't looking where I was going."

Nate is here. At my work.

This cannot be happening. What is he doing here?

It hits me like a ton of bricks.

Hadlee, his girlfriend.

He is here to see her.

Of course he would be. Isn't that what people who are in love do? They visit each other at work. Ugh, as if it wasn't already enough of a shit day.

The corners of his lips tug up into a big smile as I speak. It does nothing to stop the heat from traveling up my neck. I avert my gaze, looking down to survey the damage I caused. Coffee coats the front of his sweater. The wet fabric clings to his chest, outlining the curve of every muscle underneath.

"Oh my God. I ruined your sweater." I cover my face and its ever-growing redness with my hands.

"Vivian," he says with a laugh. "It's okay."

Still cradling my face, I say, "I feel horrible."

His rough fingertips graze my skin until he has them wrapped around my wrist. He pulls my hands down with his, forcing me to peek at his face. His *gorgeous* face. "Listen to me. It's fine. It's just a shirt. Not important." His voice is soft.

"Are you sure? Because I can pay for your dry cleaning or replace it." My breath hitches with every word as his hands remain on me, sending tingles of electricity dancing across my skin.

"You don't have to. It's fine. I promise." His blue eyes meet mine. The gaze is just as intense and intimate as it was at the bar that night.

The night he was on a date with *Hadlee.*

Fuck. How do I keep forgetting he's dating her?

He. Is. With. Hadlee.

I look away, clearing my throat. "Okay. Well, I, um...have to go." I rush off before he can get another word in, and I don't stop until I'm at my desk. Hell, I don't think I let myself breathe until the wooden surface comes into view.

Sutton is already there when I sit down. "Don't worry, V, you can breathe. Everything for the first meeting is taken care of."

I must appear to be on the verge of crying because she takes me in her arms, giving me the type of hug only a best friend can as I breathe in and out.

"Okay, I've already checked in the 9:00 a.m. meeting. It's two men, so don't panic. And besides, the younger, hotter of the two went downstairs to the coffee shop a few minutes ago."

I let out a sigh of relief, but my brow furrows as Sutton scrunches her nose, leaning away.

"I know you're having a rough morning, and you know I love you, but damn. Your breath is horrible."

Slapping my hand over my mouth and nose, I exhale, cringing as I get a whiff of myself. As if knowing what I'm thinking, she bobs her head. "Yes, girlfriend, it is rank, and your hair is...well, the hair is something else too."

This time, I cry. Not from embarrassment or sadness, but because I'm laughing so hard. Of course I would look and smell disgusting the next time I see the man who made me experience every emotion possible during one night. Sutton joins my hysterics for a minute before ushering me off to her office to use her "just in case" supplies.

Once I get to her office, I open the cabinet across from her desk to find everything I need to salvage today. Deodorant, fresh clothes, a brush, dry shampoo, and a toothbrush with toothpaste. Everything is right where she said it would be. I have zero clue what I would do without Sut. She is my little fairy godmother.

I take the time to clean myself up, changing into one of the spare sets of clothes Sutton keeps. Knowing she is out there looking after my boss and the clients, I take my hair out of the nasty bun and run her brush through it. I twist my hair into delicate and tight braids. Once I finish with my hair, I make quick work of my face and teeth. I don't look my best, but I also don't look my worst. I'm going to buy Sutton lunch for a week to say thank you for everything today.

After I freshen up to the best of my ability, I relieve Sutton from my desk, taking over. Escorting the next clients into the conference room, I offer refreshments before letting them know Mr. Tillan will be with them shortly.

Minutes later, my boss steps out of his office, laughing with a tall, olive-complected man. It must be the landscaper from Fisher's. Gesturing me over, Mr. T turns back to the door, shaking the hand of someone I can't see. Oh, that must be the younger, hotter one Sutton was talking about.

As I turn the corner to enter the office, I throw my hands up just before colliding with a man—again. He sweeps an arm around my waist, doing his best to keep us from toppling over.

Once we are steady, I look up to thank the man and am met with those same blue eyes from earlier.

And all I can think is, damn, he is tall.

How had I not noticed this before? The first time we met, we were both sitting, so that makes sense. Had I been in such a panicked daze earlier that I hadn't noticed he's a good foot taller than me? Some would think I would be used to it, seeing as I'm five feet three, but something about his height compared to mine is eye-opening. It's mind-boggling.

Still holding on to my waist, he leans forward. His warm breath brushes against the shell of my ear as he whispers, "Vivian, if we keep meeting like this, I'm going to think you like me."

My brain, still trying to comprehend the past few minutes and hours, lets my mouth spurt out the first thing that comes to it. "Have you always been this tall?"

This gets a laugh from not only him but also from the two other men I had forgotten were in the room with us. The vibration of his chest against mine is enough to shake me out of whatever trance he has me in. With one hand, I reach back, pulling his hands off my waist as I fumble away from him.

A flutter spreads through my stomach. Why is Nate coming out of the office? I assumed he was here to see Hadlee, but it hits me as I glance from him to the shorter, older man. Is he the consultation? Is Nate a landscaper? *That would explain his calloused hands.*

Clearing my throat, I run a hand down the front of my shirt while pulling myself together. "I'm so very sorry about that, sir. I didn't see you there."

"As I said before, Vivian, it's okay." He sounds sincere, but the smile on his face says something different. It screams amusement. The man is enjoying my continuous embarrassment.

Mr. T's talking breaks my train of thought. "It was great seeing you guys again." He shakes each of their hands. "I'll be in touch soon after giving the clients your designs. Vivian here will be your point of contact for everything, so don't hesitate to contact her if you have questions."

He turns to me. "Vivian, please escort Jim and Nate to the lobby?"

"Absolutely, Mr. Tillan. It would be my pleasure." I force a closed smile to my lips. "Right this way." I gesture for them to follow me as I walk them past my desk to the elevator.

We are silent as we step into the empty cab. This is where I would typically chat with the clients and get their take on how the meeting went. Or put them a little at ease after being all business. But today, I want nothing more than to keep the silence.

With two floors to go until we reach the lobby, the elevator stops to let on two more passengers, forcing me to move closer to Nate.

He turns to me, taking the opportunity to speak. "No, I wasn't always."

I peer at him out of the corner of my eye. "What?"

He smirks. "Tongue-tied, Vivian? I seem to recall that tongue of yours was very talented—with knots."

My jaw drops. The suggestiveness of his words has me speechless.

"Tall. I wasn't always this tall. I was once your size a long time ago." He looks around before leaning in, his voice quieting. "Probably when I was in elementary."

I swat his right arm with the back of my hand, moving an inch away from him. "You're ridiculous."

"I'm the ridiculous one? Am I? Because I'm not the one who ran into the same person twice, ruining his shirt one of those times," he says with a playful smile tugging at the left corner of his lips, revealing a dimple.

My gaze narrows as his words gnaw at me. "That's it. I'm paying for your dry cleaning."

He throws his hands up in the air, palms out. "I was joking. But hey, if that is what you need to do to feel better, then fine. Go for it."

"It is." I turn away again just as the elevator pings, opening to the lobby.

The three of us step out, wordlessly walking to the middle of the lobby. I completely forgot about the other man who was with him. He was quiet the entire ride down. With a polite wave, I head back to the elevator.

"Vivian, wait." Nate approaches me. "If you are serious about the dry cleaning, give me your number."

I give him a no-chance-in-hell expression.

"...so, I can let you know the damage," he adds.

"I don't think so. You can call my desk phone."

"Wouldn't that be inappropriate? To call you at work to discuss nonwork-related things?"

"Okay...Fine." I rattle off my number to him just as the doors open to a group getting off the elevator. I jump in without looking back to see if he's still standing there.

After a long, draining day, I have one thing in mind—well, two things. A hot bath and wine. Lots and lots of wine.

I throw my purse on the entryway table and stalk toward my bedroom, doing my best to avoid my bed until after I bathe because I know that the moment I touch the lush pillow top mattress, I won't be getting back up.

Peeling off my clothes, I leave them in a pile on the floor as I head into the bathroom, needing all the relaxation I can get. Carefully, I twist the faucet back and forth until I find the perfect temperature, feeling the water on my skin. As the tub fills, I search through my basket of luxury de-stressing bath goods. There are bath bombs, salts, and bubble baths. I go with my favorite scent, black chamomile and lavender.

I pour an extensive amount of bubble bath and salts under the running water. The stream turns into a fluffy, fizzing cloud on top of the water.

Before I climb into the scalding bath, I run to get my Moscato out of the fridge, not bothering with a glass because why pretend I'll only have one. I grab my phone on my way to the bathroom, shooting Sut a quick text.

> Dude. Today was total shit. You legit have no idea.

I lay my phone down on a towel by the tub after putting on my newest audiobook—a story about two men who enter a relationship with the same woman, only to find comfort with each other instead.

Turning off the water, I climb in. The water is scorching as I gradually lower myself in, letting my body adjust to the steaming water before submerging myself. With my wine still in my hand, I tip the bottle to my lips, taking a long sip. The fresh, floral aroma fills my nose as a wave of calm drifts through my limbs. Squeezing my lids shut, I try not to replay the train wreck that was me today.

I listen as the couple from my book confess their attraction to each other, my mind drifting back to those blue eyes staring at me.

Damn it, can I get one moment of peace from my own thoughts?

Just as I'm chastising myself for not being able to clear my mind of Nate, my phone dings.

I expect to find a text from Sutton, but I stare down at a number I don't recognize. Damn it, Sut, where are you? I need to vent about today.

> Hey, Cherry, did your day get any better?

Just my luck. It's a wrong number.

> Sorry, but you have the wrong number.

Immediately, I receive another text.

> I don't think I do.

With a wink emoji following. Ew, who the hell is this creep? Turning over my phone without responding, I try to ignore the sound of a new text, followed by another text coming in.

Ah, fuck. I can't. This time, Sutton did message me, but so did the wrong number. I read Sutton's response first.

> Oh, come on, V. So you were late and looked like a drowned rat. It's fine. You shall make it through this dark, dark time.

> Ugh. Why do I have a best friend who is such a dick all the time? Can't you just listen to my story without insulting me?

I pull open my other new message, finding another text from the unknown number.

I sure hope I don't have the wrong number. That means I'm stuck with this astronomic dry-cleaning bill someone promised to pay for me.

Nate...

I almost drop my phone into the water.

Condensation drips down the wine bottle as I take two large gulps, savoring the sweet, fruity taste, before placing the bottle back on the floor. Mustering up whatever nerve I can find, I type,

How much do I owe you?

Seconds later, he responds.

So it is you, Vivian.

Yes. Again, how much? And do you have Venmo?

You never answered about your day. Did it get better?

What the hell is he up to? Does he want me to pay for his shirt or not? He doesn't have to make small talk. In fact, it's better if he doesn't. What would his girlfriend, Hadlee, say?

Nate, you don't have to make small talk. I offered because it is the right thing.

With my Venmo app open, I find my username and send him a link so he can request the money from me.

> *I don't have Venmo.*

Damn it, of course he doesn't.

> *But if you want to pay me that badly, you can give it to me on Saturday.*

> *In person? Aren't you afraid I'll ruin your shoes or knock you down?*

> *You can knock me down as long as you fall with me.*

A flush of heat travels up my face. Oh my God, is he flirting with me? No freaking way. I have to text Sutton about this.

I type up a new message.

> *Sutton! Oh. My. GAWWD. If a man said that you could 'knock him down as long as you fall with him,' that's flirting, right? Is the NYE, blue-eyed hottie flirting with me? Help me, quick!*

I reach for my wine, bringing the bottle to my lips. Tipping my head back, I wait for the delicious taste of wine, but nothing happens. It's empty already. Damn, when did I finish this off?

Amid my wine stupor, my phone pings again. I glance at the screen and see that it's him. My heart beats faster and faster with every passing moment. Fingers swiping across the screen, I hold my breath as I read.

> *Hey, so I don't want to make your day any worse. But you didn't send that message to Sutton.*

A scream escapes my lips as I throw my phone onto the floor and submerge my head underwater. I did not just do that. How could I've done that?

Unable to hold my breath for over ten seconds, I lift myself from the water. Gasping for air, I pull my hands down my face to wipe off the excess moisture. This time, I am extra careful to make sure I'm on the correct person before typing out my text.

> *I. Am. Mortified. Please delete that text while I go drown myself in embarrassment.*

> *Ha-ha, what I'm hearing is you consider me as a 'hottie'?*

> *Seriously, kill me now.*

> *Vivian, it's okay to admit it. You are totally obsessed with me, aren't you?*

> *OMG. Stop, you are making it worse.*

> *"Never."*

Before I can finish reading his text, he sends another one.

> *P.S. I was flirting with you. I thought I was being obvious.*

He *was* flirting with me. Ha, I wasn't crazy. But why would he bother with me when he's with Hadlee? Does he assume I'm someone who's into cheating?

I want to ask him—want an explanation. But I'm afraid when I do, it will end. That he will stop texting me. That he will figure out the mistake he is making. As much as I want answers, I'm not sure I'll be able to handle it if he gives them and this stops.

Biting my lip, I type out my reply. *"Why were/are you flirting with me?"* I lose my nerve and erase it, then start over. My heart pounds like it might beat right out of my chest.

I can't do it. I can't. Will he think I'm flirting with him? *Am* I flirting? God, why is this so hard? Why can't I be fearless like Sut? Or hell, even like Hadlee?

"Fuck it," I mutter, channeling the spirit of all the confident women I know as I press send.

> What makes you think it was obvious?

A smile lifts my face.

Look at me, faking it till I make it.

When my phone doesn't instantly light up with a reply, I take it as a sign that I should wash away the day's dirt and grime. After draining the tub, I turn the nozzle to start the shower.

Ever since I was a child, I refused to believe a bath made you clean. Something about knowing I'm sitting in my own dirty water feels filthy. But they help me relax, so I reserve the washing for the shower.

While lathering up my hair, I listen to my "Bad Bitch" playlist that makes me feel invincible. It's a mixture of dirty and empowering music by women who are confident in their skin. Dancing, I rinse the shampoo from my hair, replacing it with conditioner. I've washed each part of my body three times, but I can't seem to pull myself out of the shower.

Something has turned my mood around. I'm not thinking about the mess I was today or how wrong everything went. No, I'm carefree and smiling to myself. Maybe it's all the wine I drank, or maybe it's the music. Or maybe it's Nate.

Mustering up some willpower, I turn off the water, wrapping myself in a towel before twisting my hair in a knot with another. Exhaustion slams into me as I dry off the last beads of moisture from my skin.

Every ounce of energy in my body seems to evaporate, my limbs growing heavier, yet somehow, I'm wide awake. I throw on a pair of underwear and an oversized T-shirt before climbing into bed and rechecking my phone to see if Nate has texted again.

Ugh, nothing.

After thirty minutes, he still hasn't responded. Did I take it too far somehow? Did I read the situation wrong? Was he only joking about the flirting?

Honestly, why do I do this to myself? Whenever I have the slightest interest in a man, I get in my head. Overthinking every single moment, word, and interaction. It's who I am—a love-life saboteur.

My eyelids are heavy when my phone lights up with a new text alert. I inhale a deep breath, swiping my finger across the screen.

> *Well, apparently, I need to step up my game if you couldn't and still can't tell that I am 100%, without a doubt, flirting with you.*

My heart leaps, reading his words over and over.

*Apparently. *wink**

Goodnight, Nate.

Goodnight, Vivian.

Closing my eyes, I pull my phone to my chest. How can something as simple as a "goodnight" make me feel so light?

Thoughts of Nate and our conversations and interactions fill my head as I fall asleep. I'm sure whatever dreams I have tonight will be of him and that dimpled smile.

Chapter Seven

Friday rolls around, and I haven't received any more texts from Nate. It leaves me to suspect he came to his senses about me, or maybe he remembered he has a girlfriend. Either way, my heart sinks whenever I receive a text and it's not from him. I try not to think about it, but the more I avoid thinking about him or how much of an idiot I was with him, the more the universe laughs in my face.

The past two days were full of correspondence and scheduling with Fisher Landscaping. FTW has used Fisher Landscaping for a few other projects in the past, meaning I have to talk to clients and coworkers about their experience with the company Nate works for. But I avoid the urge to search for any bit of information about him we might have on file.

It's becoming clear that someone in the universe hates me and loves to watch me actively suffer. As if my obsession with a taken man wasn't enough of a punishment, my phone chimes with a text from my mother.

Yep, Sally Benson reached out to me, asking to meet up for tea, knowing I don't drink tea.

Sut and I wouldn't have tea parties when we were little because even the fake idea grossed me out. Instead, we always had Shirley Temples, and they were marvelous. We loved every moment, though Sally hated making them for us. She always griped about why we couldn't have fake tea or the real deal. But Sut and I always stood our ground on it.

I agree to meet up with her this Sunday afternoon, which makes my nervous stomach flare up. As my stomach gurgles, I wrap my arms around my middle, hating my weak stomach and the gastrointestinal distress that loves to accompany my anxiety.

The last time she invited me to tea was when I dropped out of college. She and Hank were so disappointed in me. They couldn't conceive having a child who wouldn't have a college degree, as if it were the only thing worth living for. I was enrolled to get my degree in interior design. A pointless degree, in their opinion. What was the point if I wasn't getting an education in the medical, law, or financial field?

I tried to use those exact words—the same words they spoke to me when I declared my major in the arts—when I spoke to them about my decision to quit school. But Sally and Hank Benson aren't so chill with, well, *anything*.

My head is buried under a mountain of files, and I'm so lost in the dread of spending time with Sally that I almost don't notice when Hadlee delivers a small gift bag to my desk.

"Looks like someone finally has an admirer. How cute." Her tone is sweet but laced with sarcasm.

The delicate emerald bag has a gold ribbon holding the handles together. The wrapping is so simple yet beautiful. I itch to pull on the ties.

But this can't be for me. The only person who ever gets me spontaneous gifts is Sutton, and the girl wraps everything like a toddler.

My fingers curl around the smooth silk of the ribbon, pulling it off. Inside is a small dark jar, along with an envelope. I examine the jar first. There's no labeling—no sign of what's inside. Setting the jar aside, I move on to the small envelope with my name written with beautiful lines and curves across the front. I rip it open, finding the most meticulous, beautiful, simple handwriting. It is delicate and so precise, unlike my large and illegible scribbles.

"Dear Vivian, I couldn't find any with stems. I guess we will have to find another way to prove to each other how skilled we are with our tongues. -Nate."

My heart stops dead in my chest.

Dear God, is this what it's like to be flirted with? The heat in my face is akin to fire. If anyone is watching me now, they'll think I'm reading straight filth. And they wouldn't be wrong.

His words are so suggestive they make chills run throughout my body, straight to my core, causing an intense throbbing. My breathing increases with every glance I give the note. Absent-mindedly, I grab the stack of papers, using it to fan myself.

The lid pops as I twist it open and confirm my suspicions. It's maraschino cherries.

Stemless maraschino cherries.

Thoughts of him take over my mind. Of his eyes. Of that stare that makes my insides melt. But mostly, I think of his mouth. His tongue and everything he could do to me with it. I think of his tongue on my skin, imagining him taking his time with my body.

I try to fight the warmth from rising to my skin again. Desperate for a breather, I jump from my seat. Once in the bathroom, I check every stall, ensuring I'm alone. With a splash of cool water over my face, I glance at my reflection. I don't recognize the pent-up person staring back at me.

My pale skin is crimson, just as I thought it would be. But my eyes are something else. They're wild and intense. My pulse is hammering under my skin. I take a deep breath, concentrating on my lungs filling before exhaling steadily, helping to slow my heart's erratic beating.

How can a man I've only met a handful of times, embarrassing myself each time, cause my body and mind to react this way? All from a few flirty words.

The door opens, breaking my concentration as Hadlee walks into the bathroom, giving me a once-over. She laughs. "Someone has it bad." Gazing appreciatively at her reflection, she lifts her perfectly manicured hands to her long blond locks to primp herself.

I wash my hands, pretending as if I wasn't just turned on by her boyfriend. Oh my God, why do I keep forgetting he is her boyfriend? My pulse pounds in my head as my rage roars to life. I cannot and will not be like Allison. And I won't be with another Andy.

I don't acknowledge her as I walk out. Even with the extreme hatred I harbor for her, I won't do that to her. No one deserves that kind of hurt—not even soul-sucking demons like Hadlee. Once back at my desk, I pull out my phone and go straight to Nate's number.

> *Please don't send me flirty gifts. What would your girlfriend think?*

Within seconds, I receive a reply from him.

> *My girlfriend?*

Does he not think it's wrong or disrespectful to her and me to do this?

> *Obviously, you misjudged me if you think I would be interested in a cheater.*

The three little dots pop up and disappear. Is he going to try to justify his actions to me? Or lie about his intentions.

He replies a minute later.

> *Cheater? Cherry, why do you think I have a girlfriend?*

My teeth grind together.

> *Hadlee.*

> *Not my girlfriend.*

My heart is pounding again. Did they break up?

> *Since when?*

> *Since always. We have never been together.*

I type out a message, only to delete it. What am I supposed to say now?

Either he is being impatient or is annoyed by my lack of response because he texts me again.

> Vivian, I promise you I am not with Hadlee or anyone else.

> What about NYE? Were you two not there together?

> Yes and no. Can we meet so I can explain?

My heart stops. He wants to meet up with me to explain what? I don't understand what is going on.

> I don't think that's a good idea.

> Please. Tomorrow? Toasted at 9:30?

My favorite diner...I knew I was going to say yes before he mentioned Toasted, but now the urge is even stronger.

> Okay. But let's meet at 10:30. I sleep in on Saturdays.

> Thank you, Vivian.

What does one wear to a brunch date that isn't a date? Do I go super casual, as in athleisure? Or do I wear jeans and a cute top? Once again, I'm overthinking every aspect of this situation.

I decide to go with athleisure because, for one, it's perfect for stuffing my face with Toasted's delicious food. And for two, it's cute without all the effort. With my hair in a loose high pony, I head out the door to meet Nate at my favorite spot. I'm curious to know if this is his first time here or if he comes here often.

The sweet smell of pancakes and syrup wafts through the air as I push open the doors of the retro-inspired diner, making my stomach rumble. My stomach is in knots as I quickly scan the teal vinyl booths and shiny white tables to find him. Within moments, I spot him.

Uncertainty hums through my veins. I'm not 100 percent sure I can go through with this.

I could just turn around and walk out the door, delete his number, and never see or speak to him again.

I *should* do all those things.

Instead, I'm standing at the entrance, staring at him.

Unaware of my presence, he appears lost in thought, with his eyebrows scrunching together as he looks down.

I look like a creep staring at him this way from across the room. But I don't care how weird I'm being. I enjoy looking at him. The way the sunlight is catching on his curls, making them shine. Damn, do I like a lot about him.

This could be the last conversation we have. Because even if he somehow is single, I've acted like a lunatic with him, and he will probably run for the hills.

As if sensing my attention, he glances up at me, giving me a small, closed-mouth smile, which makes him look a little nervous. I return the smile, along with a small finger wave, and he matches with a shy one of his own. I take one last deep breath before walking over to

him and sliding into the booth across from him. It's only then I see
he was reading. He places the book on the table, and I reach across,
pausing just before taking it in my hands. My eyes meet his, silently
asking permission. He gnaws on his bottom lip before his head tips
up and down with a nod while he keeps his focus locked on me.

I slide the book over, glancing at the title. It's a romance novel.
Bodice-ripping cover and all. This isn't what I expected. His eyes
brighten, and his eyebrows shoot up.

Did I say that aloud?

He glances out the window, grinning. "What did you expect?"

So I said it out loud. Well, shit. How much have I said aloud to
him before this? My stomach flips because of how nervous I am
around him. "I don't know. Maybe fantasy or sci-fi?" I give him an
exaggerated shrug, hoping I didn't make him uncomfortable over
showing me his book.

He shrugs back. "Oh, I like those too. But I also like romance
novels."

"Why?" I spit out without thinking.

"Why not? They are romantic and sexy. Why wouldn't I like
that?"

I am a sexist fool for judging him or assuming men don't read
sappy books too. Ashamed for my swift judgment of his reading
habits, I look down at my fidgeting hands.

"Well, that, and some of them are like complex porn."

I can hear the grin in his voice, and my eyes snap up and widen. I
stifle back a laugh as our server comes over to take our order.

I order my usual scrambled eggs, bacon, hash browns, and pancakes without even thinking. After I say it all, I feel like a pig. But
that negative thought vanishes when he orders the same thing.

We sit in silence, staring across the table, studying each other's clothes, hair, and body language. He could have been at the gym before this, or maybe he's going after. He's wearing an old, worn-out black hoodie with a fading Fisher Landscaping logo across his chest.

Not caring what he thinks about me examining him, I lean to the side and look under the table to see what else he is wearing. Dark-gray Adidas joggers. A smile forms on my lips at his choice of footwear. Dirt-stained white Converse—the same as mine. Something about him also wearing Converses that've been well-loved warms my heart. Sitting up, I let him take his turn to study my outfit. We take turns examining each other until our food arrives, never uttering a word.

We eat in silence until he finally breaks it, setting his fork down and sighing. "What made you think I was dating Hadlee?"

I finish the bite of bacon in my hand, letting him wait for my response as I chew. His full attention is trained on me. "Because that's what she told everyone in our office. Oh, and there is the tiny fact she was all over you that night."

"I was there with her, but I wasn't there *with* her." He takes a bite of bacon. "I was being a good wingman for my best friend, Cooper."

"How exactly does letting Hadlee grope you make you a good wingman?"

Nate sighs. "Cooper has been pining after Hadlee's roommate, Sarah. She seems to be into him, but every time he wants to go out, Hadlee gets in the way."

My eyebrow cocks up. "So that's where you come in?"

"Yes. New Year's was the second time ever that I had been around Hadlee. Coop and Sarah wanted a night alone, so they suggested she take me to her work party. Coop is the best friend a guy could ask for, so I agreed. But when we got there, I couldn't handle it. The woman doesn't know how to read the room or personal space. I tried to grin and bear it, but the moment she started talking to all those people about herself or making ugly little remarks about others, I had to escape. And that's when I discovered you."

He sounds so sincere and honest. I don't know how to respond, so I remain quiet, hoping he will fill the silence with his voice again.

He doesn't let me down, taking my lack of response as his cue to continue. "I saw you, and I couldn't believe my eyes. Why would such a beautiful woman be sitting alone, hiding? I wanted to know, but also, I needed to get away from her. So I asked if I could join you, and I attempted to flirt with you until she found me."

I scoff at him. "You're trying to tell me you're interested in me but not Hadlee? I call bullshit."

This earns me a frown from him. "Yeah, Hadlee is attractive, but she isn't for me. Aside from the shallow reasons I prefer you to her, there is also the most important reason. She is one of the most narcissistic, meanest women I've ever met. You, on the other hand, are funny and smart." He pauses, flashing me a wicked grin. "As well as extremely clumsy."

My cheeks flare with heat at his words.

"Haven't you noticed I can't take my eyes off you?" He flashes me one of those deep dimples. "Oh, did I also mention bashful?"

I squeal, using my palms to cover my cheeks. "Okay, okay, let's say I believe you. What happened after I left you two alone and since then?"

"Nothing. She attempted to kiss me at midnight and tried to seduce me when I dropped her off. But that was it. The only time I've seen her since that night was at your office. And even then, I had to run downstairs to the coffee shop to avoid her."

I know from the conversation Mr. T and I listened in on that they didn't sleep together since he turned her down on New Year's Eve. But having him confirm it makes my heart beat faster with happiness. A smile forms on my lips, and across from me, Nate is doing the same. "I believe you."

"So, does this mean I can flirt with you now?" This makes my smile grow.

"I guess if you have to," I say in the flattest, emotionless voice I can muster.

"It might be hard—"

I cut him off, blurting out, "That's what she said."

His mouth drops open as he gawks at me before his face contorts, letting laughter take over. "I really like you, Vivian."

The words are like a steaming cup of hot chocolate on a winter night—they fill my heart with warmth. "I really like you too, Nate."

And just like that, we both go back to eating.

After we finish up, Nate pays for both of our meals. I offer to pay, but he waves me off, stating he knows I paid for his drinks on New Year's.

We walk out, side by side, not sure what to do next. With a small hug, we say goodbye, both setting off in opposite directions until I hear him call my name.

"Vivian?"

Turning around, I find him twenty yards away. "Yeah?" I yell back.

"Wanna go out on a date?"

I smile. "Sure. When?"

"Now?"

"Now? Now, as in this exact moment?"

"Yep, I think that is how 'now' works."

We step toward each other, and a brilliant smile transforms his face. "So, is that a yes?"

"When you said you wanted to go on a date, I never thought we would do this."

He grabs my hand, pulling me to the front of a building that reads Air-O-Line Trampoline Park. "Come on, you're going to love it." He doesn't let go of me as we walk through the doors to an open warehouse lined with trampolines and obstacle courses.

I try to concentrate on my surroundings, but all I can think about is his hand. The touch is setting me on fire.

Does he know what this is doing to me?

Better yet...Does he feel the same?

The employees force us to view a safety and rules video about the dangers of flips, flops, and running before we can get to the fun. According to this video, everything is an injury or death waiting to happen. Once the video ends, the short man in the front hands us a waiver to sign. Nate drops my hand, passing me the papers while he pays for our passes and special trampoline socks.

I scan the form. "Is a liability waiver necessary?"

He lifts his shoulders into a shrug. "People like to sue when they break their legs jumping."

"Fuck it." I sign the paper.

With a chuckle, Nate takes the pen from me, signing his form. "So, are we free to bounce to our heart's desires now?"

The man nods, adding, "You have two hours."

We take off our matching dirty-ass Converses, placing them under a bench before struggling to put on the "special" socks. They are the weirdest thing ever. They remind me of hospital socks. The ones with grips on the bottom to make sure older people don't slip. They look like that, but with toe compartments. I get mine on first and take the time to observe my surroundings as I wait for Nate.

The place is packed with families everywhere. Kids laugh, and adults smile like they just had their first bite of candy. I feel out of place but also giddy. A little girl with pigtails runs around, chasing two older kids. They are all smiles and giggles as a woman, who I assume is their mother, swoops in, doing an "illegal" double bounce, knocking all three children on their backs as their happiness grows.

I'm lost in watching this family play when Nate finishes putting on his horrible socks, joining me on the ledge.

"You ready?" he asks as if he thinks I might say no.

"Are *you* ready?" I challenge back at him.

We peer at each other before taking off in opposite directions, running, breaking the first of what will likely be all the rules. Something about the look in his eyes tells me we are both going to treat this entire experience just like the cherry stems—a competition.

My legs are light as I run up the stairs. I see him leap over the railing on the opposite side, beating me to the first trampoline. "You cheated," I grumble at him.

"Never," Nate teases as he walks backward toward a free row for us to use.

"You should be ashamed of yourself. Using height and athletic abilities to beat a small woman like me." Before he can respond, I push him and jump onto the first trampoline.

"Oh, you want to play like that?" He jumps toward me in gigantic leaps.

A scream escapes my throat as I bounce to my left to dodge his arms as they reach for me. We laugh while he continues to pursue me as I jump off and run to the nearest obstacle course.

It comprises foam blocks, a rock wall, balance beams, monkey bars, and, obviously, mini trampolines. Jumping onto the first balance beam, I glance back to find him catching up. With my arms held straight to my sides, I place one foot before the other, focusing on my steps until I reach the end. Hopping off the beam, I run to the next obstacle—the rock wall.

It's about ten feet high, blocking the way to the next obstacle in the course. Foam blocks pad the bottom of both sides to cushion you if you fall. I hold my breath as I climb, focusing on my hands while trying not to rush but still go as fast as I can.

As I reach the top, I stop to look for Nate, but I don't see him. Where did he go? Then, without warning, a hand wraps around my ankle. I scream and look down to see Nate laughing so hard he loses his grip on the wall. Trying to catch himself, he grabs at my ankle again, taking me down with him.

I hit the multicolored foam blocks a second after him and burst into laughter. He tries wiggling closer, but the power of the foam blocks is pulling him under.

"Ha," I cheer, mocking him. I push my legs into the foam surrounding me, but I don't budge an inch. "Shit. I'm stuck too. Help me," I whine with a pout on my lips.

"One sec, and I'll help you." I watch in amusement as Nate attempts to make his way to me and fails. His arms move outward while his legs sink farther beneath the surface. He claws at the foam as if it will give up and release him.

"Oh, my hero." This comment earns me a foam block to the face, and I gasp before chiding, "How dare you."

"How dare I? How dare you laugh as a handsome man drowns in this soft, cushioned pit of death?" He throws a few more blocks at my face, and I lift my arms to try to shield myself from his oncoming attack. I barely manage to protect myself from every other hit as he relentlessly wages war against me.

Soon I'm covered by blocks of blue, orange, and what I assume was once red but has now faded to pink. I wiggle my body, trying to get higher, but nothing happens. "Well, I guess this is where I die," I shout through the slivers of light peeking through the overlapping foam squares.

I'm met with silence. "Nate?"

Nothing.

"Nate?" I yell out again. Still no response. I try moving the foam blocks away from me. I'm doing it—I will escape without his stupid, handsome help. I stop my efforts, noticing I'm not getting any closer to the surface, but the blocks surrounding me continue to move until a hand pops through.

A screech bursts out of me. I attempt to slap the hand away but am slow due to being confined. When my hand hits the unknown one, it grabs mine. I let out another yelp before I see who the hand belongs to.

"Nate! What the hell? You scared me." Yanking out of his grasp, I swat at his hand again.

"Ow. I was just trying to save you from impending suffocation."

"Oh, pray tell. Because we are both still trapped in the foam pool of death."

A grin lights up his face, and every hair on my body rises. His arm grazes mine, and I have to suck in a breath to stop myself from reaching out to touch more of him. Something must have flashed across my face, though, because his smile fades. His tongue traces along his bottom lip, and heat pools in my stomach. Desire swirls in my core as I imagine tasting him, feeling his teeth graze my skin.

His breathing picks up as he leans closer to me, pushing away any remaining blocks between us. I gaze up from his mouth to his eyes, finding them locked on mine. He leans closer until we are mere inches away from touching. I glance at those perfect lips one more time before they find their way to mine.

His lips are soft and full as they move against mine. I take his top lip between mine, deepening the kiss while swiping my tongue across the seam of his lips. It's less than a second before his mouth parts, allowing me access to him. He moans as he trails his hands down my body, leaving a trail of heat burning across my skin. One hand snakes across my back to hold on to my waist while the other makes its way to the nape of my neck, tangling in my hair.

He caresses and massages my body as he takes control of the kiss. His tongue is unhurried as it enters my mouth, and I let out a whimper of pleasure. How could a kiss feel this good? It's like a whole-body experience that I don't want to stop.

I wind my hands around to his back, needing more, tugging him even closer to me. He tears his mouth from mine, moving his lips down my jaw to my neck. My entire body melts into him, my hands traveling down until I find the hem of his hoodie. Bunching the soft fabric in my grasp, I dip my fingers under, bypassing his shirt to touch his bare skin. The warmth radiating from his toned abs beneath my touch has my body pulsing with desire. As I descend lower to his waistband, a husky sigh escapes from deep in his chest.

It's all the encouragement I need. My fingers dance along the skin right above where his joggers rest, moving back and forth before dipping just below the fabric. His eyes are full of hunger. The same hunger that's coursing through me right now. The same degree of desire I have for him spills off him for me.

I'm about to move my hand farther into his shorts when a voice sounds from above us, causing us both to freeze. "Mommy said no. It's time to go."

Neither of us dares to move or make a sound when the small child's voice argues back, "But I just want to jump in one last time. Please?"

My heart stops as I stare into Nate's wide eyes.

"I said no. We are leaving now," the woman says, and I assume she walks away, being followed by what sounds like a crying little girl.

Were we just going at it in the middle of this foam-block pit at a family-friendly trampoline park? My laughter is silenced by Nate's lips fastening back on mine. This kiss is different. It isn't full of the same urgency and lust as the last. It's slow and sweet. The kind you imagine as your first kiss.

He pulls back, placing a few pecks on my lips, a smile dancing on his. "Come on, I think we have been here long enough."

I let him show me how to swim out of the pit, sneaking glances at him every other moment.

Now free of the obstacle course, we return to the trampolines, jumping and playing every childish game we can think of.

After a few rounds of monkey see, monkey do, we both pant as we collapse on the bouncy black surface. I try calming my heavy breathing, but it's an impossible task with Nate lying beside me. Placing my hands on my stomach, I fidget with my nails to distract myself from how close he is.

"I'm glad you ran into me the other day," he says, looking up at the ceiling.

"Really? Even though I spilled coffee all over you and ruined your sweater? By the way, I still haven't gotten your dry-cleaning bill."

A smile spreads across his face as he brings his hands to his sides. "Yes. I've been wanting to see you again since the moment you walked away on New Year's." He turns to face me. "And as for the sweater, I washed it myself. Nothing to pay for, and even if there was, I wouldn't let you."

My hands fall to my sides, scratching the tightly wound material beneath us. "A handsome face, and he can do laundry. How are you still on the market?" I joke.

"I don't know. Maybe I'm just waiting for the right person." He slowly moves his hand over mine. Interlacing his fingers with mine, he never breaks eye contact. Even as my breathing falters. He just smiles at me.

We lie like that, holding hands, staring, and cracking joke after joke until our time is up.

The walk back to the diner is bittersweet. Hand in hand, we take turns talking about our favorite things. We tell each other our favorite colors—mine being royal blue and his being yellow, even though he thinks it is a little ugly. But when he was little, he felt bad for the color because no one ever picked it. So, not wanting to hurt yellow's feelings, he chose it as his favorite and, to this day, refuses to change his mind. We talked about favorite foods—mine being anything breakfast related and his being anything potato related.

By the time we get back to the diner, I don't want the date to end. It appears Nate doesn't either, because he won't let my hand go as I attempt to walk away. He pulls me back to him, folding me into his arms. His warmth is almost overwhelming as my face rests on his chest, and I inhale, breathing in spice and pine. He smells like a fall day in the woods—like heaven. I know how creepy I am sniffing him, but I can't help myself. I look up, finding him with an all-knowing grin plastered across his face.

Shit, he caught me.

"Now that I'm officially a creep, I need to go find a rock to die under. So, if you will excuse me..." Untangling my arms from around him, I turn, only to be pulled right back into him as he chuckles. The vibration from his chest brings a shy smile to my lips.

"I hope you know how happy I am that you gave me a chance to explain," he whispers, resting his chin on my head.

I tip my head back to look at his face, studying the curve of his stubble-covered jaw. "Me too."

"So, does this mean you'll agree to a second date with me?"

I snake out of his hug, walking backward. "I don't know. You set the bar pretty high with Air-O-Line. Do you think you'll be able to live up to that?"

"I guess you'll have to go to find out," he calls out to me as I skip away.

Chapter Eight

The moment I get back to my apartment, I slide down the door, my hand over my heart. He will be the end of me. I just know it. My heart is still pounding from thinking about him. About his intoxicating scent. About his smile and those lips.

I moan, remembering those soft lips on mine and how he tasted like mint.

I manically start cleaning up the apartment, needing to get my mind off him—off our kiss. Some people drink, smoke weed, or sleep, but not me. I tidy up. It's something I always do when I get inside my head. I deep clean and organize.

I read an article once that said many people with anxiety will organize to make themselves appear like they have some semblance of control. Until then, I hadn't noticed I did things like this. But now it seems like I know myself better than before.

After I finish cleaning, I switch to the organization stage. It's not long before I find myself knee-deep in books and knickknacks as I rearrange my bookshelves. I remove all the books from the shelves, stacking them in one enormous pile. Fingers combing through each title, I remember how the stories evoked varying emotions, along with smiles and tears.

I flip through an old romance novel, stopping at a racy scene. The book is about a maid who is taken aboard a ship to find the vessel overthrown by pirates. Soon she is engaged in a sexual relationship with the captain of the pirates.

I let my mind wander, imagining Nate touching me the way the captain touches the maid. Imagining every caress, every thrust. Shivers run down my spine, and my breath falters as I force myself to close the book. Just the thought of him has me coming undone.

Attempting to block out the visions of Nate fucking me, I force my mind back to my chores. I sort the books into stacks by genre. Once I complete that stage, I then sort each genre by color. Soon I have a colorful line of books that reminds me of a vibrant rainbow.

Proud of my accomplishments, I curl up on my navy couch. The plush velvet fabric is like butter underneath me. I knew the moment I saw the couch that I needed it. So what if it cost two months' rent? I was in love. Its deep cushions and rich colors called my name, and I never stood a chance of resisting it.

Turning on my TV, I flip through the movies on Netflix, settling on a cute rom-com. Throughout the whole movie, my mind keeps wandering back over today. How it started, how it ended, and everything in between. The touches and kisses we shared. His laugh and smile.

Today was hands down the best date I had ever been on. I felt free, out of my anxiety-ridden head. Nate brought out my carefree side—the side that doesn't care if I look stupid. The side that is full of wonder and adventure. He made me feel alive. Made me feel seen. And that is more than I ever could have expected.

Unable to contain myself any longer, I send Sutton a text, needing to share everything with her.

> Oh my FUCKING God, Sut!

Her reply is immediate.

> What? Who do I need to kill? Is it your mom? It's Sally, isn't it? I'm not afraid to cut her down. Just tell me when and where.

> It's not Sally. It's Nate.

> Nate, as in NYE hottie? As in Hadlee's date? Coffee on his sweater, Nate?

> Yep. We met up today...

> What? Why? Tell me everything!

> He explained the entire New Year's Eve/Hadlee thing. They are not and never were a couple. He took her out because his friend was with her friend, and they needed alone time. Aka, a Hadlee-free night.

> And?

> And then we went on a date.

Vivian Marie Copper-Goddess Benson, you best tell me everything right now!

You know Marie isn't my middle name...

Stop changing the subject, Copper Goddess. What happened on this date?

He took me to a trampoline park.

What the fuck?

Yep. And Sut, it was the best date I've ever had. I felt like a little kid again.

Okay. But trampolines?

Shut up. It was perfect. And so was the kiss.

Without waiting for her response, I send another message.

I've never been so turned on by a kiss in my life. I legit almost gave him a hand job in a foam pit because it was so sexually charged.

Dayum. My little girl has grown into a horny hoe.

Her reply sends me into a laughing fit.

Leave it to Sutton to bring up masturbation. Honestly, I'm surprised she hadn't mentioned it earlier. The girl is, and has always been, the most open person about her love of "self-care."

Since my seventeenth birthday, Sutton has always gifted me some sort of vibrator or sex toy. I used to be super embarrassed by it, but now I look forward to the new toys she gives me.

Maybe a little self-care is what I need.

Climbing down on all fours in my room, I reach under my bed, sliding a long black trunk from underneath. My sex chest is full of every present Sutton has gotten me for self-pleasure and partner play. I have costumes, blindfolds, restraints, and all the birthday vibrators.

My favorite—a small jeweled, purple suction vibrator—is the closest thing to oral sex a toy can provide. I don't think I'm able to get off without it. It was life-changing for me. For the longest time, I didn't think I could orgasm. But the moment I placed the opening of my purple toy to the most sensitive part of my body, I knew. It was them, not me. I came alive, coming within thirty seconds of it suctioning onto my clit.

I place my sparkling sex toy on my plush duvet and set my laptop on my nightstand. With my favorite dirty website pulled up, I scroll through video after video. After an abundance of anal and blow job videos, my mood is almost ruined. *Almost.* But I finally see what I've been looking for.

An attractive man in his late twenties strips a brunette woman of all her clothes, kissing down her body. I imagine the man's lips on my chest, stomach, and pussy. The heat builds inside me as I place the vibrator's opening over my clit while he slams into her repeatedly. I increase the strength of the suction until I can't take it anymore, climaxing as I picture Nate's face. It hits me then how much I want him. How much I need to be with him.

Never in my life have I masturbated while thinking of someone I know. Famous people, yes. Ian Somerhalder, yes. But never a man I've met. And definitely never a man I've dated. This is new for me. The increased want and need for someone.

As I float down from my wave of pleasure, one hand settles on my lower stomach while the other rests over my slowing heart. With my eyes fluttering shut, I fall asleep thinking of the future.

The rich aroma of freshly brewed mocha latte drifts through my bedroom, stirring me awake. The promise of chocolaty coffee puts a pep in my step as I leave the warmth of my bed. I plop down on the couch, careful not to spill any of my delicious hot holy grail of caffeine. With a glance down at my phone, I discover three new texts. One from Sut, one from Nate, and one from Sally.

I read Sutton's first.

So, did you masturbate to your new lover's face last night, or were you lame?

Um, as if I would ever tell you.

So what you're saying is yes, Sutton, I did indeed masturbate to the memory of the man I hope to bone soon.

I hate how well she knows me.

Shut up.

I dread reading Sally's text.

Vivian, darling, don't forget we have tea this afternoon at The White Glove.

Fuck. I forgot I'd agreed to go to tea. It's too late to get out of it now. I'm expected to be there in a few short hours, acting like the classy, respectful daughter Sally wishes she had raised.

I'll be there.

With one text left to read, my chest tightens. Nate's name flashes across my conversation list. Everything inside me vibrates. What if he wants to see me again? The thought alone brings a smile to my face. But then the little devil on my shoulder leans into the other ear and whispers, "What if he is texting you to tell you he doesn't want to see you again?" And just like that, I'm ignoring the message, pretending it doesn't exist.

With a quick shower, I move into my closet, finding a simple dress. It's a soft-spoken lilac color that should keep Sally at bay. It has always been her favorite color. And the modest cut of the dress should be conservative enough that I won't upset her.

Fingers crossed.

I attempt to cover the dark circles with a dab of concealer on the delicate skin of my under-eyes. They are somehow always present, even after a full night of sleep like last night. With a swipe of mascara, I call it good, hoping she will be satisfied.

Her idea of what I should let my appearance portray has never meshed well with mine. She wants me to be prim and proper—a lady—at all times. While I like a more relaxed, freeing look. She would love for me to remain blond, while I enjoy the copper locks my stylist gives me. I thought I'd have more control over how I dress as an adult, but here I am, still trying to meet the demands of the impossible to please Sally Benson.

I arrive at The White Glove Tea Room at 3:00 p.m. on the dot. After telling the host I am meeting Mrs. Benson, I'm led to a small bistro-style table for two.

Nothing has changed in all the years I've been coming here with her. The elegant, feminine decor has stayed the same. Light floral wallpaper, with pastels and stark whites all around the room. The large room is full of mothers and daughters, talking with closed-mouth smiles as they sip the amber liquid from porcelain cups.

Where on earth could my mother be? It isn't like Sally Benson to be late. She's always prompt. It's one of the few things I admire about her. She may be a lot of things, but late isn't one of them.

After five minutes of sitting alone at the table, I spot the same man who escorted me in walking my way, followed by Sally. With her head held high and nose up in the air, she is the epitome of grace and sophistication. Her billowy white pants and matching blazer make her stand out while fitting in. She has her blond hair styled in its traditional straight bob, which has stayed the same since I was in middle school.

I want to pull out my phone to document this moment—the time Sally Benson was late. She would never live it down, but also, I would never hear the end of it if I pulled out my phone during tea. And God forbid I take a picture. The woman would have a conniption. So I leave my phone in my purse, giving her a small, closed-lip smile as she frowns at me from across the table.

She doesn't say a word to me but asks the host to please send over the attendant. I wait, not saying a word as she situates herself in the chair. The need to keep her appeased has me lifting my shoulders and pushing them back. With perfect posture, I'm tenser than before. I only ever sit like this when I'm with her. Anytime she catches me slouching, she has the need to drone on and on about my spinal health, as well as how unattractive and unintelligent it makes me appear.

Eventually, she clears her throat. "Honestly, Vivian, I didn't expect you to show up."

I fight the urge to snap at her. Instead, I lift my mouth into another serene smile. "I told you I would be here. So here I am."

"So you are." Her lips form a small line of displeasure. Is she angry I'm here?

The moment I open my mouth to ask her why she was late, our attendant, as The White Glove calls their servers, arrives to take our order.

"We will have a pot of Earl Grey, please, and a plate of cucumber sandwiches. Thank you." The attendant takes the menus as she places her hands in her lap.

"Yes, ma'am." He gives her a curt nod before turning to leave.

"Um, actually," I say, stopping him in his tracks. He turns back to face me. "I would love a pink lemonade and a spinach quiche, please."

He glances back at Sally. Her pursed lips pull into a slight frown. When she doesn't object, he scurries off.

"Why do you always insist on embarrassing me? Is it because of the sushi thing? Because if it is, I'm sorry. I didn't remember."

I embarrassed her? By ordering what I wanted?

And not just that; I *always* embarrass her?

Also, did she just apologize? If so, that was half-assed at best.

I bite the inside of my cheeks, attempting to rein in my anger. My eyes flicker closed, and I suck in a deep breath, telling myself the new mantra I made for situations like this. *I am calm. I am strong. I will rally. I will not cry in front of Sally.* I exhale and ready myself to open my eyes, as prepared as I'll ever be to face her stare.

"I'm sorry. That wasn't what I was trying to do. You know I've never been a fan of tea, and the quiche here is amazing."

"Hmm. So, tell me, Vivian. Has your father spoken to you about the job at his firm yet?"

"What job?"

"Oh, the girl in the front, Patty, just got married. So she no longer needs a job, and it would be an excellent fit for you."

Curious to know why my mother thinks a receptionist job is right for me, I ask, "Really? Well, congrats to Patty on bagging a man and no longer working."

"Yes, good for her. Anyway, she isn't important. It's the perfect spot for you. You will be out front greeting clients, directing calls, and maybe catching the eye of some of the more established attorneys."

Yep. There it is. I knew it. Since it became apparent that I would never amount to what she or my father wanted, she has set her sights on marrying me off. Which I guess makes me qualified to be some man's wife.

"While I do appreciate that you both thought of me for that opportunity, I am happy where I am with Mr. Tillan. And besides, being a receptionist would be a step down from my current position."

"It's not about the position or title, darling. It's about what the job might do for you."

"I understand. But I don't want to marry some lawyer and quit my job to take care of him. I enjoy working." I want to bring up the fact that I met someone. A handsome, funny man, who's a fantastic kisser. But it's too soon. And I like the thought of having him to myself. A part of my life Sally can't touch or hurt.

Before she can respond, our attendant comes over with her pot of Earl Grey and my pink lemonade, filling our porcelain cups. We both sit with our heads turned toward him as he sets a small plate of cucumber sandwiches on our table before turning to me. "I am sorry, miss, but we are out of the quiche today. I hope the cucumber sandwiches will be sufficient." He leaves without letting me respond. I wonder if they are actually out of spinach quiche or if he was too nervous about crossing Sally by bringing me both items I asked for. The smile on her face makes me think it's not the former.

We finish up our tea hour with minimal small talk. She doesn't ask any more questions, shifting to talk about the upcoming babies instead. There is still so much to be done before Rian or Amy gives birth. She goes on and on about how the twins were as babies. How she is sure their children will be the same. I interrupt to ask how I was as a baby and if I was quiet and well-behaved like them, only to be told that I was nothing like my siblings. I cried day and night.

Something about me being horrible, loud, and crying all the time as a baby makes me smile. The thought of her being miserable fills me with immense joy.

I'm lighter as I leave The White Glove, almost like I can accomplish anything. After surviving Sally's scrutiny at tea, I can handle reading a brief text. In the front seat of my car, I reach over the console, find my phone, and open Nate's text.

> *Hey, Cherry. I just wanted to let you know that I had so much fun with you yesterday.*

My stomach flutters.

> *I had fun too. I had forgotten how fun trampolines can be. Makes me wish I had a backyard so I could have my own.*

> *You can borrow my backyard, but it will be a strict BYOT situation.*

> *BYOT?*

Bring Your Own Trampoline.

Deal.

So, when should I expect you and said trampoline?

Soon. I'll want to jump very soon. Are there any other rules besides the BYOT that I should be aware of?

Well, in fact, there is.

I fidget as I wait for him to explain.

After five minutes of silence, I am desperate to know his rules—for him to text me. I clutch my phone to my chest, not wanting to do something brash and come off as clingy.

Fuck it. I send him another text.

...I'm chomping at the bit to know.

Still no response. I give my phone one last look before I place it back in my purse to drive home.

Once I reach my apartment elevator, I pull my phone back out of my purse to see that Nate replied, giving me butterflies.

Sorry, I got distracted by my sister for a moment. The rules are as follows:

•Vivian must bring her own trampoline if she wishes to jump as high as the sky.

•The owner of the yard that said trampoline will be set up in may use said trampoline if he pleases.

•No jumping between the hours of 1 a.m. and 9 a.m.

•Trampoline must be removed from the premises within one hour of jumping cessation.

•Said trampoline can't have a net. Nets are for the weak.

•Vivian will go out on a date with Nate this week.

•No one else may be on said trampoline besides the owner of said trampoline or the owner of the yard on which said trampoline resides.

•No jumping when you need to pee.

•No jumping within thirty minutes of eating.

•Kissing is allowed and encouraged on said trampoline.

Reading each one makes my smile grow wider and wider until I laugh. God, I like him.

> *I have some questions regarding a few of the rules stated above that I'm hoping you might be able to clarify.*

All questions can be answered Friday night.

> *Friday night?*

I ask, unlocking my door and dropping everything but my phone on the entryway table as I rush into my bedroom.

Yes, Friday night.

Feeling bold, I shoot back,

> *Are you asking me on a date?*

Do you think I am?

> *Well, I did, but now I am questioning all my life choices. Even the purple and teal Scooby Doo sweater I wore in third grade with pink Converse instead of purple ones. Was that a major fashion faux pas?*

Yes.

> *Yes to the date? Or yes to the fashion flop?*

Yes, you def looked like a fool in pink with Scooby's signature purple and teal. SMH.

A small laugh escapes my mouth as my stomach drops. I set my phone aside while trying to come up with something to say back, but it lights up with a new message alert before I can think of anything witty.

Nate.

I sit down on my bed, trying not to panic.

> *Oh, and also yes to the date.*

> *Ha-ha. I bet you think you are so funny. Well, I have news for you; I am much funnier. And prettier. And smarter. And a better jumper than you. So, ha!*

> *Madam, that was uncalled for. I am beyond astute, humorous, and handsome. At least that's what my mother says. Unless you are calling my mother a liar. Are you? 'Cause she is a saint who would never, ever tell a lie, but also, she will fight you. And my jumping skills are far superior to yours. You are only lying to yourself to say otherwise.*

I laugh when I read his message. He is so quick-witted. I've never texted a man who can reply with the same level of cleverness as him. He is in a league of his own.

> *You. Are. Killing. Me.*

> *In all seriousness, I would love it if you would go out with me Friday night.*

> *I would really like that.*

I place my phone up against my chest, over my heart, flopping backward onto my bed and sighing with what I am sure is a goofy grin on my face. I'm already wondering what I should wear and how I should do my hair. Loose waves or straight? Or should I wear it up? And don't get me started on my makeup. Minimal vs. all out?

I open my go-to app for everything—Pinterest—and scour pictures for date inspiration. After putting endless pins into my new "Date Night Inspo" board, I find my mind wondering about more than just outfits.

Am I ready for more than kissing?

Can I sleep with him on the second date?

I already know I *want* to sleep with him, but should I?

My heart flutters with excitement and indecision. Based on how the man can kiss, I have zero doubts it won't be anything less than impressive. But that alone doesn't mean I should. I like him. Like, *really* like him, and I don't want to rush anything. I've been down that road before with both of my exes, Ty and Andy. Soon after sleeping with each of them, their true colors came out, showing they were not who I thought they were. Both relationships brought me nothing but pain.

My mind wanders like that for the entire night, racing with nervousness until I fall asleep.

Chapter Nine

"Vivian?" Mr. T calls from his office.

Peeking my head around the door, I ask, "Yeah?"

"Come in here. I have something I want to discuss."

"Okay..." I sit in one of the oversized chairs in front of his desk.

He leans forward onto his forearms. "I need your help."

I peer at him. "Have you fallen or hit your head? When did you start having trouble remembering? Because my job is to help you."

"No, and no. How old do you think I am?" He holds his hand up. "Wait, don't answer that."

I bite my cheeks to suppress the smile itching to be set free. "Okay, what do you need my help with?"

"I need you to take the lead on some projects for me. Play liaison between them and our outside contracts."

"Which jobs?" I ask, pulling my phone out of my pocket to take notes.

"Just two, for now. Both have the structural work complete," he replies.

"Okay, which jobs, Mr. T?" I ask again.

"The Feldman's, which would be overseeing that the clients get the design they want. As well as the St. Clair project."

"The St. Clair project?" The project Nate's family's landscaping company is on...

"Yes, the St. Clair project, and before you complain, I know you and Nate had a rocky first meeting, but you will see he is great to work with. I promise."

"But, sir."

"Do it, Vivian. I promise it will be fine. You will take my place in the design meeting with the client and Fishers today. Suck it up, buttercup, and fast."

This cannot be happening. Me working on a project with Nate. The person I have a date with in four days. The man whose bones I almost jumped at a family establishment.

This is a disaster waiting to happen.

After I escort the client into the conference room, I walk back to the front. My stomach drops like I've been hanging upside down on a roller coaster as Nate walks closer to me.

He stops three feet before me, and his eyes beam down at me as he greets, "Vivian."

"Nate," I reply, fighting to keep my expression neutral. "Follow me. The client is already here."

As we walk side by side, his arm grazes mine, sending my body into a tizzy. Goose bumps form all over my arms and legs as the memory of the last time I saw him floods my mind.

Our meeting was less than thirty minutes with the representative from the St. Clair group. After getting a sense of what they want their grounds and gardens to look like, we devise a design timetable. In a few weeks, we will meet again to review Nate's design mockups, letting the client visualize what the finished product might look like.

Once it's only the two of us left in the conference room, the temperature grows increasingly hot, especially with Nate's eyes locked on me.

"What?" I ask.

The only response I get is his lopsided smile, with one of his dimples winking at me. In a sly move, he wheels his chair a little closer to mine.

"Nate," I chide, giving him a stern expression I hope hides my breathlessness from his proximity.

"Yes?" His eyes fall to my lips.

"We are at work."

"Mm-hmm. Your point?"

He leans into me a little more, and I place my hands on his shoulders. With a gentle nudge, I push him back. "The point is, everything is 100 percent professional while here, okay?"

"Okay, if that's what you want."

"Yes, it is," I lie. The moment he walked through those elevator doors, I wanted to kiss him more than anything, but I know better, unfortunately.

He walks backward to the door, never letting his gaze stray from mine. "See you Friday?"

He doesn't wait for my reply. He walks away, leaving me wishing I had let him kiss me.

The week seems to fly by and drag on at the same time. My mind is full of thoughts about Nate and seeing him again. We text every night, giving each other highlights of our days and telling each other all the stupid things our coworkers do and say. It has been the best part of my day, and I get excited to hear about the small things, like what kind of bread he used on his sandwiches—100 percent whole wheat.

Instead of doing our usual coffee breaks this week, Sutton and I hole up in her office, talking about Nate and our upcoming date. We search through the pins I saved, throwing out the crazy outfits for a few fun, flirty, casual looks.

After going over how I should do my hair and what I should wear, we change topics to Sally and the high tea on Sunday. I relay my entire experience to Sutton, and we dissect every comment and question she made that day. From the mystery of her being late to wanting me to work for my father to find a rich husband.

It's times like these that I am even more grateful for Sutton and her lifelong friendship. She knows my family; she has been around them her entire life, too, so she understands my weird relationship with them. Not only that, but she understands not having a terrific home life. But unlike me, Sutton grew up with a loving mother.

I'm bouncing out the door at the end of Friday's workday when I hear Hadlee snickering to Shelby about her weekend plans. I continue to walk until Nate's name is mentioned. I slow down, pretending to search for something in my purse so I can listen to what they're saying.

"What are you planning to do, then?" Shelby asks Hadlee, leaning on the reception counter.

"Probs the usual. Show up in something skimpy and let him drool over me." They both laugh.

"You are so bad. There is no way he can resist."

"Ugh, I sure as shit hope so. I cannot believe how hard I'm having to work for this one. Like, I don't do the chasing. Men chase me." This time, I'm the one who starts laughing. Both of their heads turn in my direction, and I cough to cover up my outburst. They eye me before turning back to each other.

"Who does this Nate guy think he is?"

"Right? Well, once he sees what I have planned for him, he'll be begging for more."

Not wanting to hear more about Hadlee's disgusting plan to seduce the man I have a date with tonight, I step into the elevator, pressing the garage floor button a little too aggressively. I try to push the thought of Hadlee and Nate together out of my mind as I race home to prepare to see the man who has taken up residence in my mind.

Once I'm through my apartment door, I rush to get ready. First, I shower my workday off, scrubbing my body with the invigorating smell of Japanese Cherry Blossom. With a quick shave, every inch of my body is ready to be touched, prepared for whatever direction the night takes.

With the outfit Sutton and I decided on laid out, I pull on my favorite high-waisted skinny jeans, doing a few bounces to get them over my thighs and ass. Growing up, I didn't know that most women had to jump a little to get their pants on. Rian and Sally never had these issues, but they were not born with these curves.

The dark denim goes perfectly with my mustard-yellow slinky top. It shows the smallest amount of cleavage; just enough to pique interest. I chose this top for the sole purpose of it being Nate's favorite color. Then I pair the entire outfit with my favorite black ankle booties.

With a quick curl of my hair, I create a soft wave. I swipe on a few coats of my favorite waterproof mascara, giving my eyes the refreshing pop they need.

Finished and pleased with my appearance, I put on a comedy special on Netflix to pass the minutes until Nate will be here. Just as I'm getting into the female comic who makes a ton of vagina jokes, a knock raps on my front door. Pausing my TV, I stand, fixing my top and jeans as I stride to the door. I peer through the peephole, knowing it's Nate on the other side, but I want to see him without having him see the visible shiver that always crawls up my skin when I first lay eyes on him.

Nate stands in front of my door, wearing a blue T-shirt and jeans. His brown curls are tame, and his face has that dusting of stubble that I love. With one last deep breath, I open the door, flashing him a closed-mouth smile. "Hi."

"Hi." He mimics my smile as his eyes roam over me, taking in my appearance.

"Come in while I turn off the TV and lights." I press the door open a little wider for him to walk through.

He nods, passing me as he roams around my living room. I head back to my bathroom, checking to make sure my iron is off before leaving, as well as taking one last glance at my appearance.

Back in the living area, I find Nate looking at my wall of pictures. With the TV off, I slip on my jacket. "Okay, all done."

He points to a picture. "Who is this with you?"

"That's Sutton, my best friend since kindergarten. She is pretty much my nonsexual life partner." His eyebrows quirk at my words.

"Nonsexual life partner?"

"Yep. We have a plan to grow old together."

"What about a sexual life partner?"

"Well, Sut and I have talked about it, but sadly, we both agree that lesbianism isn't for us." I frown.

A small chuckle escapes from him. "What I meant was, what if you find someone you want to spend your life with romantically? But now I am more interested in this talk you and Sutton had about taking your friendship to the next level."

"I'm sure you are." I tilt my head, gesturing for us to leave as I turn toward the door, picking up my bag and pulling it over my shoulders. "Maybe I'll tell you about it someday."

As we ride in Nate's black pickup truck, I'm in awe of how clean it is. It's a weird thing to be in someone else's space. For me, it's like reading their diary. You can find out so much about a person based on the inside of their car.

Take me, for example; my car is pristine. But that isn't because I care about the vehicle. My car is something I use to get me from point A to point B, and I don't think about it much after that. It's spotless because my anxiety almost constantly flares when driving or stuck in traffic.

But Nate's car doesn't have crumbs in little crevices like mine. Yes, he has extra clothes and some water bottles in the backseat, but other than that, it's clean. So he either respects his property, is a neat freak, or is the worst option...a car person. Fingers crossed, he is simply responsible.

Nate hands me his phone, breaking the silence and my roaming gaze. "Put on some music?"

My mouth drops open, gaping at him. He shakes his head and asks, "What?"

"You're just going to hand me your phone? What if I go through it and learn all your dirty secrets?"

"Do you want to know all my dirty secrets, Vivian?"

My hand flies over my chest in the most dramatic manner I can think of as I peer at him, feigning shock. "Obviously."

A smirk appears on his handsome face. "Just put on some music, please."

I force my eyes away from the side of his strong, stubbled jaw. Sighing, I turn my attention back to his phone—no passcode. Who doesn't have a password? I sneak another glance at him. How can someone so good-looking be so down-to-earth, funny, and kind?

I scroll through his apps until I find Spotify and browse through his favorite songs. His taste ranges from Elton John to Big Sean. Both are favorites of mine. "Any requests?"

Still focused on the road, he says, "Play me your favorite song."

My eyebrow quirks up. "Are you sure about that? I could be into some weird stuff."

"Maybe that's why I want you to."

I find my all-time favorite song, pivoting in the seat to face him before pressing play. A shit-eating grin accompanies the shake of my shoulders back and forth. I want to see his reaction to every note, every lyric. I want to know if he sings along. If he hates it or loves it.

The moment I tap play, I observe his face, watching his features change as he hears the first note of the song echo from the speakers.

A muscle in his jaw ticks up as if he is suppressing the urge to smile. He listens to my happy song, never turning his gaze from the road.

The song takes over the truck and me as I sing and dance along with Britney to "Toxic." I circle my hands over the tops of my breasts, mimicking the dance moves from the music video.

Nate glances at me over his shoulder. His jaw ticks as he fights the smile building, and his eyes beam as he watches me. They look like sparkling blue pools only found in a magical realm. I get so lost in thought that I forget about the song. He frowns, turning down the music. "What?"

Lost in a daydream about his eyes, it takes me a moment to comprehend that he is talking to me. "What?"

"Why did you stop?"

"Oh, that," I rack my brain for the quickest lie. I point at him. "It was time for your solo."

He turns his finger to himself. "You think I can perform at the same caliber as you and Ms. Britney Spears? Psh, you must be crazy."

"Don't 'psh' me. You know you could easily be at Brit's and my level if you tried."

He gives me a little shove. "Get out of here."

"Hey, I wouldn't lie to you." He turns to look at me as I take his hand in mine. "I never lie about star power."

He breaks out into a deep laugh that fills my body with warmth as he rubs his thumb over the top of my hand, refusing to break our handholding.

I switch up the music, finding his most recently played songs. We listen in silence for the next ten minutes until he pulls the truck into a parking lot, backing into a spot in the last row. He gives my hand one last squeeze before he lets go, hopping out of the truck to jog around to my door. He takes my hand to help me out, and his chivalry isn't lost on me.

Still holding hands, Nate refuses to tell me where we're going until he stops to announce that we've arrived.

I look up to see a sign in bright yellow lights: Puzzles The Pub. He pulls on my hand, leading me into the pub, where we are greeted with the sight of rich red and blue velvet chairs and booths. I take in my surroundings as Nate leads us to a tall table with two large bar stools with cushioned velvet backing.

I drape my jacket across my bar stool before hopping up. My eyes are still wandering around the room. The decor is beautiful. "Why is it called Puzzles?" I turn to ask him.

Nate reaches across the table, handing me a menu. I expect to see a list of drinks and food, but instead, I find categories of 300 pieces, 500 pieces, 750 pieces, and 1000 pieces.

My gaze flicks up with curiosity and excitement. "Are we going to do an actual puzzle?"

"Yep; which one should we do? I, myself, am feeling some Disney princesses tonight."

With my back against the chair, I stare at the puzzle menu. "Well, I can't say I've ever been on a puzzle date before."

"Me either."

"So it's a first for us both." I smile. "How did you even find this place?"

"My friend Coop is always discovering new, interesting places."

Our server, a petite blond girl, arrives, taking our puzzle order. After handing us the food menu, she bats her eyelashes at Nate, telling us—or should I say telling Nate, seeing as she doesn't even glance in my direction—about the drink specials.

Nate smiles at me. "Viv, babe, what do you think? Want to try a sangria swirl with me?"

She turns to me, glaring as I say, "Yeah, that sounds delicious. We'll take two. Thanks." After she walks away, I turn my attention back to my menu. "Well, someone seems to like you."

"So, you admit it, you're in love with me."

My gaze darts up from the menu. He leans closer to me, resting his weight on his forearms. The warmth from his body has a hum of desire vibrating through my body, aching to feel his touch.

I lean forward to capture his mouth in a quick kiss. I've never been this bold with a man before.

Hell, I've never been this *comfortable* with a man before. His eyes grow large with shock and awe that I kissed him.

I cross my arms over my chest, pressing my back into the chair. My face falls flat, erasing all traces of emotion, and I try to sound as unfazed as I can. "You're okay, I guess."

He shakes his head disapprovingly, mimicking my posture as he crosses his arms against his broad chest. His shirt stretches to show off every muscle beneath it.

Heat burns through my chest all the way to my toes as I suck in a deep breath. My gaze moves from his shirt, tight against hard muscles, to where his toned forearms rest. It takes everything in me to stop myself from licking my lips as I stare at his beauty.

A smug smile graces his face. "Okay, my ass." His brows lift, acknowledging that he knows I was checking him out and saw the desire in my eyes.

I shrug as my heart races, not just from the kiss but from being caught ogling him like a snack I want to gobble up. "Oh, stop with the face. You know you're good-looking."

"First, thank you. Second, I..." He's cut off by the flirty blond server bringing over our frozen drinks, along with a 500-piece Disney Princess puzzle.

Her attention is, surprise-surprise, solely on Nate. She leans over the table to set his drink down, practically begging him to stare down her V-neck shirt at her tits. His eyes glance down for a moment before widening as they meet mine. We both hold back a laugh as we wait for her to end her blatant advances on him. I can't blame him for looking because I also did. I mean, how could we not when it's being placed in our faces?

She, no shock here, places my drink and the puzzle at the corner of the table near her. "Okay, hun, what would you like to eat?" Her hand finds Nate's arm and rests there as she wiggles her eyebrows at him suggestively, making it clear she wasn't offering him food to "eat."

I'm sipping my sangria as I catch her innuendo, and I choke on my shock, causing me to do a spit take. I spew sangria across the table onto her and Nate. My hand flies to my mouth to keep myself from spitting out the drink on them. "Sorry!" I mouth across the table in their direction.

His hand drags across his face. He doesn't even bother to hide his bemused smile. "Can we get an order of hot wings, loaded french fries, and napkins? Lots of napkins. What else, Viv?"

"Um." I glance back down at the menu, reading off the first item I see. "Fried pickles and lots of ranch. Please." I gather the menus, placing them in her hands with a big smile as she walks away in disgust.

"So, what are the chances she spits in my food?" I take another sip of the frozen goodness.

"Very low, seeing as we ordered appetizers to share." My gaze bounces back to the bar where our waitress puts in our order. "She wouldn't dare screw up what she believes is her chance with all of this." He gestures with his hands down his body.

I nod in agreement. "You got me there. From now on, we will only order family-style dishes, just in case. You know, to protect me from the loogies I'm sure all your admirers want to give me."

"From now on? So there's a next time?"

"Yeah, I figured since you are obsessed with me, I would allow you the honor of seeing me at least one more time." This earns me an expression I can't quite decipher. It's a mixture of amusement, curiosity, and a bit of lust. It's times like these I wish more than ever that I wasn't such an overthinker.

He shakes the box. "Are you ready for this?"

"Absolutely. You don't know this, but I'm what some would call a puzzle master." I snatch the box from his hands and flip it open, revealing all the pieces to us.

"A master, you say. I'm ready to be wowed by your puzzle prowess." With a handful of pieces from the box, he sorts the corner pieces from the inner pieces. I watch him. To be more specific, I watch his hands. The same hands that held mine a few moments ago. I know they are rough from his landscaping job, but the way he picks up and moves the pieces is like pornographic art. It makes my mind wander further down the dirty rabbit hole it has been living in ever since New Year's Eve.

Our food arrives just as we finish finding all the outside pieces. We meticulously arrange the plates at the end of the table before we get to work on the border. It doesn't take long to figure out that Nate is a puzzle lover. The way he concentrates on the pieces and the excitement that takes over his entire body when he matches two parts or sections together is nothing short of adorable.

We continue putting our puzzle together while eating our delicious appetizers, dipping everything into the ranch. Soon we are on a roll placing piece after piece, section after section together until we have one puzzle piece left.

Nate slides it into my hands. "I want you to have all the glory."

His hand is still in mine as we hold the last piece between us. "Are you sure?"

He nods, letting go, leaving the piece in my hand. I admire our masterpiece—the princess perfection we created. That we spilled and wiped ranch off as inconspicuously as we could. With an exaggerated movement, I place the last piece in its spot. Nate lets outs a cry, "Victory!"

He chuckles, jumps off his bar stool, and walks over to mine. He takes my face in his hands and leans in for a victory kiss. When his soft lips graze mine, I snake my arm up his back to pull him closer as he takes my lower lip between his. Even with his lips cool from our multiple sangria swirls, my body heats under his touch.

A heady whine leaves my mouth as he pulls his lips off me. My eyes peek open to see why he stopped. Nate's admirer for the night stands beside our table. Well, his *other* admirer of the night.

She must have said something to us, but I was too caught up in the man before me to hear anything other than my pounding heart.

His hands fall off me as he reaches into his back pocket. I frown as he pulls out his wallet to hand her his credit card. I wait till she's gone before I pull him back. My lips find his jaw, and I brush light kisses across his skin and up to his ear. "How much you want to bet she did that on purpose?"

He huffs. "You think she'll leave her phone number on the receipt?"

My teeth nip at his earlobe as I whisper, "I would."

He sucks in another breath as his hands rest on my thighs, moving up and down. "Are you ready to go, or do you want to stay longer?"

"I'm ready."

We gather our things, waiting for Nate's card. Once he gets it back, he signs the receipt, chuckling as he shakes his head. "You were right." He picks it up to show me in bright purple handwriting, "Call me when you want to have fun. -Ashley," followed by a winky face. I roll my eyes as I throw some cash on the table for our tip, as he leaves the receipts behind.

As we make our way back to my apartment, our hands stay intertwined the entire drive and elevator ride up to my floor. Nate waits beside me, not saying a word as I unlock my door. I step backward, stopping to smile at him. "Do you—?"

"Yes," he blurts out before I can finish asking him to come inside. I waste no time stepping forward, wrapping my fingers in his shirt and yanking him closer. A jolt of excitement shoots over my skin as I tilt my head to stare into his eyes. He rubs the back of his neck like his nerves are boiling up to the surface. How can someone who looks like a Greek god be nervous about me?

With a small smile, I reach up, pulling his head down to meet me in the middle, pausing just before his lips touch mine. "Will you come inside and kiss me for a while?"

He answers by crushing his mouth to mine. His hands tangle in my hair, pressing me even closer to him. I walk backward through the door, and his tongue sweeps across my lower lips, begging for permission into my mouth. With the growing need to deepen the kiss, I open my mouth, granting his tongue the access it needs to dance with mine.

I struggle to take off my jacket without leaving his sweet kiss, causing us to knock into the arm of the couch. His arms wrap around my waist, pulling me closer to him, catching us before we fall. With his arms still snaked around me, every part of his hard body molds to mine. God, his body is lighting my core on fire. My hips circle into his, needing more pressure, more friction between us, needing to touch all of him.

A groan escapes Nate's lips, which does nothing to dampen my arousal. He lifts me onto the arm of the couch so I'm sitting with my legs around him, then brings his pelvis flush to mine.

I groan at the exquisite pressure as our breath becomes increasingly shallow.

His hands travel all over my body, caressing and massaging until he finds the hem of my shirt. Warm fingers snake underneath, and I gasp at his touch.

Nate pulls back a few inches to see my face, and his eyes are dark pools of desire and need. I reach down, placing my hands over his, helping him pull higher and higher until he takes my shirt off. He swipes his hands across my collarbones, descending until he reaches my breasts, hidden by my bra. His touch alone is enough for moisture to pool between my thighs. I want him. I want *all* of him tonight.

Moving to stand, I grab his hand and walk him to the middle of the couch. I press one last kiss to his mouth before I push him back, forcing him to sit on the middle cushion.

Steadying my nerves, I swallow down the rising need to hide my body. Instead, I let my desire for him take over. My breathing grows more ragged with every passing moment, and I bite my lip as his gaze wanders up my body. With trembling fingers, I reach behind my back, unclasping my bra. The straps fall off my shoulders, and I inch them down and off my arms. I drop the black lace that had covered me to the floor between us.

His eyes shine with desire as he remains still, watching me as I step closer to him. His chest rises more rapidly the closer I get. With my last step, I lean forward, grabbing his shoulders. I straddle his lap, trapping him between my legs.

The moment I'm seated on top of him, his control breaks. He darts his hands to the nape of my neck, bringing me closer as he coaxes my mouth open with his tongue. I sigh into him as he invades my mouth, and his hands wander down my back, sending shivers throughout my body.

He pulls back, leaving me panting, wanting his mouth back on mine. I open my eyes to see him scanning my face. Heat rises to my cheeks, and I turn my head to avoid his stare. Placing a hand on either side of my face, he turns me to face him. "Don't." He returns his lips to mine, giving me a soft, slow kiss before he pulls back again.

I wrap my hands around his wrists, keeping his hands on my face as we make eye contact.

"You are so beautiful."

A blush rises to my cheeks again, and his hands move down my neck to find my boobs. His fingers graze the tops, and the throbbing between my thighs strengthens, the intensity of my lust growing stronger as he palms my aching breasts with his rough hands.

A shy smile covers his face as he moves closer to kiss me again. Needing to feel more of him, I move my hands down his arms and across his chest and stomach until I reach the hem of his shirt. I drag it up, gliding up his naked chest as I do. Nate raises his arms, helping me remove the material.

Sinking my teeth into my bottom lip, I stare down at his bare skin. *My God, this man is gorgeous.* From his toned biceps to the divots in his collarbones that I want to lick. Hell, even the light dusting of hair across his chest has me sweating. I used to think chest hair was a turnoff, but on him, it's the most erotic thing I've ever seen.

I lean forward to kiss his shoulders and whisper, "You are the most beautiful man I've ever met" against his skin. A shiver ripples through his body as I scrape my teeth up his neck. "I mean it, Nate."

With that last sentence, we both give in to the burning desire. My hips roll against his pelvis, and I swear I've never felt pleasure so strong. He moans my name while grabbing my hips, increasing the pressure as I move against his hardening cock, our mouths colliding like lightning striking the earth.

"Fuck, Viv." He breathes between kisses. "I want more. I need more."

"Yes," I pant. "More."

With both hands on my ass, he stands, lifting us from the couch. His skin is flush against mine as he holds me, and I wrap my legs around his hips. With each step, a thrill of anticipation shoots through me. His heavy footsteps echo off the walls of the otherwise silent apartment, creating a soundtrack to our needy kiss as he walks us to my bedroom, never separating our lips.

I've never been carried by a man like this before. He stood and held me like I'm light as a feather. He made it seem so effortless. Hell, I've never been with a man who was strong enough to carry me.

The bed dips as he lays me down, kissing my neck and slowly licking and sucking every inch of my skin as he descends lower, giving my tits the same attention. He takes a nipple into his mouth, flicking his tongue across the stiff peak. A bolt of pleasure jolts through me, and I gasp. The soft curves of his lips turn up as he smiles against me, pressing a kiss in the middle of my cleavage before claiming the other with his mouth.

He bends, moving lower and lower, eyes locking on mine as his hands meet the waistband of my jeans. For a brief second, insecurity ripples through me, but the heat swirling in his blues douses those nerves, and I nod my head. He unbuttons them, and I lift my hips as he pulls them down my legs, leaving me in nothing but a tiny black lacy thong.

With a sharp inhale, I watch as Nate licks his lips as if I am something delicious. He crawls over me, bringing our lips together as our hands explore each other. My lashes flutter closed with the sweet sensation of him palming me through my underwear, his fingers rubbing the sensitive area between my legs.

He hisses as his hand dips under my panties, past the last barrier between us, finding the wetness pooling between my thighs. "You're drenched. Absolutely *fucking* soaked, Cherry, but not quite ready for me just yet."

My eyes roll back as he strokes up and down, coating his fingers in my arousal. I moan, clutching at his shoulders. Every stroke, touch, and ounce of friction drives me insane, winding me tighter and tighter, pushing me closer to the bliss just out of my reach.

Nate stops, taking his hand away, and my eyes shoot open.

"Why did you stop?"

"Because I want to show you what my tongue can do." With a hard kiss, he stands. Goose bumps pebble my skin as his hands move down my thighs before gripping them to pull my ass to the end of the bed. I gasp, and he lets out a deep, sinful chuckle. Moving to his knees, he stares into my eyes as his fingers wrap around my underwear. I bite my lip again, and he yanks them down. Wasting no more time, he suctions his mouth to that sweet spot between my legs. A shock of ecstasy shoots through me when the tip of his tongue hits the perfect spot.

The pads of his fingers bite into my thighs as he holds me spread apart, open for him to feast at my center. His tongue is like magic as he flicks, licks, and sucks at my clit. "You taste even better than I imagined. I could eat this pussy every day."

"I won't stop you," I choke out.

He laughs between my thighs, the warmth of his breath pushing me closer to bliss as he releases one of my legs, only to drag two fingers through my slick center before plunging in.

My back arches off the bed, and I lace my fingers through his hair, holding his face against my throbbing clit as my pleasure builds.

Every nerve tingles as my thighs quake, threatening to snap closed with each lap of his tongue perfectly timed with his fingers curling to hit my g-spot. "That's it, baby." He hums in satisfaction when my pussy tightens around him.

He never once lets up as he kneels before me while I ride his face to find release.

I've never been with anyone who bothered to put my pleasure first. Who not only enjoyed but loved seeing how they affected me.

I call out his name, panting as my orgasm crashes over me in continuous waves. "Nate, oh my God." My whole body floods with warmth.

He doesn't stop his exquisite torture until my orgasm has stopped. Nate's hungry gaze never leaves mine as my entire body shudders with pleasure. He groans against my center, the vibrations causing waves of aftershock to hit my sensitive clit.

A small laugh vibrates from my throat as I lift onto my elbow. "Holy fuck, Nate."

"Did my tongue live up to its reputation?" He stands, revealing how turned on he is.

I move to sit at the side of the bed. "You could say that." My voice is raspy, which makes that sensual mouth of his turn up into a wicked grin.

I reach forward to palm the erection pushing through his jeans. He hisses, tipping his head back. I take that as my cue to unbutton his pants, pushing them down his strong, muscular thighs. Climbing to my feet, I tangle my fingers in his hair as I guide him to my face. After a quick tease of his lips, I lower to my knees before him.

"Vivian, you don't—" His words stop when my tongue slides up the prominent bulge in his navy-blue boxer briefs. The want and need radiating off him are undeniable as I press a kiss on the tip of his still-covered length.

I pull down the last barrier between us as we look into each other's eyes, smiling. I brush my fingers over his twitching abs as I take in his thickness and length while my mouth waters. It's large without being terrifying or a threat to my cervix. I've never wanted to be on my knees for a man, but Nate isn't like anyone else. He is beautiful. Hell, his dick is the best-looking penis I've ever seen.

A large vein courses over the length of his shaft to the head of his cock, accentuating his erection. His cock curves up in a way that guarantees to hit all the right places inside me.

Biting my lip, I move closer, grasping him in my hands. His breathing turns husky as my hand moves up and down in a circling motion.

The sound of his breath catching is the most erotic music to my ears, and my need builds again. I lean a little closer, bringing his wet tip to my lips. With a flick of my tongue, I swipe across the top, circling, savoring how he tastes. Needing more of him, I suck him deeper into my mouth as I continue to pump. The pad of my tongue strokes down his length as I take him as far as I can. A groan escapes his mouth before he whispers through gritted teeth. "Fuck. So good. You are so good."

I continue to work on his pleasure, sucking and licking every inch I can until he reaches down, scooping me up. He pushes me back onto the bed, landing with me as his mouth finds mine in an urgent demand for my kiss.

His lips move from my mouth down my chin to my neck.

"I need you, Nate." I tangle my fingers in his hair, clutching the curls near his scalp, pinning his face to my body.

"What do you want?" He breathes into my skin between nips on the sensitive skin between my shoulder and neck.

I skim my hand down his back and around his hips, not stopping until I'm holding his heavy cock in my hand. "I want you to stop playing and fuck me already, Nate," I plead.

A groan rumbles through his chest. His eyes beam down at me, asking a silent question.

A strangled voice rips from my throat as I answer, "I'm clean and on the pill."

Without another word, his velvety soft tip is out of my hand as his knees nudge my legs apart. With one last slow, soft kiss to my lips, he presses his hard length into my opening, letting out a hiss, not stopping until he is fully seated inside me.

I adjust to his girth, allowing the stretching pain to turn into pleasure. We're both already panting, the air thick with arousal and need.

"Tell me what you need," he groans, moving his hips, sliding in and out of me with a slow, sensual burn.

"Deeper," I beg, wrapping my ankles around his waist and pulling him even further inside me.

He hooks one of my thighs in the crook of his arm, sinking deeper and deeper with every thrust. "*Fuck*, you feel so good gripping my cock with your tight pussy."

My head rolls back as I lift my hips to meet his every thrust. The pressure building in my core grows to an almost unbearable extreme, on the verge of pain as I grind my clit on him. I don't want this to end. I want it to last forever. As the walls inside my pussy contract, Nate slides a hand between us, pressing his fingers to my throbbing nub. His fingers drive back and forth, up and down, until I am writhing beneath him. Nate's pace picks up as he rides out my orgasm until his release follows.

He pulsates inside me until he spills every drop and leans down, giving me a passionate kiss. We stay like that for a few minutes, him inside me as our tongues tangle with delight until we're breathless.

Silence rings through the air when he rolls off me. I turn to face him, finding him on his back with his eyes closed, his chest moving up and down rapidly as he attempts to regain his composure. I laugh.

A grin breaks across his face as he rolls onto his side to face me. "So."

"So."

"I'm not sure if you're aware, but I really like you. I mean, reeeeally like you."

Another laugh slips out of me. "Ditto."

His blue eyes sparkle as he tilts my chin to find my mouth. He mutters, "And that tongue is exquisite."

I slam my hands into his chest, roaring with laughter as he falls onto his back. We continue this teasing game until we fall asleep with our legs tangled up in each other.

Chapter Ten

*S*lam.

The sound of a door closing in the distance startles me awake. My eyes drift open to him.

Nate.

The date with Nate.

The mind-blowing sex with Nate.

His warmth fills my entire body as he tugs me closer to him. A stupid smile overtakes my face. I find his hand and move it to lie across my chest, and I thread my fingers through his with a rush of happiness.

Never has a man made me feel this way. Never have I cuddled with someone through the night. And never, ever has a man given me not one but two orgasms.

I bring our laced hands up to my face, kissing the inside of his palm. A sigh sounds from behind me, followed by the tingling of my skin as his lips brush against my back and shoulders, finding their way to my neck.

"Good morning," he mutters between kisses across my skin. It's the simplest yet most sensual sensation in the entire world. I reach behind me to hold his head, his lips on my neck as my ass moves against his growing length.

His hand on my chest grazes my breast as he moves lower to grab my hip. The tips of his fingers dig into my skin in the most painfully delicious way. He holds me in place, grinding his hardening cock against my cheeks.

He pants a laugh in my ear. "Do you want me as much as I want you?"

Breathless, I manage, "Yes...I need you to fuck me."

He reaches between my legs, coating his fingers in the slick evidence of how ready I am for him. Fingers teasing at my entrance, he takes his time, savoring every moment until my bedroom door bursts open.

"Hey, Vivi, I wanted to know..." Sutton pauses, her smile growing as large as her eyes as she takes in the sight of Nate and me naked. *Completely* naked, barely covered by pale lilac sheets pooling at our waists. "Fuck. My bad." Slapping her hand over her eyes, she continues to stand there.

Untangling myself from Nate, I pull the sheet up to our necks. I clear my throat and mutter, "Hey, Sut?"

Still covering her eyes, she answers, "Yeah?"

"Can you leave the room, please?" I ask, not taking my eyes off her.

"Oh, shit, yeah. Sorry, guys. Sorry!" She spins on her heels, closing the door behind her.

I groan, slipping down under the sheets. "Oh my God. Did that just happen?"

Nate slides himself underneath the sheets to look at me. His face is nothing but happiness, with smile lines crinkling around his eyes. "Yeah, I think it did."

"On a scale of one to ten, how mortified should I be?"

"Vivian, don't hide from me." He pulls my hands off my face before pressing a kiss to my lips. "I would say ten, but since there are two of us, we can split it and each take 50 percent of the embarrassment, okay?"

"Is it wrong that I am more upset she got to see you naked than I am that we got interrupted?" I bury my head in his warm chest.

His body vibrates with his laugh. "Really? Cause I am dying from needing you over here."

One of my hands moves down his chest with a feathering touch. I graze his skin until I find his still-hard erection. Squeezing, I wrap my hands around the thickness, pumping him up and down. My wrist rotates between fast and slow. Tilting my head up, I watch his face as my hand brings him a torturous pleasure.

"Fuck..." He grabs my hand to stop me. Before I can question why, I am being hauled on top of him. My slickness glides up and down his length as he pushes and pulls on my hips.

My palms fall to his chest, nails digging in as I ride him, causing the pleasure to build every time my clit rubs across his hard dick from the shaft to the tip, wanting, needing him inside me. I stop, holding still as I turn my head toward the door.

"What's wrong? Do you not want to?" His voice is calm, and at that moment, if I said no, I know he would stop with no hesitation.

"Hey, Sutton?" I yell over my shoulder.

"Yeah?" she shouts back, confirming that she hasn't left.

I turn my focus back to Nate's perfect body, dragging my eyes up to his face. Tilting my chin over my shoulder, I shout, "Can you come back in a few hours?"

Nate's cock twitches between my legs.

Sutton's laugh echoes through the apartment before the front door opens and closes.

With the sound, Nate snakes his hands up my back, crossing to grab my shoulders as he pulls me down into a kiss. We stay like this for a few minutes, making out while rubbing against each other in the most teasing and tortuous way imaginable. When a moan slips out of Nate's mouth, he loosens his grip on me, sliding his hands back down to cup my ass.

He lifts me, and grasping his cock in one hand, he rubs the tip along my entrance before pushing into me in one smooth, swift motion. With long, fast strokes, his cock pushes in and out of me as he holds me in place. Needing to control the pace, I grab his hands, pulling them around to my breasts. I sit up and begin grinding my pussy into him, circling up and down, back and forth, until I can't take the intensity building inside me.

As if he senses my need for him to bring me to ecstasy, Nate flips us over. Never moving from inside me, he slides one hand between my legs, moving his fingers back and forth over my clit while pounding into me with such intensity that I have to lift my palms against the headboard to stop myself from slamming into it.

I moan his name as I come all over his dick. As he continues to fuck me with such raw abandon, another orgasm begins building before the first even finishes.

"Fuck," he says in a low growl as sweat glistens on his forehead. He pulls out, only to slam back into me, causing my second climax to take over. Not stopping, he digs his fingers into my hip, riding out my orgasm with me until his hits. His teeth scrape against my neck as he throbs inside me. He doesn't stop his relentless fucking until every bit of his cum is inside me.

With another kiss, he pulls out. Our hands continue to explore as we lie beside each other, exchanging slow, lazy kisses.

Finally getting up, I head to the bathroom to pee and clean up. After quickly brushing my teeth, I walk back into my bedroom, pulling out a pair of underwear and an oversized T-shirt. I put them on as Nate takes his turn in the bathroom to wash up.

As I hope to return to bed, Nate meets me with a massive grin. "You are so beautiful." He presses a kiss into the sensitive part of my neck. "And when you come, it's earth-shattering."

"Ditto" is all I manage to reply.

We continue to revel in each other's bodies for another few hours until Sutton texts, asking if the coast is clear. She wants to come by and talk about "the hot piece of ass" she saw in my bed this morning. Before he leaves, Nate and I plan to go out again this Wednesday for dinner.

I take a quick shower and am just stepping out when Sutton bursts into the bathroom.

"Oh. My. Fucking. God," she screeches. Her eyes are enormous as she jumps up and down. While wrapping a towel around my body,

I dry off as she begins to pelvic thrust into the air, chanting, "Vivian got the dicky in" over and over.

"Shut up, Sut." I push past her, laughing, to throw on some clean sweats.

We plop down on opposite ends of the couch, facing each other. Draped over the back of the couch is a blanket that we both pull over our laps. I meet Sut's obnoxious stare, knowing the conversation coming my way.

Sutton calms her face, looking at me as seriously as she can. "So, Vivian, do you have anything you would like to share with me?"

I move my head from side to side, looking down at the black-and-gray chenille blanket while picking at the balls of pilling fabric. "Nah. Not really."

My favorite cheetah print throw pillow flies toward me. "Liar," she shouts the moment it hits me.

My mouth drops open but then quickly closes because I want to tell her everything, and she knows it.

"Spill it," she demands, her eyes growing larger with each moment.

I blow out a long breath. "Best. Sex. Of. My. Life."

She squeals, leaning in for more information.

"Not only did he make me come each time, but I had back-to-back orgasms."

Her jaw drops. "Fuck! Like two in a row?"

I nod, raising my eyebrows.

"Wait, so the man is sexy *and* can actually please you in the bedroom? He is a damn unicorn."

I let my head fall against the side of the couch. "He is too good to be true, right? Like, no man can be this perfect?"

"I don't know, but I say ride that man as long as you can."

I give her a pointed stare and say, "I'm kind of mad at you for this morning."

Sutton rolls her eyes and swats her hand in front of her face. "Oh, for walking in on you about to bone? Get over it." When I don't respond, her face falls a little. She scoots closer to me and pulls me in for a hug. "Wait, are you seriously upset with me?"

"Kind of. Maybe. No. It's just that...I have nothing or anyone for myself, and when you walk in looking like you...It's stupid, I know." I peer down again. I focus all my attention on the blanket, picking at some invisible lint. Shame boils under my skin at my insecurity.

"What? Vivi, I don't think he ever took his eyes off you. Hell, I know it. 'Cause didn't he bring you to pound town right after I walked in?"

"Yeah. I know it's dumb, but my insecurity is unavoidable." My eyes blur with tears. I squeeze them closed, tipping my head toward the ceiling, hoping I don't break down.

"Stop thinking like that. You are freaking amazing. And hella hot. Did he give you any reason to think this?"

"No. It was actually the opposite," I tell her, confessing about our date at Puzzles and the server with her shameless flirting.

She gives me another bear hug. "See? You're just getting into your head. Don't let your insecurities push away the orgasm-giving man. Okay?"

I laugh, wiping a tear away from under my eye. "Okay."

"Okay. Now, bitch, I want you to go into extreme and nasty detail about everything he did to you. Or at least pull up some porn to show me because I need to experience it all." In typical Sutton fashion, she helps me go from crying to laughing over X-rated videos in a matter of minutes.

Chapter Eleven

T ime seems to play tricks on me as I count the days, hours, and minutes until I can see Nate again. He plans to pick me up from work on Wednesday so we don't have to waste time not seeing each other. But time, the little bitch it is, is dragging in every possible way. My days at work have felt like weeks as the anticipation of seeing him continues to build, causing me to be spacey in the most inconvenient ways.

On Monday, I forgot to cancel a meeting for Mr. T. So when the contractors started calling, furious that he didn't show up for a planning meeting, it was my ass that got chewed. Rightfully so, though.

On Tuesday, I hit one thousand copies on a twenty-page document instead of the intended ten that I needed. I was blissfully unaware of my mishap until Hadlee stormed across the ample office space, weaving in and out of the cubicles and seating areas to reach my desk and start screaming at me about using all the paper and toner. And I quote, "Earth to Bitchian." It's a play on my name that she thinks is witty.

It's not.

Then she went on, ranting and raving about how I have no respect for her time since, as the receptionist, she needs to print and blah, blah, blah. After the first minute of her standing there, I stopped paying attention. Instead, I focused on her stomping her incredibly high heels, which I assume cost her a whole paycheck, as she berated me for five minutes.

I want to say that was the worst of it, but I can't. Later that day, I got so caught up in texting Nate about his day that I might have caused a little, tiny fire in the break room.

It was a freak accident. Involving popcorn.

After putting the bag into the microwave, I closed the door and got a text from Nate, explaining to me in detail about the crazy client he is currently working with coming out to the lawn and attempting to flirt with each and every member of the crew. The woman even requested that they all work shirtless so she could admire them from afar.

While reading the texts he was sending in, I must have pressed something crazy on the microwave because the next thing I knew, smoke was billowing out of it, and the horrible smell of burned popcorn permeated the entire floor.

By the time Wednesday rolled around, I was a mess and exhausted from all the minor mistakes I kept making. But I was excited to see Nate. I pull my hair up into a simple yet stylish high pony and slip on a yellow floral dress that ties on the side, along with knee-high brown boots, giving myself a little pep talk.

"You are smart. You are sexy. You are Vivian, and you got that dicky in." As dumb as Sutton's little chant was, I can't get it out of my head. It is now a part of me. Vivian and the dicky in.

With a few swipes of mascara after curling my lashes, I'm out the door, ready to get work over with so I can see the man who has infiltrated my every waking moment.

The drive to work is short and sweet. The morning drags on but isn't full of fuckups on my part. So that's something.

Mr. Tillan and I spend most of the day on conference calls with clients, discussing their wants and needs for the future projects we are taking on. I barely have time to go to the bathroom as I focus on taking notes and setting things up to move along the projects' planning periods.

After hours of the same thing, Mr. T lies his head face down on his desk, grumbling, "Ugh, Vivian. I don't know about you, but today was...Well, shit. I don't even know how else to describe it. That's how exhausted I am."

I shake my head, chuckling at his dramatics. "You took the wordless-ness right out of my mouth."

"Go home, kid. Get some sleep. Lord knows we both need it." He lifts himself off the desk, stands, and grabs his gray jacket off the back of his chair. Sighing, he gives me an exhausted wave before walking out the door.

I return to my desk to find three texts from Nate. "Shit," I mutter as I open them up to read.

> *Hey, Viv. I should be there around five. See you then.*

I glance at the time on my phone. My eyes grow wide. It's five thirty.

> *Here. Just let me know when you're done.*

Then the last text.

> *I'm coming up to your floor because you're either swamped and don't have your phone, or the zombie apocalypse started, and you have already turned. Or you're ghosting me. Is it wrong of me to say I crossed my fingers for any of the following but the ghosting?*

"Fuck!" My heart speeds up with panic as my fingers fly to send him a text.

> *Nate! Oh my God, I'm sorry. I was busy without my phone. I'm so sorry. No zombies and not ghosting you. Please tell me you don't hate me.*

I send a silent prayer to whatever spirits or gods can help me ensure he isn't mad at me.

With my purse and phone in hand, I head toward the elevator, freezing when I hear Nate's voice. I don't see him anywhere. But that is him speaking, or at least I think it is.

I walk down the hallway, following the sound of his voice toward the break room. Butterflies flap around in my stomach at the sight of him laughing. He is the picture of relaxed as he leans up against the counter where my popcorn disaster happened just the day before.

In the doorway, I admire him for a few moments. Dressed in a dark, almost royal-blue sweater, my heart melts. My favorite color. He's wearing my favorite color.

Does he remember me telling him that? If so, did he do it on purpose, as I did with today's yellow dress and the top from the other night? The sweater clings to his body, muscles shining through to show every definition. I take in his low-slung jeans, which rest on his hips, reminding me of what lies beneath them.

I'm so caught up in looking at him, at thinking about his toned body, that I don't give any attention to the person he is talking to. He lets out another small laugh, his head turning in my direction. When he sees me in the doorway, a bigger and brighter smile graces his face. "Vivian."

Before I can open my mouth to reply, I hear her voice. *Hadlee.* "Oh, hey, Vivian. I hope you don't mind, but Natey and I were just catching up since you left him waiting forever."

Frozen in place, I shift my eyes to the side where Hadlee is sitting on the table across from him. Her pencil skirt hiked up her toned thighs.

My face falls as my eyes flicker between them. "I-I just got your texts. I'm sorry." Turning around, I walk back into the hallway, speeding up as I make my way to the elevator.

Nate calls after me, "Viv, stop. Wait up."

I don't. I press the button multiple times, trying to will them to open.

He grabs my hand, pulling me in his direction. "Vivian, stop." Like the sea's dark depths, his blue eyes plead with me to talk to him. "What's wrong?"

"Nothing. What was going on in there with her?"

His forehead crinkles as he looks back to the break room where Hadlee is leaning on the doorframe, smirking as she watches us. "Nothing. She was just talking to me while I waited for you. I promise it was nothing. You know I don't like her like that."

I bite my lip, peeking over his shoulder to determine whether her sneering ass is still staring, which she is. "Promise?"

He brings his hands up to my face, cupping my cheeks and forcing me to look up at him. His lips barely brush mine as he whispers, "Promise," before locking his lips on mine with a tender, reassuring kiss.

Seconds later, he pulls his lips off mine and laces our fingers together, pulling me into the elevator. We step to the back before he pushes me into the wall. I press my hands into the cold metal wall behind me as his mouth is soon on mine, pressing into me with an all-consuming kiss. His tongue licks along my seam, coaxing me to open. I greedily let him in, sucking and nipping at him as I do.

He groans into me as his hands find their way to my backside to palm my cheeks. He kneads my skin as if he's trying to memorize me with his hands.

Pawing at me, he takes everything he can until the elevator ding warns us that our private ride is over. The doors open to the lobby, and Nate takes hold of my hand. Lacing our fingers, he brings my hand up to his mouth, placing a gentle kiss on it.

My heart stops at how intimate that moment seems. More intimate than making out like a couple of horny teenagers a minute ago. That was pure lust. This...this is the beginning of love.

Nate opens the truck door for me, helping me in before walking around the corner to his side. Suddenly, I'm full of nerves. This feels real—like it could be something special.

Nate buckles up before handing me his phone to put on some driving tunes. Once again, I'm flabbergasted that he would give me his phone without hesitation or concern. As Sutton said, he truly is a unicorn. I put on the sweet melodies of Harry Styles, but when I look over, I catch Nate rolling his eyes.

"What?" I demand.

"Nothing," he says, staring at the road.

I narrow my eyes until I'm peering at him through slits. "Spit it out, Natey," I mimic in Hadlee's voice as I use her annoying nickname for him.

His head spins to face me. Now I have his attention. "Natey? Really?"

"What, do you not like that name?"

"Stop it, Viv. You know I don't. And if you have yet to notice, I only have eyes for you. From the moment I looked at you sitting alone, I was done for."

"Sure. Sure. That's what they all say."

"Who are *they*? Are there other men? Tell me now, because maybe they have a club I can join where we all discuss how you're the perfect woman."

I push him into his door. "Don't be an asshole."

Laughing, he says, "Okay, I wouldn't join, because I would be too jealous. You know, like you with Hadlee."

"Oh my God. You are the worst." Covering my face with my hands, I lean forward, refusing to acknowledge his speaking. "How can someone who looks like a picture-perfect gladiator be so annoying?"

"It is a gift from the gods." His fingers brush my thigh as he slips a hand between my legs, dancing on my skin. His touch sends a shot of electricity to my core. I dart my tongue out, licking along my lips, but I keep my head down as my breathing picks up. He moves his fingers higher up my leg, sliding under my dress as he tortures me with his teasing caress.

I sit up straight, trying to keep it together. Still covering my face with my hands, I'm careful not to let him know how much I'm enjoying myself.

The callouses on his fingertips make me gasp whenever they hit the sensitive flesh outside my panties. Subconsciously, I spread my thighs, giving him more room to continue his exploration. He cups me through my underwear, drifting his hand up and down with on-and-off pressure, and my panties soak through in seconds.

I sink my teeth into my bottom lip as I bite down, trying not to moan as my arms fall, uncovering my face. I keep my eyes squeezed shut as I move my left hand to find his arm. The soft, almost silky fabric of his sweater glides beneath my palm until I reach his hand. I bring it up higher until I can dip his finger into my panties. As I push his hand down, he lets me control him. I place his fingers in my slick folds, moving them up and down until they're drenched in my arousal before I move his middle finger to press inside me.

A moan slips from my lips as he takes over, moving his finger in and out of me, pressing the base of his palm into my clit. A hiss slips from my lips, and it's all the encouragement he needs to continue using his hand to torture me with pleasure.

He adds a second finger, curling them and pressing against my walls. I grip the ends of my dress as his hand brings me to my peak.

Everything inside me tightens as my orgasm crests. My back bows, and I grab his shoulder, squeezing down as he keeps finger fucking me until I'm finished.

Breathlessly, I open my left eye to peek at him.

In my post-orgasm haze, I take in every inch of him. He continues to face the road, jaw tight, but his breathing is rapid as his chest rises and falls at a gallop. I gaze down, the strain in his jeans growing as his finger lazily moves out of me, gliding up and down my wetness. With one hand, he turns the wheel, pulling into a driveway as a garage door opens.

He waits until the garage door closes behind us before he turns to me, pulling his hand out of my panties. I watch with rapt attention as he brings his fingers to his face, sticking them in his mouth and sucking off every bit of my moisture. Closing his eyes, he moans before he pops them out. "So fucking delicious."

It's the dirtiest thing I've ever seen or heard, but fuck does it turn me on. Unbuckling, I move over the center console to straddle him.

His hands fall to my hips, pushing me into his hard erection. I bring my mouth to his neck, my tongue tracing up to his jaw until he shudders beneath me.

Unable to control myself any longer, I unbuckle his pants as he lifts his hips to slide his jeans and underwear down until there's nothing between us. I reach to palm his hard length, working him into a frenzy of need.

With his thick cock in my hand, I lift, lining his tip up with my opening before lowering myself onto him. I take him inch by inch until he fills me up. As soon as our lips touch, I move my hips up and ride him. Our kiss deepens with every thrust. His breath fills my mouth as I pick up the pace, bouncing up and down his length. Controlling every moment of his pleasure with my speed and force.

A growl escapes his lips, and I take that as my cue to up my game. His head dips back in pleasure as I circle my hips in a continued assault. I press my chest to his, dropping my head into the space between his head and shoulder, whispering, "You feel so good inside me."

This lights a fire in him as a moan erupts from his throat. He grips my hips, taking control, holding me still as he slams into me from underneath. The pain and pleasure mix into an irresistible sensation I never want to end.

I move my hand between my thighs until I find my sensitive peak and rub. The back-and-forth motion as Nate fucks me hard, sliding his cock in and out of me, has my second orgasm of the night shattering through me.

The walls of my pussy contract, squeezing his dick until he erupts, pulsing inside me. His orgasm ripples through him, and he pulls me down, pressing inside me to spill every drop as he rides out his pleasure.

We're both panting, staring into each other. His blue eyes shine with a glazed-over, postorgasmic bliss, and I can't help but want more.

I take his bottom lip into my mouth, savoring his taste. A bright smile dances across his face as he closes his eyes, sighing in what sounds like contentment.

Inside, the warmth and intensity of my feelings bubble up, all for this man who makes me smile, have fun, and fucks me like no other man ever has. Within seconds, I dissolve into laughter, Nate following suit.

We sit there in his truck, doubling over in a fit of giggles to the point of tears as we talk about how we are both acting like a couple of horny teenagers. The shaking of our bodies as we giggle over hyped-up sex drives doesn't help disprove our point while I'm sprawled over his lap, with him still seated inside me.

Every shift of our bodies causes arousal to stir again. And before I know it, we are starting round two. We indulge in each other in a frenzy of erotic gratification.

When we're both satiated, Nate jogs around the truck to open my door. He helps me out before pulling me into him for a slow, tender kiss.

Pulling my hand, he leads me to a door. "I hope you know this was not the date I planned." He pauses, spinning to face me. "I didn't mean that I didn't like what just happened, because I did. I *really* did, Viv. There are no words to describe how much I loved that..."

I playfully slap my hand over his face, cutting him off.

"Nate. I get it. You didn't plan to hump me in your truck on our third date tonight." I remove my hand, pushing him forward. "Besides, everyone knows that is fifth date stuff."

He shakes his head as the left corner of his mouth pulls up, revealing his dimple. That damn dimple makes my legs weak and my heart flutter every time I see it.

We walk through the garage door, and a subtle aroma of vanilla and woods fills the air. With a deep inhale, I breathe it in. It's an instant comfort. It smells like Nate. I haven't bothered to ask where we are, but I'm pretty sure it's his house. As we step in, my eyes dart around the room, taking in a large mudroom with a bench and coat rack above. Nate leads me into the house, and I brush my fingers over the clean gray walls.

We stop at the kitchen; he observes me as I make my way around the room, touching and studying as I go. He lets me stroll the hall, roaming from room to room as I soak up his environment, all while he stands a few feet behind me. Without making a noise or questioning my curiosity, he lets me invade every room without hesitation.

His home is clean and organized. But also has a very lived-in atmosphere to it. The large living room has an oversized sectional with a chaise that's perfect for cuddling up on a lazy Sunday. A giant flat-screen television hangs on the wall above a white brick fireplace, directly across from the couch. I throw myself down on the cushions and sigh from relaxation. It's plush and deep, and just the right amount of worn in.

Jumping to my feet, I move down the hallway. The walls are blank except for a few family photos. Happiness and a tinge of jealousy take over my thoughts as I study all his framed images. From his teenage years to more recently as an adult, the love he and his family have for one another shines through clear as day.

Behind the first door, I find a small bathroom. I inspect a little more than a brief glimpse before carrying on, Nate still trailing me with insane ease. Opening the next door, I find Nate's bedroom, complete with a massive bed that must be a California king. I hop onto his bed face down. A small chuckle sounds from behind me. Not answering, I plant my nose on the first pillow I can find and inhale the sweet essence of Nate.

I know, once again, my habit of smelling him is creepy, but I can't help it. His scent is irresistible to me. Hell, everything about the man is enticing. From his face to his perfect penis, I cannot get enough.

With one last deep sniff of his pillow, I roll across the bed, clutching the fluffy bag to my chest. Nate catches me just before I fall to the ground. He holds on to my waist, smirking while asking, "You almost finished, little bloodhound?"

"Maybe, maybe not." I press his pillow between us. "I guess that all depends on what you have hiding in the last room."

His eyebrow quirks up as he walks backward, pulling on the pillow I'm clinging to with him. "Do you want to see my deepest, darkest secret?"

A giddiness takes over me as I bounce out of the room. "More than anything."

When we reach the door, Nate stills, his face becoming serious. "Promise me you won't tell anyone what you see in this room, okay?"

My mind races with all the theories of what could be in there. At first, I thought it was an office or a home gym based on his lickable body. But now I'm leaning toward a sex dungeon or the room where I'm to be murdered. Fingers crossed for a kinky fetish.

But then he opens the door, and I scan the room. "I can honestly say this is not what I was expecting."

He bites his lip as his eyes follow me, looking nervous for the first time tonight. He didn't look like this when I rifled through the other rooms. He seemed amused by it. But here, he appears vulnerable.

Drawings cover the walls. They range from pictures of dragons and unicorns to flowers and families. Over at the tall desk table, I lift myself onto the bar stool like a chair. Placing the pillow on my lap, I notice a black notebook. I still just before opening it, glancing at Nate. He gives me a curt nod, which I take as permission to view inside.

Beneath the cover are more drawings. This time they aren't the cute and cuddly creatures he has on the walls. Inside the book are erotic fantasies that make my insides churn with desire.

I am in awe of the attention to detail in every picture. Every curve and every muscle is defined and showcased with skillful precision. I swivel around in the chair to face him once more. "These are all yours?"

"Yep." His gaze focuses on the floor as he shifts on his heels.

"I...I am in awe."

He lifts his gaze to meet mine, a soft smile appearing on his lips as he asks, "Really?"

I drop his pillow on the floor as I walk over to him. Putting my hands on his cheeks, I cup his face. "You." I press a chaste kiss on his lips. "Are." A second kiss. "Amazingly." Another kiss. "Talented."

He exhales as if he was holding his breath this whole time.

"I'm serious, Nate. Have you ever thought about being an artist, or is it something you like to do for fun?"

Nate goes to close the book before taking my hand to walk me back into the living room. We sit on opposite sides of the couch, facing each other.

"It's both, actually," he voices after a few minutes of us sitting in silence.

I don't answer, waiting for him to elaborate. He gets up again, strolling to the kitchen. He digs through the fridge, gathers food, and walks to the French doors attached to his dining area. Hands full of food and ingredients, he opens one door and steps outside.

I follow him out and am immediately hit with the beauty of Nate's patio and backyard. Flowers are blooming everywhere, which is insane, considering it is winter. He has a pergola covering a fire pit, with wicker chairs circling it.

"Wow," I whisper to myself as I walk to follow a stone path that leads to where Nate is setting up a grill. Wrapping my arms around myself, I rub my hands up my arms, trying to stay warm in the chilly night air. Once I reach him, my face must show my complete shock and awe at the breathtaking surroundings because he takes one look at me, and his face lights up in delight.

"Do you like it?" he questions as he turns on the gas to the grill.

"Are you kidding? This place is magical." I spin in circles with dramatic effect. "I love every part. Did you do it all?"

"Yep. Well, me and my dad."

"Well, aren't you a jack-of-all-trades?"

"I dabble."

Moving closer to him, I place my chest on his arm. I graze his skin with my tits as I lift onto my toes to whisper in his ear. "You can dabble me anytime."

A small exhale from his nose lets me know he did note my boob graze and suggestive wording. Inside, I am doing a little victory dance to celebrate my achievement.

Grinning, he shakes his head. As he reaches for the tongs sitting on the counter to the left of us, his hand sweeps across my breast, not just when he goes to grab the tongs but also when he brings his hand back toward the grill. My body stills at his touch. That cheeky bastard is playing the game better than me. With the tongs in his hand, he places some raw chicken and steak onto the sizzling rack.

Watching him grill our dinner fills me with more awe for this man. "You know what you are?" I ask.

He glances at me with a slight tilt of his head.

"You are a damn unicorn." Sighing, I fall back into the hammock he oh so kindly pulled over for me a few minutes prior.

Confusion washes over his face. "A what?"

"You heard me." I throw my arms out to my sides. "A *damn* unicorn."

He leans against the counter. "Pray tell, madam, how am I a unicorn?"

A bubble of happiness and desire forms in my stomach as he talks to me in a Southern accent. I didn't think I could like this man any more than I already do, but then he goes and speaks to me in my native tongue of dumbass. A wave of emotions floods through my veins. He is the person for me. I feel it in my bones, somewhere on a molecular level. I know he and I are soulmates. Twin flames.

With a big, dumb, goofy smile, I peer into his eyes across the small distance between us. Putting up my hand, I count on my fingers. "He can draw, garden, build things with his bare hands, cook, and give chicks multiple orgasms. You are what some call a unicorn, or in layman's terms, the total package."

A flush grows along his cheeks, covering his face with a coy expression. "A unicorn, you say." He snickers to himself before continuing, "Well, it is pretty magical how horny you always make me."

My jaw drops at him in shock before I bust out laughing. I laugh so hard that I topple out of the hammock, falling face-first into the grass, which doesn't help because it makes my laughing grow more intense. With my vision blurring with tears, I stare at where Nate was standing before I fell to find he isn't there.

I don't see him anywhere, but I hear him. I follow the noise to find him rolling on the ground, grabbing his crotch.

Wiping away my tears as I attempt the impossible—catching my breath—I ask, "What are you doing?"

Gasping for air as he rolls around, he answers, "I'm about to pee myself."

So much for my composure. Another round of cackles hits me harder than the first as I watch him struggle not to piss himself.

Able to keep a morsel of self-restraint, I get up and move over to him. Beside him, I pull my legs in a crisscross applesauce position. He is the epitome of an idiot writhing around on the ground, trying to keep control of his bladder. A handsome idiot, but an idiot, nonetheless.

Before I know it, the words slip out of me. "You make me crazy happy."

He freezes as his laughter dies down. He stops rolling back and forth, stops holding his manhood, and pushes off the ground to match my posture, resting in an identical position. "You make me so fucking happy, Viv. Whenever I'm with you, I smile more than ever. And I come harder than I ever have."

I push him back down. "Why do you have to ruin everything with your nastiness?"

Forearms braced on the ground, he grins up at me. "You love my special flavor of nasty. Especially my mouth and all the tricks it can do."

"God, you're such a perv." Once up, I brush my butt off before offering my hands to help pull Nate up.

His hand folds around mine as he pops up to his feet, pulling me into him. With a quick hug before pushing me back, he commands, "Now go get us some drinks from the fridge while I run to the bathroom before I piss myself."

I reach out, swatting his ass as I head back into the house. It takes me less than five minutes to whip up a pitcher of frozen margaritas for us. I had no problem finding all the supplies and ingredients because Nate is an organized freak.

I head to the living room with two beer mugs full of frozen tequila goodness, queuing up Netflix and settling in. My body sinks into the cushions as I cuddle up on the comfy sectional with a blanket from the back and a pillow from Nate's bed.

The rest of the night is full of jokes, drinks, eating food Nate grilled, and snuggling on the couch while watching a movie.

As I drift off to sleep, Nate asks me to stay the night. Against every fiber of my being, I decide to go home. The ride back to the office is quick, so I take advantage of every minute with him, sitting curled up on his side as he drives.

It's a struggle, but I force myself to wake up enough to drive home. I don't even register until I'm parking in the garage at my apartment that I still have Nate's pillow, now sitting in my lap. Bringing the pillow up to my face, I breathe in his scent again. The comforting smell washes over me and stays with me as I go to sleep holding the pillow to my chest.

Chapter Twelve

I silence my alarm, lying back in bed to look at my phone. A new text from Nate pops up on my screen, and I shimmy against the mattress.

> *Good morning, Cherry.*

As I type out my reply, my heart leaps.

> Good morning, Unicorn.

His response is instant.

> *Did you sleep well?*

I take a quick picture of myself, pressing my face into his pillow and smiling like an idiot.

> Oh yeah, I slept like a coma patient.

> *You're welcome.*

> *Excuse me? For what?*

For granting you the use of my pillow, laced with the magical, intoxicating scent of me…

> *A little full of yourself, don't you think?*

Says the girl who stole my favorite pillow.

> *Stole? You shoved it into my arms and made me take it home.*

Liar, liar, pants on fucking fire.

I prop myself up against my headboard, laughing.

> *I hate you.*

Nope, more lies. Admit it, Viv, you're obsessed with me.

> *Takes one to know one.*

Good comeback.

> *Thanks, I practiced all night.*

Lol, in all seriousness, I had a great time last night. I especially enjoyed it when you fell off the hammock and humped me.

My heart gallops in my chest at his reply.

I also enjoyed the humping part. But I think my favorite part was when you peed your pants.

I didn't pee myself…I almost peed myself. It's not the same.

I'm like a thirteen-year-old girl teasing the boy she has a crush on.

Sure, sure. That's also what I would say if I peed myself and didn't want to embarrass myself in front of the sex goddess who keeps blowing my mind.

That's not the only thing she blows.

Truth.

Ugh, stop it. You are turning me on by admitting you've blown me. Distract me so my boner goes away.

How do I do that?

Talk to me about very nonsexual things.

Out of bed, I force my sleepy self into the kitchen to start my coffee machine. I see the best, most nonsexual item in the fridge next to my creamer.

Okay, okay. I got this. Milk.

Nope, won't work.

Why not?

Milk makes me think of breastfeeding, which makes me think of tits. So nope. Try again.

You are disgusting. I don't know what I see in you.

Ugh, men are gross. I stir creamer into the filled-to-the-brim mug, enjoying the sweet mocha aroma that fills the surrounding air.

You are about to see a dick if you don't help me!

I imagine the dick pic coming in, and my intrigue piques.

How would he pose?

Would he be grasping his dick? Or maybe he would be jacking off? Would it be a standing or lying down photo? How would the lighting be? I hate to admit this, even to myself, but just talking and thinking about his hard penis has me needing a cold shower too.

Fine, fine. Don't get your boner bent out of shape.

Ha. Ha. Ha. SOOOOOO funny, Vivian.

I know, right? Okay, here we go again. Poison ivy.

Are you even trying?

What! What's wrong with poison ivy? How could you possibly find itching and oozing sexy?

And just like that, I douse the flame of arousal growing in me.

Across the room, I put my mug on the coffee table. I sit on the couch, curling my feet up underneath me, and wait for his reply as the three little dots appear on my screen.

It's a long story, but it involves poison ivy finding its way to a very sensitive spot.

Laughing, I take one last drink of my coffee before walking to the bathroom. As my shower warms up, I sit on the toilet and text him back.

Oh, Nate, this story sounds very embarrassing.

Oh, Viv, it is.

Tell me everything. No detail is too small.

I step into the shower, letting the hot water wash over me, giving me that little extra perk for the day. I'm barely in the shower for a minute before my phone buzzes, but it doesn't stop after its usual text sequence. Looking to the counter, I realize he is calling.

Giddiness fills me as I step out of the shower and grab my phone, bringing it with me as I step back into the lovely oasis of steam.

"Hello," I say, wondering if maybe he butt-dialed me.

"Okay, so it was my senior year of high school. My friends and I went to this secret wooded lake place for a party—"

"Wait, are you telling me the highly embarrassing story? Right now?" I ask, interrupting him.

"You asked for it. So back to the story; we all went to—" He stops. "Vivian, are you in the shower?"

"Yeah, why?"

He groans in the background, muttering, "This boner will never go away now." He exhales loudly. "I can't with you. Back to the story again. So we were partying in the woods as all high school kids do."

"Correct, go on."

"Okay, so I had been seeing this chick for a while now, and I thought that night was the night."

"Oh my God." I wish I could see his face.

"Yep, you guessed it."

A laugh builds in my throat as I choke out, "You got poison ivy on your penis?"

He sighs. "Mm-hmm, sure did."

"So, did you guys do it in a bush of it or something? Oh...Did she have it in her vagina? Because shit, that is a whole other level of uncomfortable."

"Wrong and wrong."

"Wha—how? Okay, what exactly happened?" With my phone on speaker, I set it down on the ledge, out of the shower's stream. Pouring my favorite body wash on my loofah, I wash my body as he tells his tale.

"We didn't end up having sex. So no vagina rash."

"Whew."

Chuckling, he adds, "But she gave me a handy."

Once again, I'm laughing as he details how it showed up on her hand, and when their moms were talking together at a school soccer game, the two moms put two and two together. They were both grounded, and she broke up with him, but that's not all. He wasn't the only guy with a case of the poisoned pecker. It turns out, his so-called girlfriend gave two guys at the party her rash.

When he finishes, I'm to the point of tears.

And from the sound of it, Nate is too.

I turn off the shower, wrapping myself in a towel before stepping out. "Okay, poisoned pecker, I have to get ready now."

His laugh is howling through the phone as he says goodbye.

The day was an extension of this morning, teasing and laughing as we text nonstop throughout the day. We take turns telling embarrassing stories, attempting to one-up each other with every cringe-worthy detail.

Yep. Nate Fisher is not just a unicorn. He is my unicorn, and I'm falling hard.

At the office, everything is business as usual. That is, when Nate isn't here. Working with him to make the client's vision a reality for the St. Clair project is exhilarating. We could and do spend an hour on the phone talking.

But we keep it professional, mostly. Sometimes we are anything but professional. He makes me feel like a child again with how much I laugh.

But when he is here, it's another story.

The man's imagination is like nothing I've ever seen. How he can build an entire world—well, landscape and garden—in his head has me in awe. Not including his ability to put those ideas onto paper. His artistry is in a league of its own. It has quickly become one of my favorite things about him. I could watch his hands for hours as he creates his vision.

He is light in his movements as his hand grabs the green pencil. With a flick of his wrists, he makes it seem like the easiest thing in the world.

I stand inches behind him, peering over his shoulder as he makes flowers, grass, vines, and more appear out of nothing. He is putting the client's edits into the design, causing my heart to stop as he erases parts of his masterpiece. How can he stand doing that?

"Is there something you need, Vivian?" he asks, his voice thick with amusement. But his gaze is still on the drawing in front of him.

"Oh—I. Your art, it's so beautiful."

His body tenses at my words, and a crimson blush steals over his cheeks.

"I'm sorry. I didn't mean to crowd you. I'll go." My feet carry me a few inches backward before his hand catches around my wrist, hauling me back to him.

His eyes flicker up my body as he skims my wrist, sending a trail of goose bumps up my arm. A small gasp escapes my lips as his other hand grips the back of my thigh.

With a devilish smile, he stares at me, his eyes screaming with lust. His lips twitch as he pulls me even closer to him.

"Nate," I chide in a hushed tone, looking around. "Someone could see."

His blue eyes are dark and bright all at once. "So?"

"So? I don't want to be the topic of office rumors this week."

His face drops a small amount as his hands loosen their grip on me. "Do you really have to deal with that?"

I try to conceal my emotions, tilting my head down.

"Vivian, that's shitty. You don't deserve that." His touch turns from serious and full of want to a light caress of concern. Sensing the unease building in me, he lets me go, backing away.

The loss of his touch leaves me cold. I've never needed to be linked with someone whose every graze sets my skin on fire. "We need to remain completely professional while you are here, for both our sakes."

As he gives me a nod, his lips form a shy smile that makes my chest ache. I can't take it. That expression of disappointment is complete torture.

"Fuck it," I say, bending over and caging his face with my hands, pulling his face up to mine as my lips stray to his. The kiss is brief but full of emotion. With his eyes still closed, I pull away.

His hands find mine where they rest on his face. He covers them as I step backward, pulling him up to stand with me. Our fingers lace together for a small, blissful moment before he sits back down and finishes the design.

Chapter Thirteen

"Ugh, do I have to?" With her bottom lip sticking out, Sutton crosses her arms, turning her back to me to face the window, whining into her reflection.

"Yes, my sweet best friend, you do." I tap my fingers on the steering wheel as we drive to what will most likely be the dullest time of our lives. Sutton agreed to be my emotional support animal weeks ago, but until today, she hadn't comprehended what all that would entail.

As we pull up to The Kensington, a bougie hotel in the downtown area, we glance at each other. My eyes grow bigger as we talk through stares, no words.

We stop at the front doors as a man in a deep-blue jacket steps up to our car. The man is not a man, but a boy no older than nineteen. His chin has patches of hair growing in, and his limbs are lanky. But he walks with such lightness in his almost airy steps. Sutton and I sit in silence as he breezes over to us with the confidence and ease of having been alive for decades.

As he sidles up to the side of my car, I open my door, swinging my legs to the left. My feet hit the pavement as I force myself to stand on the thin heel supporting my body. "Good afternoon, ladies. Welcome to The Kensington. My name is Mark. May I take your keys?"

I blink slowly at the elegance in his tone. I can't fathom how this youngster could have more class than Sutton and I combined. "Ugh." Is all I get out before I hear Sally yelling at me from the large glass doors ten yards away.

"Hand the young man your keys already, Vivian. God." She huffs, yet still sounds like pure class. And I hate her for it.

I slip my keys into his outstretched hand and move to the sidewalk, trailing behind Sutton, who has the gifts in her hands.

Another man in the same regal blue remains at the entrance, holding the door open for none other than the woman who gave me life. Sally looks over at us with the corners of her lips curved slightly down as she arches her eyebrows. Sutton and I have had enough experience with my mother to know what that face means. It is a silent order—a signal to follow her that instant. We share yet another wide-eyed stare as we follow her.

The Kensington is far more than I could have ever imagined. It screams wealth and luxury. It is beautiful, from the sleek stone counters to the grand wingback chairs. It is the finest hotel money can buy. So it makes sense that Amy and Rian would have their baby shower here. Better yet, it makes sense why Sally would *plan* their showers here.

"Fuck," I whisper to Sut out the side of my mouth.

The over-the-top, enormous ballroom has me in complete and utter awe. It is amazing. A light mauve and pastels cover the room, rainbow arches gracing each table. Above us, fluffy clouds hang, looking delicate and calm.

"Wow." Sutton spins, her eyes roaming the room. "It's so beautiful. And fancy."

Unable to find the words to describe it, I shake my head up and down in agreement.

Her hand wraps around my wrist, hauling me to her side. Slightly turning her head down, she whispers, "Was there a dress code?"

"What? No." We both chose our outfits with perfect caution. Nothing low-cut, nothing short, nothing shiny. We both went for floral wrap dresses with nude high heels. But as I inspect what the vast number of women in the room are wearing, I understand why she said it. "Oh my God."

"Right?"

I examine my dark-green dress with golden flowers speckled all over. I'm entirely out of place. Except for my other half, the women in this room all wore neutral colors. Whites and nude dresses and pant suits fill the space. "They look like they walked out of a high-end, designer business-casual catalog."

"They look like they use dry cleaning." Her lips turn up into a half smirk.

"They look like they pay someone to do their taxes." We get into our rhythm and begin our tradition of trying to one-up each other. We have become entirely reliant on it in situations like this.

The first time was at a birthday party when we were thirteen—our first boy-girl party. We were so uncomfortable and insecure that we started a competition to see who could come up with the best secret-backhanded compliment. Sutton and I ended up sitting in a corner the entire night laughing. Soon, our little compliments and jabs became a routine for us. Anytime we felt out of place, we started up the game.

With her finger in the corner of her mouth, she twirls it up. Her finger lifts into the air, pointing up. "They look like they take their car to get serviced regularly."

My jaw slaps shut, causing my teeth to grind together. I suppress the smile trying to form. "They look like they belong to a country club."

She slaps her hands together as she jumps. "That's it. By George, I think you have cracked the code."

Across the room, Sally shoots a glare at us to stop. While trying not to laugh at Sutton or at Sally's attempt to hide her disdain for us, I choke on my spit.

I try to catch my breath as I wave off the concerned glances aimed my way.

As my eyes rim with tears from the continuous coughing, Sutton runs to grab me some water.

On her way back, she bumps into the table of gifts.

It was like time slowed as gifts for Rian and Amy fell. It's a train wreck; I didn't want to see it happen, but as it was unfolding before me, I had to watch.

My sights are glued to Sutton as she scrambles to grab the gifts, causing more to fall in her failed attempts.

When the last of the elegantly wrapped gifts fall to the floor, Sutton's eyebrows shoot up to her hairline. I can't tell if she is about to cry, laugh, or both. Her shoulders lift in a defeated shrug. Speaking loud enough for everyone watching the debacle to hear, she says, "C'est la vie."

I can't help myself. A loud cackle blurts out before I slap my hand over my mouth. I try to cover with a cough, but the damage is done. I don't even have to glance up to know what is coming Sutton's and my way.

Sutton returns to place a glass of ice water and two champagne flutes on the table. Ignoring the water, I reach straight for the champagne. With a light touch, I press my fingers upon the delicate long stem, lifting it to my mouth.

The first sip of the golden liquid is sweet as it hits my tongue. I lift the glass higher, emptying the drink in an instant. A small sigh escapes my lips, not out of satisfaction or pleasure but out of the exasperating realization that we are about to get our asses handed to us.

I set the beautiful, stupid-expensive glass down and raise my head, correcting my posture as Sally arrives at the table.

The face she is giving us is enough to make me feel like a teenager again. She peers down at me, her jaw tight as her lips form a thin line. Nostrils flaring, she seethes through her teeth, "How dare you two?"

"It was an accident. I'm sure no one bought the babies glass presents, so I think it will be okay." I'm surprised by how steady my voice sounds. Because inside, I'm trembling.

Her palms come down on the table as she leans forward. "You think this is all about the gift table?"

There is no need for my reply. I know she is going to tell me what else we did wrong.

"First, you two show up looking like"—she gestures toward us, moving her hand up and down—"that."

A frown forms on Sutton's face. "What's wrong with our appearance?" It leaves her mouth before she thinks. I give her a little kick under the table to thank her for giving my mother more to say to us than she was already going to.

"Well, for starts, you two look tacky in those over-the-top prints. I told you it was going to be an elegant shower. Not some trashy party where we smell diapers. Then there's the laughing and coughing. Do you always have to be the center of attention, Vivian?"

I'm taken aback by her words. I can't help myself. I pitch forward, staring directly into her still-squinting eyes. "Center of attention? When have I ever been the center of attention?"

"Oh, please, spare me the dramatics. You know you always ruin everything for your brother and sister, as well as your father and me. The only person you don't seem to do that for is Sutton here. It's embarrassing."

Tears prick my eyes. It was the second time she had said that I embarrass her, and I have to fight like hell to keep the water forming in my lids from spilling. "If that is all, please excuse me." I stand, walking away from the table. From her.

I need to find a bathroom before breaking down in front of the room. Someone tugs at my hand. Thinking it's Sutton, I turn around, prepared to tell her we need to make a break for it. But it's Rian.

She's in a long, flowing white dress with ruffles near the bottom. It reminds me of something I would wear. It gives a bohemian vibe, with her hair softly tied back. With one hand on her pronounced belly and the other folded in mine, she whispers, "Come with me. I know somewhere private."

A tear slips down my cheek as she leads me out of the party and into the hallway. Rian stops at the first door we come to on our left, using a keycard. She unlocks the door, and we slip in. Arms wrap around me awkwardly, with her belly between us as she rubs circles on my back. "You can cry. It's okay."

And I do. I can't stop the tears once they start. She lets me hold on to her while I sob for about five minutes before pulling back to see my face. "Any better?"

I pull out of her hold, reaching my fingers up under my eyes and wiping away any last straggling tears. "A little." It's nothing more than a whisper, but she nods.

"Want to talk about it?"

My lips tremble as I will myself to control the tears building back up. "No. I just need to get myself together. Sorry for pulling you away from your party. You can go back. I'll be fine."

Her lips turn down and her eyebrows pull in as if she isn't sure what to do. "Are you sure? Because I can stay with you."

"I'm fine. It was a brief breakdown. I promise I'll stay quiet in the back and not ruin any more of your shower."

Her shoulders fall. "You don't have to do that."

My lids snap shut as I inhale a deep breath to calm my out-of-control emotions. I exhale, releasing some of the tension in my limbs. As if I've let some of my hurt feelings go.

The door clicks behind me, and I'm alone.

Peeling my lids open, I glance around to see where I'm at. It is a lavish dressing room of sorts. There's a modern charcoal gray couch with two indigo blue barrel chairs across from it. I assume this is where they put up the brides-to-be and mothers for their big events. The bathroom is larger than my living room. I'm almost scared to find out how I look, but other than some red puffy eyes, it's not that bad.

I make a mental note to thank whatever gods might exist for creating waterproof mascara. It's moments like these that it was invented for.

With a splash of cold water on my face, I prepare to return to the shower. I'll find Sut and move us as far away from the center of action as possible. And we can bounce after we have been here for an appropriate amount of time.

Back in the ballroom filled with clouds and wonder, I instantly spot Sutton in the crowd. She is sitting in the back at a table closest to the door we came in through. Maybe Sally was right about us and our outfits. We stand out. Across the room, I could see Sut's colorful dress among the sea of neutrals. My fingers run through my hair as I weave through the gathered group of women.

I make it to the table, having snagged two more glasses of champagne. Setting them down, I slide into the seat next to Sutton's.

She lets out a small chuckle when she sees the drinks.

"What? I'm confused. Since when do you not want to drink free booze, Sut?"

"Blasphemy," she declares, leaning to the side and ducking her head under the table. When she sits back up, she holds two more golden-filled flutes. "Great minds think alike."

"To great minds," I say, raising the two glasses I brought.

"To being badass bitches, not sad-ass bitches." Her two glasses tap against mine with a clink before we down each.

Warmth swims through my veins as Sutton and I snatch up every bit of champagne we can find. Before I know it, the party has died down, and there are twelve empty glasses on the table. Or at least I think I counted twelve.

"I'm going to tell Amby—no, that's not it. Amby. Damn it. A-me. Ha! I knew I could get it. Goodbye. Okay?" I walk away before Sutton has the chance to say anything.

I find both Amy and Rian at once, and I feel like I've just won the lottery. How did I get so lucky?

They both glance at each other and laugh.

"What is so funny, baby mamas?" My head tilts to the side as I wait to be let in on their fun.

"How much did you drink, Vivian?" Amy smiles at me. She is such a pleasant woman. I hate how Sally makes me feel like I'm in fifth place—how she likes Shep and Amy better than me. Oh, and now they are all going to have sweet little babies, which I already love more than anything, but they will be two more people my mother will love more than me.

"Oh, just a few. How many have you had?"

Laughing, Rian comes closer and wraps me in the second hug she has given me today. And it's maybe the fourth hug she has given me since I was seven. "You know, you were just talking about us out loud when you walked over."

I squint, leaning back in disbelief. "Sure I did."

Amy gives me a big nod, adding, "You said you felt like you had won the lottery finding both of us together."

My mouth drops open. "Fuck. I said that out loud, not in my head?"

"Yep," they say in unison.

"What else did drunk me say?" My nose scrunches. "Never mind, I'm not sure I want to know."

They're both cradling their bellies, already being protective and loving mothers to their unborn babies. "Ooh, who is he?" Amy wiggles her eyebrows while her gaze goes straight behind me.

I glance over my shoulder, and my pulse quickens. My skin tingles with energy when his eyes meet mine. Even from across the room, there is a magnetic pull between us. The corner of my lips itch to turn up as Amy lets out a dramatic and somewhat erotic sigh while watching Nate saunter closer. I stifle a laugh by biting my bottom lip.

Unable to contain myself any longer, I leap into Nate's arms once he is a few feet away and wrap my arms around his neck. He pulls me into him, spinning us around before setting me on my feet. I stand on my tippy toes and pull his face down to mine, capturing his lips before slightly leaning back.

His lips turn up in a grin before he presses another soft kiss to my mouth. "You taste sweet."

"I thought we already established that I'm sweet enough to eat?" I wink at him.

He throws his head back, letting out a loud laugh. "I meant you tasted like sweet alcohol, but you are right." His lips brush my ear, sending jolts of desire to my core as he whispers, "You have the sweetest and tightest pussy I've ever experienced."

Heat rushes to my face as I think about his dirty words. It was exactly what I was referring to a few moments ago, but damn, if there isn't something that feels so right about Nate saying it. Everything about him, from his laugh to his kiss, has me licking my lips in anticipation.

The need to cool off hits me hard. Fanning my face with my hand, I hear a loud clearing of someone's throat from behind me. I spin in Nate's arms. My sisters are waiting with the most insanely giddy expressions to grace pregnant women's faces.

"Vivian, who is your friend?" Rian asks as her eyes dart between Nate and me with a huge grin plastered on her face.

With a playful nudge in my side, Nate says, "Yeah, Vivian, introduce me." A mischievous smirk rises on his face as if he is daring me.

"Nate, this is Rian and Amy. Rian is my older sister, and Amy is married to my brother Bailey, Rian's twin. They are both very pregnant, as you can see. And Amy, Rian, this is Nate, my—" Unsure what to call him, I pause, my gaze wandering back to his face, to his shimmering blues. He beams down at me, his baby blues glowing with adoration and amusement. I swallow down my nerves. "Boyfriend? Yeah. He's my boyfriend."

The moment the words leave my mouth, Nate's body relaxes as his palm skims my lower back. He finds my waist and grips me, helping to pull me even closer to his side.

"What? You didn't tell me you were seeing anyone." Rian's eyes gleam while her mouth sets into a frown.

"Well, in my defense, we don't text very much, and the shower hardly seemed like the right time to acknowledge my sex life."

Amy chokes down a giggle as Rian's face lights up. "You've been sleeping with this walking erotic fantasy?"

Nate's chest vibrates against my shoulder as he tries to contain his amusement. "Yep, it's true." I gesture for them to come closer. Once they're only a foot or two away, I lean forward. "Have you ever fucked a unicorn? Because it's orgasm heaven. I mean, the things this man can do with his co—"

A rough hand clamps down over my mouth as Nate's arm snakes around my stomach, lifting me off the ground. "Okay, that's enough from you and your tipsy lips." He backs away with me still in his arms. "It was nice meeting you both. I'm going to take this one home."

I make a lewd gesture with my hand toward them. He adds, "To sleep."

My sisters' laughter fills my ears as he carries me to where Sutton and a handsome stranger sit.

He presses a kiss into my hair before sitting down beside the man. "Nice to see you again, Sutton. Hopefully, you won't judge me too harshly based on the first time."

She smiles into her glass. "Oh, honey, trust me when I say you made a *huge* impression. And I won't forget it." She empties the last of her champagne. Beside her, I reach for another of the last bit of champagne left at the table. "Oh, no you don't, you beautiful, boozy bitch." Sutton swats my hand away as the man beside her picks it up and empties it.

My lips form a pout as I glare at them. "Who is this, and why do you both want me to be miserable?"

Sutton clasps my hands with a sigh, turning my attention to her and her alone. "Babe, you're trashed."

I open my mouth to protest, but she begins again. "But so am I. I called Nate off your phone to get us since we're both far beyond the point of driving."

I rest my hand over my heart. "My unicorn came to our sloppy rescue. Awe."

"And it turns out he was out with his friend Cooper, so here is the plan: Nate is going to drive you and your car back to your place or his. No one cares which one. And Cooper here is going to take me home in Nate's truck."

I agree with the plan, and then it hits me. "Oh my God, Cooper? As in thee Cooper? As in Coop? As in Nate's nonsexual, or at least I don't think, life partner?" I stand up, walking around to stand between Nate and him. I take my place in Nate's lap and bounce with excitement as I think of questions to ask him.

Cooper has to be at least six and a half feet tall. He is at my eye level while I'm sitting on Nate's lap. His dark-brown eyes shine back at me from behind black-rimmed glasses.

He is nothing and everything like I imagined. I imagined him nerdy and attractive from how Nate described him as a high school math teacher. But in real life, he blows my imagined Coop out of the water. He is scruffy like Nate and has a calm, relaxed presence. The grin that's been plastered on his face since we walked over is of genuine joy. Not like the creepy smiles Sutton's boyfriend's friends wear.

"I like you." Propping my arm on the table, I rest my chin on my hand.

Cooper does the same. "And I like you."

Nate wraps one arm around my waist, pulling me back into his chest as his other hand travels down my leg. I slap his hand away. "Stop it. I'm trying to get to know your Sutton." I pull myself forward. "Tell me every embarrassing story you know about this one behind me. Because I need to knock him down a peg, you know? Like, I need him to be a skosh less attractive."

Coop scoots closer, his stare twinkling with excitement. "What level of embarrassment are we talking about? Like, called the teacher "Mom" or masturbation stuff?"

Under his breath, I hear Nate let out a "Don't you fucking dare." I'm unsure if he meant it for Cooper or me, or hell, for both of us.

Either way, I don't care. I turn to Nate, planting a kiss on his lips with a loud "Mwah" before looking into Cooper's shimmering amber pools and responding, "Masturbation."

Chapter Fourteen

The sound of the shower starting wakes me. I wince as I open my eyes to beams of sunlight peeking into the dark room. Looking around, I realize I'm not at home but at Nate's. In his huge-ass bed with gun-metal gray sheets and a comforter that matches. I roll over, trying to cover my head with his blanket and go back to sleep. But his seductive smell has every part of my body awake.

I remember how Nate picked me up last night and took care of me when I was sloppy drunk. He got me food and made me drink water. Hell, he washed my face and helped me brush my teeth. It made me fall even harder for the guy. He wouldn't do anything more than kiss me. Well, that's a lie. There was some dry humping started by me, but it was anything but one-sided.

Uncovering my head, I find a bottle of red Gatorade—my favorite—Tylenol, and a note on the nightstand. "For your head." He had drawn a small picture of a brain with a heart floating around it. It's things like this that make me think his feelings match mine.

I hurry, taking the pills and gulping down the bottle of electrolytes, hoping to get rid of the extreme thirst that has taken over my body. Dragging my feet, I shuffle down the hall to the guest bathroom to take care of my business. I return to the bedroom and smile as Nate sings in the shower. My heart swells with adoration for the man. I grasp the ends of the oversized shirt Nate had given me to sleep in, yanking it off as I step out of my panties and walk into his bathroom.

Steam fogs up the mirror and air. As I step into the shower, he turns under the spray of water to see me standing before him. His chest heaves as his eyes grow darker, taking in my naked body. We both remain silent, moving closer until our bare skin is touching.

The water drips from his head down to his delicious chest.

"If I wasn't hungover..." I take him in. Glancing up and down, I dart my tongue out to lick my lips.

Nate chuckles, dragging me under the cascade of scalding water. He hands me his loofah, presumably to wash myself. But just because I can't handle a good fucking right now doesn't mean I can't play a little. I flicker my water-drenched lashes up at him as I take the loofah and wash his chest, moving painstakingly slow down to the cut V of his groin. I stop just before reaching for his now-twitching dick and circle around to his back. His breathing becomes shallow as I start the slow torture again, washing him from top to bottom.

"How did I go so long without you in my life?" I ask.

"I've been asking myself that same question," he says with a light chuckle, snatching the loofah from me. He takes his turn to wash and study my body.

Nate hands me a pair of sweatpants and another T-shirt after we finish our shower and dry off. They are crazy baggy on me, but I don't care. I love how his clothes smell like him and make me feel like I'm wrapped up in his arms.

From the hall, I yell, "You know you will probably never get these back. They belong to me now. Let's call it the girlfriend tax."

A faint laugh travels through the kitchen, and I find myself face-to-face with two strangers. Well, not strangers. I recognize them from the pictures on the wall. Nate's parents. His mom and dad are standing before me as my hair is still dripping from the shower, and I am wearing their son's clothes with no bra on. *Great.*

My gaze moves to Nate. Water still clings to his dark curls as he frowns, mouthing, "I'm sorry. I didn't know they were coming over."

I plaster a friendly smile on my face and introduce myself while trying to shake off the shock. "Hi. You must be Mr. and Mrs. Fisher. I'm so happy to meet you both. I'm Vivian, Nate's—"

"Oh, honey, we know who you are. You are Nathaniel's girlfriend, and if we didn't know before, we could have guessed, as you both just got out of the shower."

Heat floods my cheeks as Nate yells, "Mom!"

She shoos him away with her hand, then hugs me before leading me to sit with her on the couch. "I'm beyond delighted to meet you, Vivian. He is quite taken with you, did you know? Of course you knew. I mean, you don't shower with someone who isn't."

From the kitchen, Nate shouts, "Stop it, Mom, you'll chase her off."

She shakes her head and grins while replying, "Oh, hush, Nathaniel. No one is talking to you. Anyway, if she hasn't bolted yet, I think it's a good sign she won't."

Over my shoulder, I see him shaking off her words with a bright smile. It takes nearly all of my almost nonexistent acting skills to keep me from showing how mortified I am, as well as how deeply I'm falling for the amazing man she raised. Delia, as she soon demands I call her, is a petite woman full of spunk, from what I can tell. Her chestnut hair is in one long braid hanging over her left shoulder, with wispy bands poking through the bandanna she uses as a headband. She reminds me of a free spirit. The complete opposite of Sally in every way. For one, she is wearing long denim shorts with a tank top that shows the outline of her sports bra. She gestures with her hands and hugs me like a mad woman while telling me how excited she is that Nate has such a pretty and nice girlfriend.

On the other hand, Sally would look at me and comment on my lack of decency. She would tell me I look destitute wearing a man's clothes and that I was in no way dressed appropriately for company—especially not for meeting a boyfriend's parents.

Nate's father, Miles, touches her shoulder, announcing, "Delia, stop blabbering the poor girl's ear off. Can't you tell they were in the middle of something? Something that doesn't involve us."

Heat rises along my neck, making its way to my face. Lifting my hands to hide my blush, I peer at them through my fingers.

"Jesus Christ. Can you two not play it semi-cool by pretending to be oblivious for five minutes?" Nate grits through his teeth as he flops down into the seat next to me. Our hands find each other, interlacing. He gives my hand two tight squeezes to ground me before setting our joined hands on his thigh.

With my focus on Delia and Miles, bickering over whether or not they are embarrassing, I lose the battle between my will to stay composed and the need to smile. I scrunch my nose as my lips turn up as high as they can. Scooting closer to Nate, I mutter, "Are they always like this?"

His head tilts toward me, his gaze never leaving his parents. "Always."

A huff of laughter escapes through my nose as I study him. Nate relaxes, watching his parents nag each other about boundaries. The corner of his lips twitches as he fights the smirk that threatens to break his rigid demeanor. The love he has for his parents is something I want. It's something I admire.

My head falls to his shoulder, and my free hand curls around his bicep, needing to keep him close to me. I've never been affectionate like this. Not in private and especially not in front of anyone else, let alone parents.

His thumb rubs my hand in a slow sweep. We sit like this for a while, staying silent, just enjoying the other person's touch. Delia and Miles switch from arguing to making a grocery list for the barbecue Nate is now having.

With a loud clap, Delia slaps her hands together. "Okay, so it's a plan? While we grab some odds and ends, you two will fire up the grill and make drinks."

In unison, Nate and I both let out a "Huh?"

"Damn it." Miles pulls out his wallet from the back pocket of his khaki cargo shorts and pulls out some money. He holds it out, gesturing toward his wife. "Here's your five bucks, D."

It hits me then how much Miles and Nate resemble each other as he dips his head to hide his grin from his wife. The two men are both tall and handsome, but their mannerisms make it obvious they are father and son.

I glance at Nate to find he is wearing the same expression of confusion as me.

As if I'm in school, I lift my hand into the air. "I have a question."

They both turn to us. "Yes, Vivian dear, what is it?" Delia's voice is full of sweetness and warmth, everything I imagine a mother should sound like.

"I'm confused. Did I miss something?"

She lets out a loud chuckle, sitting on the coffee table in front of us. She places a hand on each of our knees. "Nope. I bet Miles that you two were too wrapped up in each other to pay attention to what we were discussing, but he didn't think so. He lost."

"My God, I'm mortified." I lean forward, propping my elbows on my knees.

"Don't worry about it, honey. We both understand what it's like to be young and in love." Before I can react, she walks to the door with Miles, calling out, "We'll be back in about forty-five minutes with your sister and some sides, okay? Don't forget to start the grill and make margaritas. All the supplies are in the fridge."

We stay sitting there for a few minutes, not saying anything. Unable to stand the silence any longer, I say, "So those are your parents."

His head bobs. "Yep. Those are my parents."

There is something almost flustered about him.

Maybe he is worried that his parents might have scared me off. In my past relationships, that might have been true, but this, with him, is different. It's more intense, more intimate, emotional, and physical than anything I've experienced.

Cupping his face with my hand, I rub my thumb across his cheek before pressing my mouth to his, sucking in a breath. He parts his lips, deepening the kiss. Moaning, I draw his soft upper lip between mine, savoring this moment with him.

I end the kiss, opening my eyes to find his still closed. My chest burns, knowing he is scared I might end this or that I could or would ever cause him pain. With one last light kiss, I whisper, "I like them."

His eyes open, pleading as he stares into mine. "You do?"

The couch dips as I crawl into his lap to straddle him. Thrusting my fingers into the curls at the nape of his neck, I pull his head up to mine and rest my forehead on his. "Duh. They are so funny and sweet."

"You aren't embarrassed or upset?" His gaze flutters all over my face as he inspects me for any signs of emotion.

"Have you met me? I'm embarrassed by everything. Hell, I'm still embarrassed by the time I peed my pants in the second grade. And now that I've told you that mortifying fact about myself, I must threaten your life. But that doesn't mean I don't like them, and it doesn't affect how I feel about you."

His eyes soften as worry falls from his face. Nate clears his throat, opening his mouth before closing it again, hesitating. A frenzy of butterflies flutter in my belly as I anticipate his next words.

He folds his arms around me, dragging us down to lie on the couch. I brush the runaway strands of hair off his face, and his eyes close at my touch. A quiet sigh slips from his lips as he lifts his lashes to meet my gaze.

At this moment, he is the definition of gorgeous. I want to keep him in this moment with me forever, but I settle for taking a mental snapshot, memorizing every line, curve, and freckle on his face. It is the moments of nothing, the small touches and affection, that make me realize I am in love.

I love him.

I'm feeling too much, too quick, so I stand, walking toward the kitchen. "We should work on the drinks before they come back."

I get out the meats and veggies his parents had already prepared for the grill when he responds with a quiet "Okay then."

"Shit." I wince, looking down at the almost empty bottle of tequila in my hands. The other half of its contents are now swirling through the blender. Did I really just pour half a bottle of tequila into the blender? Yep, I sure fucking did.

It's a skosh more—okay, a lot more—than the recipe calls for, but as far as I am concerned, recipes are just guides and not the rules. I make two different margarita pitchers while Nate fires up the grill. One is your basic, run-of-the-mill, everyday marg. And the other is a strawberry-mango marg. Not wanting to discuss anything heavy, we both start drinking.

Nate follows my lead. Or maybe he wants to avoid our deep feelings too. But either way, we both end up being two and a half drinks deep when his parents arrive, followed by a tall woman with a bleach-blond pixie cut, wearing a sports bra and sweatpants.

On the counter beside the grill, I observe Nate, taking another sip of my almost-finished drink. He grins, mouthing, "Sister."

My fingers snap into a finger gun, and I point at him, clicking my tongue. "Got it, Uni."

She sets down more food in the spare space beside me on the counter. Nate's sister, whose name has escaped me, looks at me, puzzled. "Uni?"

His body swings in our direction as he says, "Don't," with his finger wagging at both of us.

She bounces on her toes. "Oh, now I have to know. I'm Audra, by the way. Nate's cooler, smarter older sister."

My gaze shifts to him. "Is this true, my unicorn? Am I dating the uncool, and dare I say, dumber Fisher sibling?"

He waves his hand down his body. "It's true. All those things are a part of this pretty little package right here. Take it or leave it."

I take another sip and mutter, "Don't you mean an enormous package?" A blush rises to his cheeks as his eyes dart up to mine. I throw a wink his way before finishing my drink.

"Ew!" Audra gags as she covers her face, laughing with us. "You did not just make a big-dick joke about my little brother."

I wince. "Too much, too fast?"

She leans on the counter. "Never. You already fit right in with this family." Her words hit me like a ball of energy to the chest. Warmth radiates through my entire body, making me feel welcome and wanted. "Now, come to your new Nate whisperer and tell me about this unicorn thing. Unless it's a sex thing? Is it a sex thing?"

I'm about to answer when Nate takes skewers off the grill, causing Delia, who is across the lawn, to announce, "Food is ready."

Under her breath, Audra mutters, "No shit, Sherlock."

I wasn't prepared for her to say anything like that. Mid-sip of yet another margarita, I choke. My eyes water as I try not to spit it all over the food.

Audra stares at me with an innocent grin while a concerned Delia comes up behind me to pat my back.

Nate places the remaining food on the patio table before sitting beside me. Dismissing Delia from choking duty, he rubs circles on my back.

The table is full of conversation and jokes as we eat and drink.

"So, Vivian, Nate tells us you work for FTW?" Miles asks.

With a smile, I say, "I do. I'm one of the head architects' assistants."

Delia's eyebrows pull together. "Is it normal for assistants to be so involved with the design process?"

"Mom," Nate and Audra chide in unison, giving their mother a pleading look to stop.

"Oh, I didn't mean it like...What I mean is that you must be very talented and trusted." Her face flushes as she catches my gaze.

A knowing grin forms on my face at her words. "I would like to think that is true, but maybe it's because my boss overextended himself and was desperate for help."

Nate chimes in, "Nah, babe. You are great." He turns his gaze to his parents. "Viv here has been helping me create the designs for the clients."

"Really?" Audra says, sitting up a little straighter.

"Just a little, nothing huge. Nate here is the talented one. His ability to draw the designs for the clients is amazing."

Miles's and Delia's smiles grow wider as they glow with pride for their son. "He is pretty amazing not only with the artistic side of the business but with the financial aspects as well. Which is more than a father could ever ask for when his son takes over the family business," Miles says with such sincerity that it makes my heart melt.

Nate's shoulder sags a little. Not enough to be obvious, but enough that I notice and want to be there for him.

My need to comfort him is overwhelming as I reach my hand out to hold his. With small strokes of my thumb, he relaxes, bringing my hand to his lips, gently brushing a kiss against my knuckles. For a moment, I forget how to breathe as the significance of the gesture registers with me.

"Ahem," Audra says, pretending to clear her throat as she pulls us out of our very public, private moment.

A blush rises in my cheeks as I sip my glass of water, trying not to look at the people around us who have witnessed our intimacy.

The rest of the day with Nate's family flies by. We eat, drink, and play card games. But mostly, we joke. I've never been so comfortable with a boyfriend's family. Hell, I never knew it could be like this. I want this—to have a fun family who jokes and shows affection. I want this family with Nate.

Chapter Fifteen

As the evening went on, it became more apparent that I wasn't leaving tonight. Nate and I freely indulged in multiple margaritas with his family. So much so that there was no way either of us would drive tonight. But it isn't the actual reason I'm not going home. The real reason is that I'm madly in love with this goofy, charming man, and I don't want to leave. I want to stay with him.

I climb into the huge plush bed that could fit a family of four without them ever touching. We curl up next to each other, facing one another, and my hands hold my head as it rests on another of Nate's pillows I claimed as my own.

Halfway drunk, we lie there in the quiet, staring at each other while we tell stories of embarrassing moments with exes. I tell him about my high school boyfriend Andy, who dumped me for the girl I thought was my friend, and how the entire experience has scarred me for life and away from sushi for all eternity. I let him in on the secret that every year since and still to this day, Andy texts me, begging for forgiveness and a second chance. I tell him about how I prank call Sally every few months with Sutton for shits and giggles.

He fills me in on how one of his girlfriends in high school agreed to let him touch her boobs one night. He was so emotionally and physically excited that he came in his pants the moment he held one in his hands. And I now know all about the time a girl he was seeing in college walked in on him watching porn and rubbing one out, then accused him of being a sex fiend and told him she would pray for him.

We exchange sleepy smiles, both perfectly content to stay up talking for a while longer. With each memory we share, we give each other a bit of ourselves.

Nate fidgets with my shirt sleeve, sighing. "So, what did you think of today? Of my family?"

My voice grows quiet as I admit, "I really liked them. They are so fun and welcoming. It was a pleasant change from what I'm used to."

His eyebrows scrunch together, forming a line between them. "What do you mean?"

"My family—they aren't like yours." I shrug. "They have never been the welcoming kind."

"So if you brought me home, they wouldn't treat me like one of the family?"

"No, they wouldn't." I clear my throat, trying to push away the looming emotions. "Although, they don't treat me like I'm a member of their family most days either."

He slides his hand down my arm with a light graze before taking my hand in his. Pulling it up to his mouth, he kisses my knuckles softly.

I wipe away an escaped tear. "Sally, my mother, has never been too fond of me. But the twins are my parents' whole world."

"I'm sure it feels that way sometimes, especially with the babies on the way."

He peers at me, sounding hopeful that this is what I mean. Optimistic that I'm being sensitive, not that my family sees me as the black sheep.

My chin trembles. "I wish. Sally told me a few weeks ago, and again yesterday, that I am an embarrassment to her and the family." Warm drops roll down my cheeks as Nate wraps his arm around me, dragging me into his body. With my face pressed into his chest, I cry. I tell him about growing up with unaffectionate parents. I fill him in on the baby shower. How Sally talked to me and what led to my drinking so much.

He holds me, letting me talk and cry with no judgment. He makes me feel safe.

Safe to express everything that's hurting me and explain why it stings so much.

Once all the tears have dried, we're both straddling the line between being awake and asleep. With his head still resting on mine, he whispers, "I love you."

I take a deep breath as his words sink in. They take hold of my heart. The heart that belongs to him in every way. I smile into his shirt and mumble back, "I love you too."

His arms tighten around me, acknowledging my words. As his body relaxes further against me, I fall into a deep sleep with a stupid-ass grin fixed on my face.

A couple of days later, Sutton and I agree to meet with Cooper and Nate at some shady, hole-in-the-wall bar downtown. Once we walk in, we discover it is surprisingly nice inside. The floor is sticky like every bar but isn't nasty like we assumed.

After we score a table, I text Nate, telling him where we are. They are sitting beside us within moments.

"Where are we, Coop?" I ask, still in awe of the hidden gem of a bar.

He gives me the side eye as he replies, "A bar. Have you been drinking without us?"

Sutton rolls her eyes as she pushes him. "Don't be an asshole. You know what she meant."

Laughter bursts out of him. "I'm sorry, but do you not remember the other time we've all been around each other? You were both hammered at a baby shower. A *baby shower.*"

"Whatever. Why are we here again?" Sutton asks while shooting Coop a glare that would cut me down if I were on the other end.

Coop looks over to Nate. With a nod of approval, he announces, "For Trivia Night."

We both stare at them. Why would they think we'd want to do a trivia night?

"Now, now," Nate says, taking hold of my hand. "You haven't found out the night's theme yet."

"I'll bite." My eyes narrow in on his beautiful face. "What's this marvelous theme that will weaken Sutton and me at the knees?"

Nate and Coop glance at each other, sharing the best friend nonverbal communication that Sutton and I have. They drum their hands on the table.

"Late '90s and early 2000s teen movies," they both announce with jazz hands.

After multiple drinks and high fives, Sutton and I walk out of the bar as champions. Our obsession with Freddy Prinze Jr. and Shane West has finally come in handy.

"Don't pout, boys. It's not our fault you can't remember the poem from *10 Things I Hate About You*," I say while sprinting off down the sidewalk toward Sutton, humming the tune of "Can't Take My Eyes Off You."

Behind us, Nate and Cooper chuckle at our winners' antics.

I enjoyed a night out with Nate and our besties. Sutton and Cooper are pure fire together, even though they both refuse to admit it. The constant back-and-forth bickering is full of sexual tension whether they cop to it or not. Even if I could get one of them to make a move, there is still the problem of their current "significant" others. Both are in toxic relationships that sadly don't appear to be ending anytime soon. But until they can get their heads out of their asses and stop dating losers, my playing cupid is lost on them.

The Uber ride back to Nate's from the bar is quick and full of kisses. We've spent these last few days in a love bubble, basking in each other's bodies and minds. Wanting to know everything we can about the other. Taking time to learn every like and dislike. What annoying habits we might have.

Nate's, I've learned, is not putting the toilet seat down. Growing up with an older brother, I thought I would've learned not to go sitting down in a man's bathroom blindly. But alas, my many years of living with women or alone have left me with a false sense of security—one where I didn't have to worry about falling in a fucking toilet.

As for my annoying habit, according to him, it has yet to be discovered. I call bullshit on that, although it makes me happy that he loves me so much that he doesn't want to hurt me. That, or he is blinded by all the "lovemaking." Let's be honest. It's primarily straight-up fucking. Nasty, raunchy fucking. And I love it.

But I also love those rare moments amid the frenzy of pleasure that're full of real intimacy and adoration. The moments when I stare at him and can tell, with his slack expression and gentle caress, that he truly understands what I feel.

That this is more than lust.

More than a crush.

That this is real. The type of love you see in movies. That you dream about.

Chapter Sixteen

The moment I step out of the Uber, a cheeky smile rises as I walk up the sidewalk to the ugly yellow door. It is awful but wonderful simultaneously. I can't imagine anything different from this.

I pick up a package waiting on his doorstep while Nate unlocks the front door. He holds it open for me before moving to disarm the alarm system threatening to go off any second. I look at the box to see if I can tell what is in it before glancing at the shipping label. Nothing obvious there. But the name on it catches my attention.

"Hey, Nate, this package isn't for you. It belongs to a Neil Bloom." I bring it to the kitchen, where he's leaning against the counter, gulping down a bottle of Gatorade. "How weird. It has your address, though."

He says nothing, just drinks his blue sports drink with his eyes shut.

I place the box on the table, walking over to the fridge to grab water. "I can swing by the post office tomorrow morning on my way to brunch with Rian."

He looks at the floor, mumbling into his bottle, "No, it's fine."

"It's no biggie for me to do it, babe. I don't mind."

"I said I'll handle it, Vivian."

"Are you sure? 'Cause I am—"

He cuts me off by letting out a loud sigh as he pinches the bridge of his nose. "Yes, Viv. I'm sure. Now, will you drop it?" The heat of his anger radiates off him as he grinds his teeth.

"What's wrong?" I ask, taking a step back.

"Nothing. Drop it."

"I don't understand why you are being such a dick right now?"

"I'm not being a dick," he says, grabbing the box and taking it to his art room office.

I rear back, sure the shock is visible on my face. I'm speechless, my mouth agape as I glare at him in disbelief.

"Okay...Why are you getting so mad then?"

"Maybe because it's none of your business, Vivian," he grits through his teeth.

Snapping my head away, I focus my gaze on the wall, trying to control my emotions—to stop the reaction that's threatening to take over.

I clamp down on my lower lip as my head bobs. Unsure what to say next—unsure of what I did wrong—I push off the counter I was leaning against across from him. With my head and shoulders high, I trudge past him, making my way to my purse. At the door, I freeze, pausing with my hand on the knob. I wait to see if he is going to say something or try to stop me.

Silence.

He doesn't bother. My eyes water as the sting of whatever just happened sets in.

Screw him and his childish reaction.

Once in my car, I grip the wheel as tight as possible before falling forward to rest my forehead on it, giving myself a moment to process before I bottle it up to make it home.

I stay like that, practicing my breathing, until a knock rattles my window.

Nate stands there staring at me, his Adam's apple bobbing while his shoulders are slouched, giving him a slight hunch in his spine. His expression is full of defeat as he opens my door, kneeling in the space.

His hands rub across his weary face. "I'm sorry. Please come back inside."

A tear threatens to fall as I turn my face to the windshield.

"Please, Vivian. I don't know why I did that. You were right. I was acting like a dick, and you don't deserve that."

I sniffle, wiping my nose with my hand. "No. I don't."

His hand finds mine and squeezes. "You don't. It wasn't about you. That was all about me, getting in my head. I was an asshole. I know it, and I'm sorry."

"I-I just don't understand."

He takes a deep breath, focusing on our touching hands. "Will you come back inside for me to explain?"

"I don't know, Nate. Maybe...Maybe we rushed this. Maybe we need to slow down."

His face crumbles. "Is that what you want?"

My shoulders lift into a shrug. I hate how emotional I am getting. My hands tremble as I wipe away a falling tear. "You can't even open up to me about a package; I just feel stupid right now."

His rough palms find my face as he brushes away the moisture pooling under my eyes with his thumbs. "You aren't stupid. I'm the stupid one. Please, Vivian, come inside. I'll explain it all...Please."

I dip my head forward in agreement. He helps me out of my car, clasping my hand as we walk up the sidewalk as if he doesn't want to let go or is scared that I might change my mind and leave.

Once inside, he moves ahead of me, stopping at the end of the hall. I expect him to take us to his bedroom. But he turns to the left, pulling me into his art room office and motioning for me to sit in the chair.

Wiping my sweaty hands on my dress, I settle on the ground with my legs folded crisscross applesauce. A small smirk crosses his face at my defiance before he moves into the closet to retrieve a black plastic container.

He takes his place across from me on the cold hardwood floor, placing the tub in the middle of us. I wait for an explanation, but all he says is "Open it."

I remove the lid, keeping my eyes on him. He looks like he did after his mother and father left to go to the grocery store last weekend. His face is unreadable, almost a little lost.

"Go ahead."

In the container, I find children's books and nothing else.

"Those." He points a finger at the large picture books. "Those are my secret."

I pick one up. The cover has an illustration of a large flower with a wasp sitting on it. The name of the book is *The Wanna-Bee*. Next is a book called *The House Dragon*, which depicts a dragon curled up on a couch beside a small boy. I pick up the following three books, which are children's picture books. But that isn't the sole thing that connects them. Under the title, after the author, each book lists Neil Bloom as the illustrator.

My gaze darts to him as he nods, giving me a shy smile. As I flip through the pages, I admire skillfully drawn pictures. Some are of nature. Others are fantastic creatures. All bright, all colorful. "You drew these?"

"Yeah. It's my dirty little secret."

"Why?" I flip through the pages of details. "Why keep this a secret?"

"It's hard to explain. It all has to do with my responsibility to my family and the business."

"What does that have to do with your art?"

"Everything. My parents expect me to take over the business soon while Audra takes over the florist shop. My time and energy are supposed to be spent making the family successful, not drawing for children's books."

"I still don't understand. You are so talented, and you obviously love it. Why would they be upset by this?"

"They may seem easygoing and supportive, but there is a limit to their support. They worked their asses off to make the landscaping and florist business what they are today. And they raised Audra and me to take over. As kids, they supported our hobbies—Audra with her dance and me with my art. But as we got older, I was told my art could never be more than a hobby; that it isn't a career. My parents paid for my college degree for me to run the business. If I pursue my art, they will have wasted their savings on me for nothing, and I can't do that to them."

"I doubt they see it that way."

"You don't know them like I do. So I publish my art under a pseudonym."

"Do you want your art to be your career?"

"It doesn't matter. It can't happen. Too many people depend on me."

My hand grips his wrist. "It matters. It matters to me. And more importantly, it matters to you. Do you want to be an artist or a landscaper?"

His gaze lingers on mine. "An artist. It's been my dream since childhood, but some things aren't meant to be. So I hide it from everyone. I keep my passion a secret."

I wrap my arms around him, pulling him into me. "Thank you for telling me. I guess I forgive your dickish behavior. So, is this what was in the box?"

He nods. "Yeah. A few copies of the latest book with my illustrations." With a wary smile, he continues, "I'm sorry again for being a dick and freaking out on you. I've been keeping this a secret for so long, and I panicked at the thought of someone knowing."

"You never have to hide anything from me. I love you. No matter what."

His lips find mine, pressing together in a tender kiss. "I love you."

I smile against him before kissing him back.

"What is your dream?" he asks.

"My dream? You mean besides having a breathtaking, handsome man give me glorious orgasm after orgasm?"

A groan escapes his throat before his mouth moves to my neck, kissing a trail along my jaw, down to my collarbone. "That dream will be a reality as soon as you answer the question."

"Stop torturing me. Why can't I have the sexy reality and tell you later?" My ass circles around in his lap as he shifts underneath me.

He finds his way back to my mouth, hovering his lips an inch away from where I crave them. My body tilts forward just as he leans back. A smile dances on his face as he says, "Tell me or this"—he gestures from his lips to his crotch—"is off-limits."

I cross my arms and narrow my gaze at him with a glare. "Really?" The gall of this man.

With a twinkle in his bright blue eyes, he says, "Yep. Tell me your hopes and dreams, or kiss my erotic mouth goodbye. Metaphorically, because, as I said before, kissing will be off-limits."

I concentrate on the container with his books, avoiding eye contact. This man right here doesn't even know how phenomenal he is. He is lucky to have something he loves and is talented at. Having the option to pursue his passion is more than I could ever imagine.

But I don't have anything like that. Yeah, I love interior design—making a space special and beautiful. But I couldn't hack it in school. It wasn't meant to be. But now, working with Nate on his designs, I get a brief glimpse of that future I could have had.

He brushes his fingers across my jaw and pulls my chin up, dragging my focus back to him. "Viv, why won't you tell me? I shared. I was open with you about something my family doesn't even know about. Why can't you do the same?"

"I don't know." My words come out as a whisper. Clearing my throat, I try again. "I haven't thought about these things in a long time. So I don't know my answer."

His eyes drill into me as if they could make me give a different answer. After about thirty seconds of lingering silence between us, he sighs. "Okay."

I lean back, raising my eyebrows, hesitant to ask, but I do anyway. "Yeah?"

"Yeah. I trust I'll be the first to know when you figure it out."

I wrap my arms around his neck, pulling myself against his warm body.

"Besides," he says, "There is no way you are lying to me because I know you can't resist this bangin' bod."

His laughter fills my ears as I unwrap myself from him at lightning speed. "Oh my God, you asshole." I shove him and end up toppling onto the floor with him.

We lie shoulder to shoulder, laughing, our backs pressing into the floor. "In all seriousness, though, thank you for letting me explain or attempt to explain my...secret."

"Well, if that is your only deep, dark secret, I think we'll be okay."

"What if I have more?"

"Do you?"

"Maybe." He wags his eyebrows.

"Hmm, are you secretly a murderer?"

His brows draw together. "No."

"Do you smuggle drugs in your body across borders as what is referred to as a 'drug mule'?"

"Negative."

"How many times have you and your"—I raise my hand to make air quotes around—"'best friend' Cooper fooled around?"

He places a hand on his chin. "While we've been together?"

"Yes."

"Ah, yes. Nada."

"Okay then, how many times before we were together?"

"Now you're asking the juicy questions. Let me think." With his hands up, he draws into the air, calculating his answer. "Okay, I think I have the answer."

I hop up onto my knees, leaning forward in anticipation. "Ooh, tell me."

"Nil." He grabs me by my waist to pull me onto him before rolling to land on top. "No other secrets, dark or dirty."

"You know what some people might call you? Boring. Not me, though. I would never. But I know other people would."

The lopsided grin from a moment ago is gone, replaced by a look of pure lust. With his lips parted, his gaze grows in intensity, and the look ignites my arousal.

We spend the night worshipping each other's bodies until we have spent every drop of energy, passing out in each other's arms.

The following day, we sleep in, getting up with just enough time to shower to make it to lunch with Sally and Rian.

Maybe it's the love bubble or the post-multiple-orgasm hangover, but I enjoyed my time with them. If Sally made any unsavory or backhanded comments about me, I didn't notice. Maybe the new babies will change our family in ways I didn't know was possible, bringing us closer.

Chapter Seventeen

Time seems to fly between spending time with Nate, work, and trying to build a relationship with my family before the twins have their babies. These positive changes in my life make me nervous. These things don't happen to me. I'm the black sheep—the perpetually single chick. Not the woman who is going to lunch and shopping with her family. Or even the woman who is in a healthy adult relationship.

I'm a walking definition of Murphy's law at all times. Well, I was, until as of late. If something could go wrong in my life, it would. So now that I appear to have my shit together, it's scary. I don't know which part of my life will implode or if every aspect will.

I agree to a girls' day with Rian as her one last hurrah before she becomes an official mommy. We invited Amy and Sutton along, but neither ended up being able to make it.

Amy planned on coming with us, but she felt run down last night and not herself, then ended up vomiting all over Bailey later that evening. Fun fact about Bailey: as kids, if Rian or I would get sick, he would panic because if he even smells—let alone sees—puke, his gag reflex takes over, and he ends up throwing up as well. So he and Amy had a disgusting night. Oh, what I wouldn't give to be a fly on their wall at that moment.

Sutton's excuse could have been better. She accompanied her loser "boyfriend" Dillon to his band's gig at some spring music festival. I say boyfriend loosely because, for one, he's a tool. And second, they break up every other week. Last time she went to support the band, she was their roadie and found Dillon and some girl making out. Sutton claims he was so drunk he didn't know what he was doing. But I call bullshit as a proud member of team Dump Dillon the Douche.

Rian arrives to pick me up, appearing the most undone and down-to-earth that I've seen her since becoming an adult. She is wearing black leggings and Shep's old high school football hoodie. Her hair is piled on her head in a giant messy bun. Face free of makeup, of perfection. The pink tinge of her skin shines through, along with the dark under-eyes of a soon-to-be mother.

With a burst of laughter, I finish taking in her whole appearance, loving how she looks like me.

Thinking of relaxation and comfort, I chose my favorite stretchy leggings and an oversized sweatshirt with the name of my favorite book boyfriend—Mr. Darcy—on the front. Without a stitch of makeup, my face is dull and puffy, and my knotted red hair is heaped on top of my head without a care.

"Don't be a bitch, Viv." She brushes past me to the bathroom, not bothering to close the door behind her. "You better be ready to go because our appointment is in thirty minutes, and once I get all the damn pee out of me, we are booking it."

"I'm basically ready to go. I just need to grab a book and my phone." I find the copy of the latest romance novel I'm reading buried in my sheets. I stash it in my bag, along with my phone, before meeting her at the door.

She glares, shaking her head. "Fuck, we look like we did this on purpose."

"Who cares?" Placing my hands on her upper back, I push her out the door with me. "I thought you were all about twinning."

The spa day Rian booked is unlike anything I would have ever booked for myself. It is over the top. I have zero words to describe the quality of massages we received. I'm more than relaxed and rejuvenated as we leave the spa and the fantastic hands it employs.

Ri and I are all smiles as we head to a few local baby boutiques. We shop, shop, and shop. By the time we get to the third store, I'm drained. My legs are as heavy as concrete while I keep up with Rian. The post pampering glow I was sporting has faded, but somehow Rian's is burning stronger than ever.

My sister is buying everything she "claims" to still need and more. She bought baby clothes, even though she is waiting to find out the baby's sex. Her explanation is that Amy has to be having the opposite sex of her baby, so none of it will go to waste. She bought bibs, bottles, blankets, and other things. I didn't know one tiny person could need more than one or two.

The latest store, and what I hope is the last store, is full of nursery decor and furniture. I stumble onto a plush white rocking chair, which I'm baffled by. Why would you ever have white with children around? I know I'm no expert on kids, but I know they are messy as hell and are stain magnets.

I fall back into the chair, and there's an instant release of pressure as my feet get to revel in the moment of relief. I moan as I tip my head back in the chair. With my toes, I pull myself and the chair forward and let go, relaxing as the chair rocks smoothly.

The subtle rocking movement has my body melting into the cushion as a lightness rolls through my veins. "Rian?" I call out.

Her head pops out from behind a shelf overflowing with tiny stuffed giraffes and horses. "Yeah?"

I wave her over. "Do you have a rocking chair yet?"

"No. Shep and I agreed we didn't need one."

"Wrong. You're both so wrong." With a hop, I'm out of the chair. "Here, meet this bad boy and tell me you don't need it."

She rolls her eyes but allows me to help her sit in the chair that I'm considering having a baby for. Her hips wiggle, moving so her back is flush with the chair. Her mouth drops open, and a bark of laughter shoots out. "Oh my god, Viv. I want this chair. No, I *need* this chair."

I squeal, jumping up and down, unable to hide the triumph I feel from being right about the chair, while also celebrating the chance to somewhat have it in my life. Clapping my hands together, I ask, "Want me to find an employee to ask about it?"

Rian attempts to get out of the chair, rocking back and forth, trying to fling her body up with force. Unsure if I should offer my help or let her struggle, I walk closer to her. As soon as I do, my question is answered as she pushes her hand out to me, and I help heave her to her feet. "Phew," she says, pushing her hair off her face.

"So?" I ask.

"So what?" Rian's eyes flit around the place.

"Do you want me to go find someone who works here to ask about buying the chair?"

Her face lights up as if she has found what she was looking for. "Oh, yeah. You do that while I pee." She scurries off toward what I believe is the bathroom.

Looking around the store, I spot the woman who greeted us as we walked in, though I can only see her back. Based on her movements, I can assume she is speaking to someone out of my line of sight. I can't tell if it's a customer or an employee, because her body is blocking them. Not wanting to be rude and interrupt, I wait for what seems like forever.

After five minutes of pretending to examine pacifiers and all the weird accessories for them, I decide enough is enough. Moving closer, I glimpse the person standing in front of her. Recognition hits me as I duck behind a shelf.

"What the hell is that she-devil doing here?" I whisper to myself. I inch closer until I can peek over. There is no doubt in my mind now. From the platinum blond locks to the tone of her over-the-top, nasally voice, Hadlee Harrison is here.

"Is this your first?" the woman asks her.

Hadlee smiles brightly. "Is it that obvious?"

The two laugh. "No. No." She waves her hand. "You just have the glow I see with first-time mothers."

My mouth falls open as my eyes drift down Hadlee's body to discover her hands on her stomach, cradling a bump. My hand flies up to cover my gaping mouth.

Hadlee is pregnant.

Hadlee. Is pregnant with a baby.

A small rush of excitement claims me as my heart pounds in my chest. This day just got a little interesting.

Rian waddles over just as I lean back into my eavesdropping position. "Did you find someone?"

Not looking at her, I place my finger over my mouth. "Shhh."

"What in the hell are you doing?"

"I'm listening. That's my bitchy coworker, and apparently, she is pregnant."

She stands up tall, a smile curling her lips with excitement. "Ooh, juicy gossip material. Count me in." She tries to match my spying stance, but her baby belly won't allow it. She rolls her eyes, stepping out from behind the shelf. "Why am I hiding? She doesn't know me."

"You're right! You can listen closer and relay everything to me. Go," I say, shooing her away.

Rian stops a few feet away by an assortment of nipple cream. She flips the jars over, furrowing her brow as she pretends to read the product information. I know she isn't because she told me about them in the last store. But damn if she isn't putting on a good show.

A few minutes later, Hadlee walks away, moving to the cash register. She pays for the items in her hands before leaving. I turn back to my sister, who has grabbed the woman's attention.

The two talk as Rian leads her over to the chair. With her hands clasped, she nods for me to follow her to the register. Once she pays for the chair and infant toys she found, we rush our way to her car, not speaking until we're inside. We turn to face each other, and she spills everything she's learned.

Chapter Eighteen

I spent my weekend on the couch, binging HGTV and picking apart the designs the TV show hosts create for the unfortunate client's home. Half of them don't learn what the people want or what would be appropriate for their lifestyle. Again, I'm brought back to the white-in-a-home-with-children thing. Why? Just why?

At some point, Sut joins me after returning from her time with Dillon. I knew how it had gone when she unlocked my door and walked in. She threw her stuff down, walked over, and sat at the opposite end of the couch with a tight-lipped frown and a shrug. I threw her the other half of my blanket, and we both enjoyed the renovations of some overpriced houses we wish we owned.

After ordering Chinese delivery, we both break the silence, spilling our guts about our weekends. She told me about how Dillon left her alone the whole time. He only talked to her when he wanted help unpacking or packing back up. Sutton's face is red while tears fill her lash line.

I tell her about the relaxing time at Serenity that she should have been a part of and the juicy bit of gossip that Rian and I have. She lights up like the Fourth of July when I tell her about Hadlee being pregnant.

"Hadlee?"

My head flies up and down like a bobblehead. "Yes!"

She sits on her knees, bouncing. "Pregnant? Hadlee Harrison?"

"Jesus Christ, *yes*. Hadlee Harrison, the bitchy receptionist we work with," I shout at her.

"Damn, that explains a lot."

"What do you mean?"

On her fingers, she counts Hadlee's behaviors that could be attributed to a bun in her oven. "Well, first, she has been dressing differently. Have you even noticed she isn't wearing skintight dresses anymore? She has been wearing flowy clothing for the past few weeks."

"I don't pay any attention to her, Sut. All she ever is to me is mean."

"Which is even more reason you should have noticed. 'Know thy enemy' is a saying for a reason."

"Point to you, madam." My hand flows in the air as I pretend to write a point in Sutton's column.

"Thank you. Now back to the strangeness with Hadlee. She hasn't been drinking at happy hour like usual. That one should have signaled that something was up. Then there is the biggest thing."

"What?" My body leans closer to her, waiting to hear the last obvious sign we missed.

"She has been...nice."

"Bullshit. Hadlee isn't going to have a personality transplant because she got knocked up."

She shoves some noodles in her mouth. "I'm serious, Viv, she has been. I sat by her two weeks ago in the break room, and she offered me some fruit. Oh, and I heard her telling Shelby the other day that your hair looked pretty, and she wished she could braid hers like you."

I rear back a little. "You're kidding?"

She shakes her head and gets up to pee, and I'm left alone with my thoughts. Hell, I don't know what to think. Could having a baby make someone a decent human, or are these fluke moments?

She comes out of the bathroom laughing.

"What?" I ask, shaking my head.

"Some poor man out there will be attached to Hadlee Harrison for the rest of his life." The moment the words leave her mouth, she slaps her hand to cover it. "I feel like an asshole now."

"Why? You didn't say anything I wasn't also thinking."

"It's just that we don't *actually* know her. We see work Hadlee, and yes, she is a bitch, but that might not be who she is all the time." She sighs. Her face has fallen, and her lips are turned down. "I feel like we should rise above our cattiness right now. Because we don't know her or anything about her life."

I pull my knees into my chest, wrapping my arms around them as I think about what she said. Heat flickers up my cheeks as the shame sets in. It's like she scolded me.

"You know I would never deliberately be cruel to anyone, right?"

"God, yes. Yes, I recognize that. I didn't mean to make you feel bad or imply that you would be hateful. I just...I realize she has been horrible to you, and it might be nice to see her not thriving as she usually does and to bask in it. But I recognize what it's like for women like her. My mom was her. And everyone bullied her because of how they perceived her. So, when I said that comment about her, it broke my heart because that's what people said about my wonderful mother."

"Oh, Sut." I move to her, wrapping my arms around her and snuggling her against me. "I completely understand where you're coming from. And you are right about everything. The joking and assuming we have the facts about what's going on in her life isn't okay, and I wouldn't want people to do it to me. So we won't. We are better than this."

She rests her head on my shoulder. "Are we? 'Cause we were pretty quick to talk shit on her."

I draw circles on her back as I listen.

"Yeah, we were, but we also realize how wrong it is. We can work to change that behavior in ourselves."

"Sounds good to me." We stay there, embracing for a few more moments before pulling away. "You realize this is why people always ask if we are sleeping together?"

Laughter fills the room as we find our way back to the couch to waste the day, binging TV while eating everything in sight.

I take what Sutton said to heart and try to be more aware of the fact that everyone, including Hadlee, is still a person who deserves respect. Over the next few days at work, I do my best not to make snarky comments or roll my eyes whenever Hadlee talks. Baby steps, right?

I find myself more aware of her than ever. Like I'm suddenly fascinated by her. It's not that she is pregnant or that I want to identify who the father is. But because she has kept a secret. I mean, come on; the girl has loose lips. She gossips more than anyone I know.

Maybe Sutton is right. Maybe there is more to Hadlee.

I push aside the thought, trying to get back to business as usual. But between thinking about Hadlee's secret, the two babies about to bless my siblings, Sutton and the dickwad, and of course, the person who's been taking up all my thoughts for months, Nate, my mind is a little preoccupied.

I haven't seen Nate in what feels like a lifetime, but in reality, it's been closer to six days. He's been working on an extensive project with his family's business and has been worn out every night once he gets off work. Aside from the few texts throughout the day, we have spoken little since the Neil Bloom incident. I know we talked about it, and I said everything was fine, but I don't know if that is true. It feels like this distance couldn't have come at a worse time.

Even though I know he is working his ass off, creating a beautiful space for someone, I feel like something is off. Maybe he wasn't okay with everything. And telling me his secret was too much. Maybe he isn't sure if I was the right person to tell. Or if I will be in his life long term.

All of my doubts continue to creep into my head while I work. Thank God it's Friday because I don't think I can handle another day of work in my current state of overthinking. And I'm not sure Mr. T would want me there, anyway. The moment the clock strikes five, I sprint out the door.

Once home, I hop in the shower to wash off the day. In my favorite ratty sweatshirt and underwear, I crawl into my bed. Turning on my TV, I go to my happy place—*The Vampire Diaries*. This show always brings me back to a simpler time in high school, when most of my worries and overthinking were about grades and trendy clothing.

Two episodes in, Damon pines after Elena while she dates his brother. My phone dings with a new text message from Nate, stealing my attention from the gorgeous brothers.

Hey, Cherry. I miss you.

A flutter of happiness fills my chest as a smile takes over my face.

I miss you too, my unicorn.

What are you doing?

Sitting in bed, watching TVD.

TVD?

Pausing my TV, I type out an explanation.

The Vampire Diaries, duh.

Never heard of it. Can I come over and watch it with you?

Wearing the stain-covered cat sweatshirt Sutton bought me for my birthday ten years ago, I consider changing for a split second before pushing that idea out of my head. I'm far too lazy to care at this current moment.

> Yes. But forewarning, I look like a drowned rat right now.

Oh, please. You could never look like a drowned rat.

> Oh, but I do.

Prove it with a picture...So I can debate whether I want to spend my evening watching TVD with you or not.

I snap a photo of myself in bed. I have wet hair, no makeup, and my cat sweatshirt's stains are on full display.

Nope. I was right. You don't look like a drowned rat. A dumpster cat, maybe, but not a drowned rat.

> I rescind my invitation to let you watch TVD with me.

Too late.

> Nope. It's taken back. You snooze, you lose.

I'm already here, so you snoozed, and you losed. Open the door, Vivian.

What the hell? He wouldn't. Would he? Jumping out of bed, I rush to the door. Unlocking it, I pull it open to find Nate with a takeout bag in one hand and a single red tulip.

I can't help the stupid smile that takes over my face. His mussed-up chestnut curls cause my heart to pound. He is wearing a navy-blue sweatshirt and gray sweatpants. And the smirk on his face highlights that damn perfect dimple.

He walks me backward, closing the door before leaning in to kiss me. It's greedy and promises to lead to bigger and better things until Nate breaks away. His mouth lingers less than an inch away from mine. Our breath mingles as he says, "God, I've missed you."

I give him a quick peck before taking the bag of food into the kitchen to see what he brought. The metal container smells rich with an Italian food aroma. Unable to contain the grumbling of my stomach, I open the container to find lasagna. A cheesy perfection of lasagna. We sit at my kitchen bar with our plates full of the delicious Italian carbs.

I moan on the first bite. "I am in heaven."

He laughs, but the moment his food hits his tongue, he sighs. "Damn, I've never eaten something that makes me feel so good. I want to marry this lasagna."

I take another bite, giving him a sideways glance.

"You jealous?" he asks.

"Don't be ridiculous." I bring the plate to my face, giving him a sharp stare. "I'm going to marry the lasagna."

He scoffs. "I beg to differ. It most definitely would choose me."

"Ha," I shout, "Anyone in love with lasagna would know you don't call the lasagna it. The lasagna is a he. Obviously."

His brows pull together. "Oh, is that so? How did you get to that insane assumption?"

I wait to respond until he takes a sip of the drink in his hands.

As he lifts his water to his mouth, I say, "It's meaty."

Water spits out of his mouth all over the counter. He chokes, coughing uncontrollably on whatever liquid was still in his mouth. His eyes are full of tears as a smile tugs at his lips. "Shit, are you trying to kill me, woman?"

With a slight shrug, I grab another bite of the food with my fork. I grin while shoulder shimmying with every bite.

Once we finish stuffing our faces with Italian food, Nate and I head to my bedroom, turning off the lights as we settle into the bed. He curls up next to me, and I turn on the first episode of *The Vampire Diaries*.

The rest of the night consisted of Nate asking questions about why Elena is identical to the old girlfriend and why the brothers are fighting so much. As annoying as it was, I loved sharing one of my obsessions with him. He never complained. Instead, he let himself get caught up in the show's magic. It made me love him even more. We didn't have sex or even fool around, which is crazy because we act like sex-deprived teenagers when we are with each other. But tonight, we just enjoyed each other's company.

Chapter Nineteen

My chest fills with warmth when my lids flutter open, finding Nate still asleep beside me. I climb out from underneath the duvet, careful not to wake my sleeping unicorn.

I grab my phone before tiptoeing out of the room.

> *Hey, Sut. Soooooooo, can I make a slight change in our plans today?*

After five minutes of waiting, I get a response.

> *Ugh, what is it?*

> *Can Nate and Cooper come along with us? Also, before you say no, know that I already told them they can.*

I hold my breath as those damn three little dots pop up.

> *What the fuck, Viv?*

Shit. She's mad.

I hesitate before sending another text. I need her to say yes. How can I get her to say yes?

> I'm sorry. I just missed Nate so much and wanted to spend time with him, and he was going to be spending the day with Coop. And I love you and want to spend the day with you too. We can be one big happy family.

> Fine, but if your boyfriend goes, mine does too.

I groan.

> Really?

> Really.

Sutton shoots back.

> Fine. Invite Dillon, even though you'll have more fun without him.

I stand, walking back and forth, pacing along the length of the couch.

> Not true.

I'm afraid to ask, but I send it anyway.

> So, 1 p.m.?

> Yep. See you and your lover then.

A screech of joy flies from my mouth while I move my hips from side to side, shimmying as I do. My hands fly up, wrists moving in circular motions.

"Is that your happy dance?" Nate's voice asks from behind me.

I jump at his words, letting out a scream as my hand flies to my chest. "You scared the shit out of me."

He chuckles, shaking his head as he finds his way to me. His arms circle me as he stoops to kiss me. "Good morning."

My chest swells with warmth as I breathe in the familiar smell of pine, and a hint of vanilla fills my nose, sending a tranquil presence over me. "Morning."

"So, what was the dance for?" He leans back to see my face.

"I told Sutton about you and Cooper coming with us today."

"I'm guessing the happy dance meant it was okay with her."

"Kind of." I tug on my bottom lip with my teeth. "She said okay, but now she is inviting Dillon."

He beams with excitement. "I get to meet the infamous Dump Dillon the Douche?"

"The one and only."

"Babe, I know you aren't happy about it, but you don't realize how much this just made my day." He laughs, jogging off to the bathroom to get ready.

While Nate is showering, I order delivery from Toasted before changing my clothes for the day. Athleisure, naturally.

The doorbell rings before Nate is out of the bathroom. I'm expecting it to be the delivery guy with the food, but I open the door to find Cooper with a duffel bag over his shoulder.

"Hey, Vivian." He grins, giving me a small, one-handed wave. "You ready for this?"

"I've been preparing since I was a wee little child."

His eyes roam the room as he waits for me to lead him farther inside.

Nate catches my attention as he walks into the room with nothing but a towel around his waist, causing my heart to speed up. His face lights up when he finds his best friend in front of him. "Hey, you bring my stuff?"

Nodding, he hands over the duffel bag. "Here you are, my lord," Cooper says, giving him a bow.

Nate dips his head, replying in a British accent, "Thank you, kind squire, for retrieving my clothing. I would have smelled quite rank today if not for your bravery and service."

My attention darts between the two. "Holy fuck," I whisper to myself. Or at least I think I did, but both turn to me with questioning looks.

"You two"—I wag my finger between them—"are Sutton and me, just with penises."

Coop throws his head back in laughter, placing a hand on Nate's shoulder. "Are you dating yourself?"

Nate and I both answer him with "No."

"No, he's dating you with a vagina."

Cooper laughs so hard that he falls onto the couch, grasping his stomach in pain as Nate nods. "Yeah, I think she's right."

Against Nate's wishes and pleas, Coop and I sit in the back together on the way to our destination. We swap stories about growing up, discovering that Cooper and I are incredibly alike. We're both the youngest in our family. Neither of us likes the taste of beer. We both believe we would win the show *Survivor*, even though we have zero outdoor or survival experience. We've both seen Nate naked. Needless to say, we are the same person.

We carry on like this for the thirty-minute drive to Extreme Lasers. Nate ignores us as we tell each other the cringe-worthy things he does. Every once in a while, he pipes in with a "Shut up," "Seriously," "I hate you both," or my favorite, "Why do I even hang out with either of you?"

When we pull into Extreme Lasers, we're all bubbling with anticipation. I hop out of the truck, bouncing up and down as I wait for Nate and Cooper to get out.

I spot Sutton's car, and as I bound over to her, I notice not one but two other people in her vehicle. She steps out, giving me an "oops" look, scrunching her face.

"What?" I mouth before the back door closest to her opens, answering my question. My jaw clamps down, teeth grinding together as a wave of anger washes over me.

Jake.

She brought Dillon and Jake.

I was right earlier when I assumed I pissed her off. This proves it.

My body is rigid when Nate and Cooper walk up to me. Nate's hand finds mine, giving me a tight squeeze. He peers down at me, eyes darting across my face as he tries to gauge what's wrong.

With a glance, I shake my head at him. His gaze drifts over to Sutton's car, where the three of them stand together.

Nate elbows Coop. They both grin at each other, making me guess that Nate told him all about Dillon and his douchey tendencies.

We don't move, standing still so they have to come to us. Sutton and I match, but instead of camo, she wore purple leopard-print workout tights and a black sweatshirt with matching shoes. When my gaze lands on Dillon and Jake, I can't help but compare them to Nate and Cooper. The two groups of men couldn't be any more different. Cooper and Nate both opted for dark joggers and long-sleeved shirts with old sneakers and ball caps from their old high school. The two dickwads across from me wore cut-out white muscle tees with jeans and brand-new white shoes.

My disgust for both of them floods to the surface when they reach us. "Who the fuck wears jeans to play laser tag?"

A small smile dances across Sutton's face before she clears her throat. Neutralizing her expression, she introduces the guys to each other. To their credit, both sets of men made good small talk with each other as the six of us walk into the building to begin our tactical mission.

As we walk in, we're greeted with black lights and swirling neon colors. Nate's face lights up as his gaze roams the room. He is in complete awe of the lobby alone. I cannot wait to watch him light up like a little kid when we play.

I head over to the check-in desk. "Hi, I need to check in a group of six, please."

We all fill out the waiver and pay our game fee, then follow a woman into a dark room for a lesson on the equipment and the game.

The woman teaches us about the tactical vest we'll wear to keep track of our hits and how to use our laser guns. She tells us about the three-level course we're about to play. It's guaranteed to be a sweaty, fun, adrenaline-filled time.

We split into two groups, the same ones we arrived in, going into our group command center. After coming up with a group name and plan to destroy Sutton's team, Coop, Nate, and I put on our gear and take a few group pictures before starting our mission.

The course is dark and hazy.

Our guns and vests light up with red as the buzzer rings. Each of us takes off in different directions. I run toward the stairs, taking them two at a time. I search for cover, settling my claim on the space under the staircase to the third level, and positioned in a low crouch, I wait for the blue lights of the other team to appear.

If it's Sutton, I've already decided I won't shoot. I've got bigger fish to fry—like Jake and Dillon.

It's not even five minutes into the game when blue lights pop through the slats of the stairs below me. Whoever it is, they are running fast. The blue light darts by, followed by a flash of red behind them. I snicker as I hear the yelling coming from downstairs.

As I run to find higher ground or one of my teammates, I see someone in blue drawing closer. My heart races as I get caught up in the game. The rapid breathing of whoever is chasing me reaches my ear. I hoist my gun over my shoulder, attempting to shoot without success.

Once I'm behind the corner, I attempt to catch my breath as I look around. Shit, I've run straight into a dead end. As I prepare for my impending death, with my back against the wall, Jake appears a few feet away with his laser gun raised.

I lift mine quickly, and we both shoot at the same time. Both vests light up as our shots register, taking us both out of the game. I smirk as Jake frowns.

I attempt to move past him, but he steps in front of me to block my path, knocking my gun out of my hand.

"So, Vivian, how have you been?" he asks.

I ignore him and hoist my weapon up.

"Come on, Vivian. I'm just asking how you've been. It's not like I'll tell your boyfriend about that passionate kiss we shared on New Year's."

My eyes dart up to him. "Excuse me?" I grit through my teeth.

He moves a little closer, stopping near me. "I haven't stopped thinking about it since that night, or how your lips would feel great on another part of me."

Before I know what I'm doing, I shoot my hand up, slapping him across the face. "Don't you fucking speak to me."

"You little bitch," he yells as his eyes water from the stinging on his left cheek.

Nate must have heard my hand slapping Jake's left cheek, putting him on high alert, because when Jake yells, Nate is at my side in an instant. His presence helps to calm me as my body shakes with rage.

"What did you just call her?" Nate asks from beside me.

"She fucking hit me, all because she led me on."

"Fuck you, Jake. I would never," I spit back at him.

"You lying little slut." He leans forward, attempting to land another blow against me. "You weren't even my first choice that night, but seeing how desperate you were, I thought I would throw you a bone."

Nate lurches forward, but I throw my arm up to block him. "Don't. I can handle it."

Nate's body stiffens behind my arm. I hold my chin high, letting a sneer fall over my face as I stalk toward Jake.

He shifts on his feet, eyes roaming my body with a skeevy smile on his lip. "Why are you coming closer, Vivian? You want another taste?"

My throat burns at the memory of his lips being forced on me. Cringing, I lean forward. "You disgust me."

"Sure I do, sweetheart. That's not what your mouth said that night; don't you remember?"

With my hand on his shoulder, I run my other up his chest. "I remember throwing up on you moments after you forced yourself on me."

His face turns bright red. As my words hit him, I seize my opportunity. I clamp down on his shoulders just before I let my knee sail upward, colliding with the one thing Jake cares about most.

He slumps forward, falling onto his knees and panting. I crouch down to stare at him. "Don't you ever touch me or talk to me again. Or else next time, I'll cut your dick off," I threaten before jumping up and strutting over to where Nate stands.

He takes off his cap, running his hands through his hair. "Well, aren't you a vicious one, Viv?"

I give a playful shrug with my shoulders before grabbing his wrist and dragging him away from Jake's whines as I smirk. "I'm full of surprises, my precious unicorn."

"That you are." He laughs as his arms encase me, pulling me into him. His lips find mine with a tender kiss as his thumb rubs circles on my back, sending tingles through me.

As he pulls away, I shake my head. I rake my fingers through his strands, loving the feel of his hair as I pull his head back down to mine. Just as I get him less than an inch from my lips, he catches something out of his peripheral.

He turns his head, and I look to see what has taken his attention off kissing me. A huff slips from my mouth as I pout. Cooper comes stomping down a ramp. Far behind but following is Sutton, with her head hanging low and her arms crossed against her chest. That's weird.

My head tips to the side when I see Dillon on her heels with a shit-eating grin. Even weirder.

Nate's eyebrows draw together as Cooper steps closer.

With a stiff nod, Cooper slides beside us with a scowl etched on his usually smiling face. "You guys ready for round two?" His voice is tight.

Nate opens his mouth to say something, but nothing comes out.

I put my hand in his. "Yeah, just let me go grab the guns."

We play for another two rounds, lasting thirty minutes each. By the time we finish, we are all sweating out of control, and Cooper is still frowning, even after winning the last two games.

While Nate and Coop head to the car, I check us out, texting Sutton.

> Hey, Cooper is ready, so we are going to take off. Sorry today didn't go as planned.

> K.

A one-letter okay...Shit.

An "Okay" means everything is good.

An "Ok" hints at annoyance.

But a "K" means straight-up anger or hatred.

> Are you mad?

The three little dots appear and disappear.

I hold my breath, thinking back to talking to her earlier. There wasn't any weirdness between us at all. The dreadful dots appear one more time before her text comes through.

> No. Well, yes, but not at you.

> I can stay.

> No, it's fine. Go hang with your hot boyfriend, and I'll talk to you later tonight.

The ride back to my apartment is silent—well, mostly. This time I sit in the back by myself since Cooper is driving, and Nate looks like a lost puppy whenever he glances at his best friend. I couldn't have split them apart even if I tried.

"So?" I say after thirty minutes of silence. "Did you guys get any good hits out there?"

"You could say that," Nate replies, not turning to look at me in the back seat.

I wait for him to show us, but he doesn't move or say anything else. "Well, don't leave us waiting in suspense."

"Let's just say this one in the back"—he gestures to me with his thumb—"Is a bit of a vicious lady."

"*Nate*," I squeak.

"Oh, come on. You don't want me to tell him all about how you slapped the shit out of Jake right before you demolished his chances of ever having kids with your knee?" His hand slaps over his mouth. "Oops. I guess the cat's out of the bag."

"No shit?" Cooper exclaims, "Vivian, our Vivian? Who is sitting right behind us?"

"That's the one," Nate says matter-of-factly.

With a bright big smile, Cooper turns his head to me. "Well, I'll be damned. I got to say, Viv, I did not see such violence coming from you."

I scoot closer so they both can see me. "What can I say? I'm an enigma."

A scoff leaves Nate's mouth, and I glare at him. "Excuse me. Do you not agree?"

"Nope."

"Oh?"

"An enigma? More like an exasperation," he says with a twinkle in his eyes.

My jaw drops, and I glare. "Asshole." I hit his upper arm.

"See," Nate says to Cooper. "She is a vicious, violent one."

They both break out into laughter, and soon I'm joining them.

Chapter Twenty

Back at my place, the plan is to take a quick shower and grab an overnight bag to stay with Nate before we go out again to meet Sutton for some drinks.

The activity might have been a bust on the bonding front, but I got to slap and knee the shit out of Jake, so that was a plus. A cackle slips from my lips at the memory as I scrub the remaining sweat off me.

With my hair wrapped up in a towel, I attempt to dry off the rest of my body before heading back into my bedroom. I hear the familiar sound of "So Good" by Big Sean, Rian's favorite song, blaring from the pile of clothes I had stripped out of earlier. I dig through the sweat-covered clothing to find my jacket until I see my phone.

I don't bother to look at who is calling before answering, "When did you change my ringtone?"

"Is that any way to greet your older, very pregnant sister? Also, it happened when we were shopping the other day. Don't worry, you prude. It's just for my calls." Rian's voice is light and bubbly.

I put my phone on speaker, set it on my bed, and continue to dry off. "My bad. How are you, my oh-so-pregnant sister? Are you well?"

"Thank you, my darling Vivian. I'm, like, nine months pregnant, so how do you think I am? I'm in hell. Every part of me hurts. I can't walk from my bedroom to the kitchen without being out of breath. My ankles have become the same size as my calves. My face is splotchy and broken out. I'm a hideous troll monster. I need this to be done and quick."

"First, you look amazing. And second, nine months pregnant or not, you are still in insane shape. I'm serious. You are in better shape than me. It's very annoying," I exclaim, hoping to make her feel somewhat better.

She lets out a laugh. "Ah, Vivi, I forgot how great of a liar you've always been."

"That right there is a bald-faced lie."

"Sure, sure it is. Anyway, that isn't why I called. I wanted to learn more about the mean girl from work."

"I see. You called for some gossip. What's wrong, Rian? Are people already treating you like a mom and not the rumor lover you are?"

"Yes! And it's horrible. Please let me live through you. Tell me all the juicy details you've learned," she begs.

I throw on a pair of sweatpants and an oversized T-shirt from my dresser. "Okay, well, be prepared to be disappointed."

Rian whines into the phone, "What? How could there be nothing newsworthy about the mean girl in your office being knocked up?"

"Well, no one but you, me, and Sutton know about her. And I've taken the high road by trying not to be a dick to her about it."

"Boooo! You aren't any fun."

"Tell me something I don't know."

"Ugh. Well, if you have nothing to entertain me with, I'll take my second nap of the day."

"Okay. Bye, Ri. It will be over soon enough, I promise."

"Yeah, yeah. Bye," she says before hanging up on me.

I grab my comb, running it through my tangles. Nate is sitting silently on the couch with his face in his hands, his shoulders low and defeated as I walk into the living room.

Sitting on the empty cushion beside him, I graze his forearm. "Nate, babe? What's wrong?"

He tilts his face to see me, his lip curling in a forced smile. "Nothing." He lowers his gaze again. "I'm just tired."

His expression makes my stomach quiver as uneasiness fills me. He looks upset, and his hand shakes as he runs it through his hair.

Pressing my lips together, I try to push away the nagging knot in my stomach that something is wrong. Not wanting to push him on the subject, I'm unsure what to do next. "Okay. Do you want to sleep here or go home?"

"I'm fine," he says before bending over. His hand brushes my cheek, causing my eyes to flutter closed as my breath hitches. My lips part as he cradles my head and gently presses his lips to mine.

The kiss is tender and simple, yet it's filled with so much love, adoration, and sadness.

His throat bobs before he asks, "Who were you and Rian talking about a few minutes ago?"

Still lost in the emotions of the kiss, I slowly peel my eyelids open. "Huh?"

"You were talking about someone at work being pregnant." His voice sounds strange, almost strangled.

"Oh, yeah. You'll never guess who Ri and I saw while buying baby stuff the other day. Hadlee."

His face pales as his eyes fix on the wall. "Hadlee's pregnant?"

"Yep. Apparently, she is pretty far into it."

"How far?" He presses his palm over his mouth.

"I don't know because she hasn't told anyone at work. But Ri heard her say something about the baby kicking, which starts at around sixteen to twenty weeks." Uneasiness fills me as I tell him. I shift in my seat as his body goes rigid.

His eyes rise to find mine, and my heart stops. His hand trembles as it presses over his mouth. My eyes grow wide as tears threaten to form.

"Vivian, I—"

I hold up a hand to stop him.

Every insecurity or doubt that has ever crossed my mind about me or our relationship comes rushing in as I turn to him. "Did you sleep with her?"

His jaw tenses as he lowers his gaze back to the ground. He doesn't deny it.

My hand moves to my throat, stroking down my neck. "Oh my God." I choke down a sob as the tears fall.

Nate squeezes his eyes shut.

"When?" My voice trembles as I fight to keep my emotions in check.

"Viv—"

I interrupt him by asking again. "When?"

"Before I met you. I swear." His voice is wobbling as his eyes plead with me.

"So, you lied to me?" I face him so he can see the devastation he's causing.

Nate reaches out to touch me, wincing as I move out of his reach.

"You might be the father of her baby."

His voice is a whisper as he admits, "I don't know. Maybe...It was just one time, but it's possible."

My fingernails dig into the skin around my collarbone, just above my heart, as the pain of its breaking sets in. My chest feels as if it's caving in on itself.

Nate and Hadlee...

Nate and fucking Hadlee might be having a baby.

"I'm so stupid." My voice hitches as I tell him, "You said nothing ever happened, and I believed you. I'm such an idiot. For thinking any of this was real. That this was an actual relationship." I get up and storm into my bedroom.

"Vivian, stop. This is real. My feelings for you are real."

My back is facing him as he walks into the bedroom. I can't even look him in the eyes. The eyes that have filled me with such warmth and promise until this moment. How could I not notice that the eyes I've been staring into every night for months were full of lies?

"I'm so sorry I lied to you. But I just wanted you to give me, us, a chance, and I knew you wouldn't if you found out that she and I had slept together."

My hands shake as I wipe away the fallen tears. "You could be having a child with *her*, and that—" Choking down the pain forming in my chest, I admit, "It's too much for me to take."

"What are you saying?" His breathing turns ragged.

My vision blurs, clouding everything as painful thoughts assault me.

Hadlee. He slept with her. Of course he had. She was just his type.

I was never going to be the one for him. I didn't fit that mold, and this proves it.

If the baby is his, I have no doubt what would happen. He would choose her. It might not happen the right way, but eventually, he'll choose, and it won't be me.

I thought I knew heartbreak before. But nothing I had ever been through compared to this. This felt like he had reached inside my chest and gripped my heart with his hands as tight as possible, causing crack after crack until it had no choice but to shatter.

"It's over."

"You don't mean that." His voice shakes as his eyes fill with tears. "Please, Vivian. Please don't do this. I'm so, so sorry. I won't ever lie to you again. Please give me a chance to fix this."

My chin trembles as the tears roll down my cheeks.

Nate grabs my hands. "Please, Viv, don't do this."

My head rocks back and forth. I can't bear to look at him.

"You are all I want. I love you." His voice cracks as the first tear falls from his eyes.

My heart breaks even more with every word, his voice pleading with me.

But the sight of him breaking down, crying, just about sends me crumpling to the floor.

"Love shouldn't be this painful." I rip my hand from his grip, somehow finding the strength and force to push myself through my weak knees to the door. My hand stills on the knob, and I gather everything I have to open it.

I glance back, finding him crouched close to the ground. His palms press into his eyes as he lets out a groan.

This time I'm the one begging, "Please, Nate. I need you to go."

After a few moments, he stands, picking up his jacket and keys as he walks toward the door, pausing as he reaches me.

"Please," I cry, "I can't breathe, Nate. It hurts too much."

His eyes squeeze shut. I hate the look on his face. It's pure agony.

Nothing about this is okay.

It's wrong—every part.

He nods, looking back at me one more time before walking out the door and closing it behind him.

The magnitude of what just happened slams into me. I slide down to the ground, a sob escaping from me as I gasp for breath, unable to stop.

Chapter Twenty-One

I'm a wreck.

Both physically and emotionally, having spent the last thirty hours crying nonstop. My eyes are puffy, and the skin around them burns from the tears that won't quit coming. Bloodshot eyes stare back at me through the mirror, examining the aftermath of my heartbreak.

After Nate left yesterday, I cried by the door for a good hour before moving. I ended up in my bed, lying under my blankets, letting the pain drag me into the darkness of my mind.

Whenever I think about Nate, my chest feels like it's caving in as aches tear through me. And whenever I even think about Hadlee, knowing how he kisses, how his hands would have felt on her bare skin, and what it's like to be with him, my stomach hardens, and nausea fills me.

I've never experienced this level of pain before.

No one has ever loved me as he did. But no one has ever hurt me like this either.

That we built our entire relationship on a lie. The lie that there was nothing between them—that when we met, he wasn't linked to any woman. Not romantically or intimately.

If he lied from the beginning, what else did he trick me into believing? Did he fake his feelings?

No, I know that's not true. I experienced it every time his fingers grazed mine, every time he held me in his arms, and with every kiss and joke. I know his feeling are—*were* real. You can't fake those kinds of emotions. The kind I saw on his face when I said it was over. When we broke each other's hearts.

My head throbs as I stand in my bathroom. Probably from the combination of crying and dehydration. Still, I look like death in the sweats and oversized band T-shirt from over a day ago. My hair is matted, and my pale skin is riddled with splotches of a red rash, the majority of it concentrated on my cheeks, neck, and chest—the places where the moisture from my tears pooled.

I strip out of the clothes that I'm sure smell horrible. My heart pounds, and heat creeps over my skin. I want to set those clothes on fire. I want anything associated with that memory to burn. I stoop, finding an old grocery bag in the cabinet, shoving the clothes into it as I place it near the door.

I know two places where I could start a fire and burn things: my parents' house and Nate's. Obviously, one of those options is an automatic no. But maybe, just maybe, I can do it at my parents'. Hank has always loved a good bonfire. He would let me, but I would have to pass the bloodhound, Sally. She would question everything and most likely judge me for it.

If I can't burn them, I'll have to toss them. Stepping into the shower, I turn the handle. Cold, frigged water shoots out, plastering my skin. It's almost painful. Which, in a way, is refreshing—something physical to take away the internal pain. I wait under the stream with a shiver racking my body as the cold water beats down.

The porcelain is hard beneath me as I sink to the shower floor, waiting for the growing warmth to wash over me. And I let it. With my knees tucked into my chest, I hug myself. *This will be it.* No more uncontrollable crying, no more letting the hollowing heaviness in my chest break me. I have to move forward.

I stay under the spray of water until the heat turns back to cold, leaving my skin pruned with wrinkles. Lazily, I rub soap over my skin, not caring if I miss any spots. Once I'm as clean as I'm going to be, I turn off the shower, grabbing a towel and my robe. I wrap myself up, drying any part of me still dripping with water.

My phone is still where I had placed it after talking with Rian just before the breakup. Dead.

Grumbling, I plug it in as I settle on the couch.

Waiting.

The silence is deafening. I can't stand being left alone with my thoughts. The comparing myself to her. If he liked the way she moved more than me. If she made him feel things I didn't. Imagining them as a family. Hadlee having his baby, and them giving their family a real shot. It all hurts. I want to drown it all out.

I contemplate calling Sutton, having her come over to comfort me. But I know what she will say. She will bash him. Tell me everything that is wrong with him. Say he is horrible. Or that he doesn't deserve me. But I'm not there yet. It hurts like this because he *isn't* horrible. He is wonderful, inside and out. I love him more than anything, which is why I'm so broken. To have anyone say negative things about the person I love dearly, no matter what has happened, will cause me even more pain and suffering.

My phone lights up as the battery charges, allowing me to see the flood of texts and calls waiting for me. It doesn't hit me until this moment that I didn't go to work. I let myself get so caught up in my misery that I forgot all about time. I wish I could say I cared more, but I don't. This is my first no-call, no-show. A glance at the window shows the sun hanging low on the horizon, which means I let another day slip away from me in favor of a heartbreak hibernation. I expected my anxiety would have taken over by now, but it hasn't. My mind and heart are too far gone to worry about missing work.

I try my best to ignore the unread messages from Nate. I can't read them; not yet.

I find a text with Mr. T's name.

> *Hey, Vivian. I was so worried when I hadn't heard from you by 10:00. But Sutton let me know how sick you are. Don't worry about work. Take a few days to rest and get better.*
> *- Mr. T.*

Classic Sutton. Covering for me even when I haven't spoken to her. I find not one or two texts from her; I find twenty. From Saturday night and ending an hour ago.

Saturday:

> *Vivian! Where are you?*

I thought you were coming out tonight?

Fine. I bet you are too busy sexing up that hot boyfriend of yours to remember that you have a hot best friend.

Are you really going to make me hang out with Dillon and Jake all night?

Fine, just know that I hate you.

Sunday:

So…you missed an interesting night…

Jake said some crazy stuff about you and the laser tag.

Did you slap him?

What about kicking him in the balls?

He also said it was because he rejected you. So that's a lie. But I could definitely see the handprint across his face.

Oh my God, text me back.

Okay, V, I'm getting worried. I'll assume you died if you don't text me soon.

Later that day:

I'm going to call Nate.

Vivian…Are you okay?

I called him. He told me you broke up with him. What happened? I asked him, but he wouldn't say. He sounded devastated. I know how much you care about him. So please let me in. Let me be there for you.

I love you and will be here when you let me.

Monday:

How are you?

Vivian, please talk to me.

Are you coming to work?

Mr. T was super concerned when you didn't show or call. So I told him you might have strep and have been throwing up all night. That you must have been too out of it to call.

Call me, please!

Her messages bring a pang of guilt for making her worry and for having her lie for me.

Her response is instant.

I don't deserve a best friend like her.

I go to my closet and throw on a sweatshirt and leggings as I slip into my Converse before grabbing the bag of clothes and my car keys.

I catch a glimpse of myself in the rearview mirror. Somehow, I appear even more unpleasant now that I'm clean. I blame the wet hair mixed with the puffy dark circles under my eyes.

Once I put the key in the ignition, my mind flips to autopilot. I am trying to remember the drive as I pull in. The large two-story house with the white privacy fence looks the same as always.

My childhood home.

Sally and Hank will be home by now. What was I thinking coming here? They will never let me start a fire pit to burn tainted clothing. They aren't those parents. My mind flits back to Miles and Delia. I bet they are the parents to buy their kids ice cream and give them a baseball bat and an old TV to hit when they are heartbroken.

As I sit in the driveway, the living room curtains move as Sally peeks out. Her gaze fixes on my car, eyebrows pulling together as she disappears. Moments later, the front door opens, and she stands at it with her arms crossed as if I made her come to the door. With a pinched expression, she motions me in.

I step out of my car with my plastic bag, walking past Sally with my head hung low. My ability, hell, my motivation for acting put together is gone. Right now, I want to run to my old bedroom, crawl under the covers, and never come out.

"Vivian, what in the hell has gotten into you?" Her eyes widen as she takes in my disheveled appearance and puffy eyes.

"Oh, you know, just having my heart ripped out of my chest. But that's nothing you would care about." She rears back at my words. Turning away, I walk toward the kitchen.

Sally stomps after me. "What on earth is that supposed to mean?"

"Which part?"

"Both."

"Well, I broke up with my boyfriend, hence the heart being ripped out. And you wouldn't care because I'm not one of the twins, and thus, I'm rendered worthless."

She stills. "Is that what you think?"

"No, I don't think that." I lift my gaze toward her. "I know it. You've made sure of that."

She steps closer, her voice low as she says, "Vivian, I—" She stops when Hank walks in. He freezes mid-stride when he sees I'm there, followed by a double take of my overall appearance.

"Vivian, you okay?" he asks, searching my face.

"Does it look like she is okay, Hank?" Sally grits her teeth at him as her eyes burn a hole through him.

The tension builds as they engage in a stare down. Both look as if they are trying to communicate something with the other, but it's being lost in translation.

I turn away from them, glancing out the kitchen French doors leading to the beautiful backyard that used to be one of my favorite places at home. With my sight set on the fire pit, I tighten the hand holding the plastic bag with the clothes in it, catching Hank's attention.

He breaks eye contact with Sally and turns his gaze back to me. "Whatcha got in there, Vivian?"

"Clothes." My voice is neutral and matter of fact.

"Clothes?" Sally's eyebrows shoot up. "Why do you have a bag of clothes? Are you planning to stay the night? And is that what you use as an overnight bag, Vivian?"

"No, this is not what I would use as an overnight bag. And no, I'm not staying here." I pause, looking between them before settling my gaze on Hank. "I want to use the fire pit."

"Why?" Hank asks.

"To burn something."

"What? No. Absolutely not," Sally exclaims.

Hank shakes his head, and I think that's it. They've denied me the one thing I need right now. But just as I'm about to let the hurt consume me again, Hank says, "Let's get that fire started."

"Excuse me?" she challenges, blocking our path to the doors.

"God damn it, Sally. Let the girl have one thing." Raising his voice, he shocks Sally and me, if not all three of us. He brushes past her to get to the backyard, gesturing for me to follow. I glance at Sally once more. Her expression is one I've never seen on her before. Her mouth is open, but nothing is coming out, baffled by his tone and words.

I trail after him, feeling like a child again. Hank isn't tall, per se, but he still towers over me. I almost have to jog to keep up with him without him realizing it.

It's always been like this, even when we were kids. Bailey, Rian, and I would make a game of it, seeing who could walk as fast as Dad or keep up with him the longest. He never seemed to notice us panting while keeping up with his stride. If he did, he never let on or slowed down. It's something I've grown to admire about him. He is the same person he has always been. Quiet, full of thought, a man of few words. The difference between then and now is that he was affectionate and playful when we were younger but still quiet.

He leads me to the back of the fenced-in yard where he has built his fire pit. Surrounded by chairs, the hole is halfway in the ground with bricks circling up. He motions for me to take a seat while he heads back toward the house. Veering to the right, he stops at the little outdoor supply shed he has. With a wagon, he gathers everything he needs.

I watch him from my seat as he takes the twigs from his wagon, placing them inside the circle until he has built a pyramid. He stands, leaning back to admire his masterpiece. A slight grin tugs at his lips, and his hard hazel eyes sparkle with enjoyment.

I say his name twice to get his attention. He glances in my direction as his smile dims just a little. With a loud clap of his hands, he says, "Ok, kiddo. Let's get this fire going so we can let some stuff go up in flames. Sound good?"

My head bobs as I move close to him, letting him walk me through the steps of starting a fire like he has done a dozen times before when

I was younger. It doesn't take long before I hold an old piece of wax-dripped lint rolled in parchment paper to a lighter. With Hank's homemade fire starters in the pit, I place them strategically under and around some small sticks. He blows on the small fire with a light force, causing it to ignite. It slowly grows larger until it's ready for my emotional purging.

I start by throwing my shirt into the pit. I watch as it catches on fire at a snail's pace. Tears blur my vision as I light the last memories I have of Nate up in flames. I toss in my old sweats, shedding a few tears. My mind is so preoccupied with the fire and Nate that I barely register an arm sweeping around my shoulder, pulling me closer. Hank holds me. His hand moves swiftly up and down my arm, giving me the comfort I didn't realize I wanted or needed.

I bury my face in his T-shirt, letting the tears and pain flow out of me. His free hand finds the back of my head, holding me close, letting me weep into him.

"Shh. It's okay, Vivian. You let it out," he whispers, stroking the hair at the back of my head.

In between sobs, I say, "It hurts. It hurts so much."

He squeezes me tighter to him. "I know, baby girl. I know."

We stay like this until there are no more tears left to be shed. I tell him about my fight with Nate and so much more. I don't know if he understands my words as I cry them into his shirt, but he listens. And that alone means the world to me.

As we pull apart, Hank wraps an arm over my shoulder again, leading me to the back patio to sit on the bench. I rest my head on his shoulder as the flames dwindle out from afar.

Chapter Twenty-Two

"Vivian."

The sound of Hank whispering my name wakes me from the first peaceful slumber I've had in days. Blinking, I glance around as my vision adjusts to the dark night sky above.

With a thin-lipped smile, Sally peers down at me. "You fell asleep, dear. Why don't you stay the night in your old room?"

Yawning, I'm unsure if I'm awake or if this is a dream. The exhaustion of letting my emotions out has taken hold of me. I tilt back a little. "I'm sorry. What did you say?"

She takes a seat on the bench beside me, taking my hand in hers and turning to face me. "I said you must be exhausted. You should stay here tonight, and I'll make you your favorite breakfast in the morning. How does that sound?"

"Fine." I rub my eyes, pushing off the bench to move away from her. "But I doubt you even know what I like. It's not like you ever bothered to pay attention to me."

I walk away before she can respond. Once in my old bedroom, I pull off my shoes and climb under the bright floral quilt. Sleep claims me within seconds.

The delicious aroma of bacon wafts through the air, and I crack my lids open at the scent, taking in my surroundings. It takes me a second to remember where I am, but after images of last night's tearful fire flicker through my brain, I pull myself out of my childhood bed. Yawning, I head downstairs to the kitchen, finding Sally with a spatula in her hand and her back to me. My mouth waters at the combination of smells. She's making bacon, scrambled eggs, and hash browns. All of my favorites, minus pancakes...

She looks up the moment I walk in. "Good morning, Vivi. How did you sleep?"

My nickname rolling off her tongue makes me cringe. I grab a coffee mug from the cabinet before answering, "Good. I passed out the moment I laid down. So that's something."

"I thought you might after the night you had."

With the mug I got Hank for Father's Day last year, reading "Father's Day Equals Fathers YAY!" in my hands, I turn to face her. "What's that supposed to mean?"

"Nothing. I just..." She adjusts her already perfectly placed blouse before finishing her sentence. "I just saw how hurt you were, and I know how exhausting that can be."

"I doubt it."

"Why?"

"Because we both know to be hurt you have to have a heart and care for others."

She slams down the spatula. "*Enough.*"

My body goes rigid.

Her nostrils flare as she spits out, "I've had enough of your jabs, Vivian. I've been trying to help you, to be a good parent, but all you do is insult me, over and over."

"You've been trying to help me? To be a good parent? Bullshit!" My hands ball into fists at my sides. "You've hardly been a parent to me. Do you even acknowledge I exist to others? Every time you see me, you make it very clear I'm the least important person in your life. How you couldn't be more disappointed to have me as a daughter."

"That is not true."

"Yes, it is! You've made sure I've felt unloved my entire life. Never good enough or worth your love and attention. You've made it to where I not only doubt myself but also that anyone could ever love me."

"Is this truly what you think? How you feel?"

"Yes."

"I—I didn't realize," she whispers.

"Why would you? You've never noticed me or cared before?" I say through gritted teeth.

"That's not true." Her face crumples. "I care about you so much."

"Really? Is that what telling me I'm an embarrassment is? That's you caring? What about giving everyone thoughtful gifts, but I get a gift card to a place where I had my first heartbreak? To a place where I'm allergic to the food? Is that love?"

"I'm sorry."

Pivoting on my feet, I turn back to the Keurig to make my coffee, taking out the old English breakfast tea pod to toss. I find a pile of burned and crumbled-up pancakes in the trash.

I look around back at the stove. She made all my favorite breakfast foods. Even attempted to make pancakes.

She did all this for me.

I pile food on two plates before taking a seat at the bar next to her.

Her lips turn up in a slight smile. "Thank you."

After taking my place beside her, we sit in silence. We both eat slowly so as to take in the moment, in case it's the only decent interaction we will ever have. I savor every bite of the food she made special for me. This. *This* is the type of mother I've never known.

"Thank you for breakfast. It was delicious." I move to put my cleared plate into the dishwasher before leaving her to finish her breakfast alone.

I'm jolted awake by a knocking on my bedroom door. I groan, patting around the bed until I find my phone. Glancing at the time, I scoff, pulling the blankets over my head. Only a thirty-minute nap, nope. That won't do. I need a good forty-five to an hour to feel rested.

I close my eyes, fully prepared to let sleep claim me once more, when the knock comes again.

"Viv, could you come into the living room?" Hank asks. What is Mr. Workaholic doing here? He never misses a day of work. Not even when he was sick with the flu one year. The man just pounded back Mucinex and acted like nothing was wrong. Maybe it has something to do with last night. Or perhaps this morning with Sally. Either way, it makes my stomach roll and my pulse quicken in fear of the unknown.

Sally and Hank are both already there, sitting side by side. Sally is wringing her hands together in her lap while Hank gives me a small smile before looking away. I decide on the seat across from them. Every nerve in my body is on fire with the tension hanging around us.

"Why aren't you at work?" I ask, eyeing him suspiciously.

"I could ask you the same."

"Psh. We all know why I'm not at work." I gesture to my puffy face.

He softens. "I took the day off. Figured we could have a talk."

I'm afraid.

Afraid of what they could have to tell me.

Is one of them dying? Which one is it?

Oh god, what if it's both?

My mind continues to fly to the worst-case scenarios until Hank clears his throat. "Vivian, your mother and I have something we have been wanting to tell you for a while but could never bring ourselves to do so." His tone is cautious.

"What is this about?" I ask as my eyes flicker between the two.

Sally shifts in her seat, looking more and more uncomfortable by the second. "Before this goes any further, you need to know I love you. I always have. The fact that I have you questioning it is beyond heartbreaking. And I'm sorry. That is my fault." She wipes her palms down her thighs. "My actions were—*are* inexcusable. I've made excuse after excuse for why I've gotten so distant with you. Colder than I was with your brother and sister. You were so independent; you didn't need me like they did. You didn't like me, so why bother? Those excuses might hold some truth, but I made them that way with my behavior."

"Okay." I watch both of their faces sink.

With tears threatening to escape from his eyes, Hank says, "When the twins were a little younger than two years old, your mother and I split up. We couldn't make it work anymore. The stress of having two children and a husband who was more invested in his career than his family was too much for her to bear. So we called it quits. A few months later, I started seeing someone in my office. Nothing serious, but she ended up pregnant."

His words crash down on me as I put together what this means. I'm not Sally's daughter. My entire world has been shattered days before, and now what is left is drowning. I can't breathe as I ask, "So I'm this other woman's child?"

The tears Sally had been holding back fall so hard she is unable to speak.

"So, my entire life, you two lied to me?" My teeth grind together as I stare at them. "This is why you've always treated me differently? Why you've always been cruel and denied me the affection you gave Bailey and Rian?"

Now in full-on sobs, Sally's hand clamps down on her mouth.

"Answer me! Why even keep me if I'm another woman's child you hate so much?"

"No, it isn't like that, Vivian. I swear, I love you. I always have, from the moment I saw you. And when you were little, there wasn't a part of me that treated you any differently from the other children. It was when you got older and looked like her that my biases slipped through. Which has everything to do with me, and nothing to do with you. But unfortunately, you became my punching bag, and I am so sorry. I don't know how to fix this." She sobs.

Not wanting to look at her anymore, I look toward Hank, asking, "Why did you guys make me believe Sally was my mother? What happened to my actual mother?"

His gaze shifts from me to his hysterical wife, then to the floor. "When she was in her late trimester, she suffered from headaches that seemed to get worse and worse until she suffered a stroke. The doctors did everything they could to save her, but she was brain dead. Your birth mother, Jennifer, was on life support for two days before her family agreed to the C-section. She died within hours."

Agony rips through my chest as I attempt to process everything they've told me. "So, real mom's family didn't care about me? They just handed me off to her, and that was it?"

"No, they gave you to me, your father. Sally and I ended up back together after she helped me care for you. It felt natural for the five of us as a family. But your grandparents loved you. They kept coming around until they couldn't handle it anymore. Their grief was too much to bear, especially when you were a momma's girl. They kept in contact all these years, checking up on you. Setting up a trust for you to buy a home or retire on. But they looked at you, and all they saw was Jen."

My voice shakes. "But why didn't you guys tell me?"

Finally able to speak through her tears, Sally says, "We thought it would be easier. I loved you like you were my own...and you are. You are my daughter, Vivian. No matter what DNA says, you are mine. I may have a crappy way of showing it, but I never wanted to hurt you."

"I don't know what to say. Why now, after all this time?"

Hank leans forward to grab my hand. "After everything you told me about Nate and how he might have a baby, I couldn't help but see the parallels in our lives. We made the mistake of keeping this from you long ago and got scared when you were old enough to understand. But I had to let you know whether the baby is his, whether you two get back together, you needed to understand what happened in your own life."

My trust in the world is gone. Broken by the people who should have protected my heart but instead destroyed it.

Nate fractured me beyond repair with his lie. But this—this is so much more. They built my entire life on deceit. How am I supposed to cope with this pain? With the fact that the people who claim to love me have betrayed me.

Without another word, I leave them both sitting there. Sally with her head in her hands, her shoulders shaking as she cries. Beside her, Hank is still as stone, with his head hung low between his shoulders.

I don't slam the door to my room. No, I close it with a soft click before making my way to my hiding spot. Tucked away in the darkness of my closet, I let my tears fall again.

Sally didn't give birth to me.

Sally isn't my mother.

I have so many questions. Mostly I want to know why?

Why did they lie? Do Rian and Bailey know?

A knock rattles on my bedroom door. I freeze, even though I'm hidden in my closet.

"Vivian?" Sally asks as the door creaks.

Her steps pad closer. From my spot on the floor, I see her feet beside my bed as she sits down.

"She'll never forgive me—forgive us," she says with a sniffle.

Hank's feet join hers on the floor as they sit on my bed.

"She will."

"No, she won't. Did you see her face? It was the last straw."

A beat of silence passes before she adds, "I did this. I'm the reason we never told her. I wanted to be her one and only mom. But I didn't treat her that way; worse, I didn't even recognize how it hurt her. All I cared about was my own damn feelings, and now I've broken our baby when she needed us to be the glue that put her back together."

"You didn't do it alone. I was right there beside you the whole time. We both fucked up, honey. We can't change that. But what we can do is be there now. Commit to being better, to standing beside her through it all."

"Do you think she'll ever forgive us?"

"I don't know, but I'll wish for it every day and do everything and anything in my power to make it happen."

My head rests against the wall, listening to him comfort her with words I can no longer understand.

I stay in my closet until they leave, unsure of what I'm supposed to be feeling.

Should I be angry with the lies?

Or should I mourn the loss of a woman, a mother I never knew?

My chest aches from being ripped to shreds from every angle.

My trust in them should be shattered, blown to pieces beyond repair. But you can't break something that was never there to begin with.

For the first time, everything makes sense.

Am I shocked? Yes.

Am I beyond hurt that they lied to me? Fuck yes.

I don't know if I'll ever get over the lies, but as crazy as it sounds, I feel closer to them than ever.

It's like the weight that had been straining our relationship has lifted.

I don't feel as if my identity has been torn from me. It's like they have given my identity back to me. I feel as if I finally know who I am.

I'm no longer a mystery.

I have bits and pieces of the story. Now I need to put it all together.

Chapter Twenty-Three

I spent the rest of the day and night at my parents' house again. After some much-needed time to mull over everything they had revealed, I went downstairs to find them huddled together on the couch, waiting for me.

We talk and talk, even agreeing we could all use therapy to restore our relationship, specifically Sally and me.

They even pull out a memory box full of pictures and things of Jennifer's she would have wanted me to have. After looking through the photos, they take turns apologizing. And Sally leaves to let Hank tell me stories about the woman who brought me into this world.

In a time when my heart is tearing to pieces, it's a little ironic that the two people who I've always felt the furthest from emotionally are the ones who ended up being what I needed.

The hurt they caused is still there, but I at least understand where they were coming from.

I broke down, calling Sutton from my parents' home phone. The turn of events stunned her, and I spent the rest of the week with her at my side after she came over Wednesday night, staying until Saturday.

She held me while I cried about Sally and Jennifer, Nate, and my life. She even called into work for me. She claimed to have the same illness as me. Sut was a jolt of electricity that I needed. She made me feel alive again when all I wanted to do was curl up into a ball and die. We joked and laughed, but mostly, we talked and cried.

Returning to work on Monday is exactly what I need. It's time to get out of my head and house and return to my regular routine. In the elevator at work, I'm hit with the realization that I'll see her. Hadlee. The woman who may or may not be carrying Nate's baby.

A wave of lightheadedness passes over me, and my mouth fills with saliva. I breathe through my nose, mentally repeating the phrase, "You are okay. You are okay. O.K.A.Y." But the moment the elevator doors part, I rush out, sprinting to the nearest restroom. Shoving open the stall door, I fall to my knees in front of the toilet. Vomit spews out of me, tears stinging my eyes as my whole body aches.

I wipe my mouth with the thin toilet paper before flushing it down with the rest of my stomach's contents. My hands shake as I dab under my eyes. Under the fluorescent lights, I'm paler than usual. My eyes are bloodshot from the force of throwing up, and my skin is slick with sweat. I look sick, which is a good thing, seeing as that's the lie Sutton and I have been spinning about my recent absence. I attempt not to appear so revolting by applying a fresh coat of mascara. Here's to hoping it will balance the worn-out look my face is sporting.

On my way back to my desk, I'm thankful to find that Hadlee isn't at hers. After setting my things at my desk, I head back downstairs to the coffee bar, grabbing the usual for me and Mr. T.

With the coffee in my hands, I step into the elevator and am met with an empty car. After I press the button for my floor, the doors start to close, with only a few inches left before it reopens. I lift my gaze to see what's going on or who is jumping on, only to find it's the one person I wanted to avoid with every fiber of my being, Hadlee.

She is wearing a long, flowy silver dress. She freezes the moment she steps on, realizing who is in the car with her. The silence is deafening. The tension between us growing thicker and thicker until I can't take it anymore. She slaps the stop button, causing the elevator to halt with a jerk.

"What the fuck, Hadlee?" I yell, "Are you out of your goddamn mind?"

"No, but obviously you are," she says, spinning to face me.

"How am I the crazy one in this situation?"

She scans me up and down. "Don't play dumb, Bitchian. I know, you know. Nate told me you saw me at the baby boutique the other day."

Everything inside of me halts to a stop. I hold my breath, picking a spot in the corner to stare at—anything to avoid looking at her or talking to her.

"Are you really going to ignore me? Even after your boyfriend called me, begging me to meet up with him tonight?" She rubs her baby bump, her cheeks rising as her lips curl into a vicious smirk.

I clench my jaw; heat rises from my neck to my face. I try to block her out and close my eyes to ignore her jabs and taunts. But the sound of my heart pounding in my chest roars in my ears. The urge to scream fills me. I want to hurt her. I want her to feel what I'm feeling—the anger, pain, and devastating emptiness. But I won't.

With a deep breath in through my nose, I push it out of my mouth. I repeat these steps until a slight release of rage flows out of me.

As I open my eyes, I see the self-satisfied expression on her face as she tosses her hair back with an arrogant laugh.

I step forward, and her body stills from her previously confident stance. She glares at me as a shudder runs through her. I move closer, keeping my eyes locked on hers as I press the button to get the elevator moving again.

She lets out a breath that I don't think either of us realized she had been holding in. A sneer forms on my lips as I study her up and down. Seconds later, the doors open, and she darts out.

I set the coffee down and pull out a compact, but the damage is done. My face is the color of my hair. There's no hope of hiding how I felt in that elevator. No matter what I do to mask my emotions, my skin always sells me out.

It's at this moment that I know what I need to do.

With Mr. Tillan's coffee in hand, I head into his office. From his desk, he beams a smile my way. "Good morning, Vivian. I hope you are all better."

I give him a curt nod, handing him his coffee. "I'm getting there. And I think I know what will get me back to 100 percent."

"That's great. I'm so glad to hear it."

"Thank you. I would like to put in my one-month's notice, effective immediately."

He leans back as if I hit him, eyes narrowing as a frown settles in. "What do you mean by one-month's notice?"

My legs shift beneath me. I force my head and shoulders to remain high for the illusion of poise. "I'm handing in my resignation."

"Is this a joke? 'Cause it isn't funny, Vivian." He puffs his chest out as his shoulders become rigid.

"It's not a joke." My voice is flat and matter of fact. "I understand how this must seem sudden to you."

He huffs, cutting me off. "Sudden? Sudden, Vivian? This is completely out of nowhere!"

I purse my lips, my body stiffening at his reaction. I had expected him to be upset or maybe even confused. But I never expected him to be mad at me.

He squeezes the bridge of his nose. "I just—I don't understand."

"It has nothing to do with you, the company, or even the job itself. It has everything to do with me. I need a change, and I need to grow." My voice comes out steady and full of certainty, which seems to shock him. Hell, it surprises me too.

"Okay, is there a reason this 'growth' can't happen here?" he asks.

"Yes."

"Are you going to tell me?"

"No...It's personal. But I'll help to find my replacement and train them to be everything you are used to."

A sigh leaves his mouth, and his body sags in his chair. "Well, damn it. I hate to lose you."

"I'm sorry."

He steps around the desk, wrapping me in his arms. "Don't be, kiddo. You deserve whatever you are looking for. I'm sorry I couldn't provide it for you."

I squeeze him tightly. My chin rests on his shoulder as I whisper, "Thank you."

"But without you here, who will help me prank the office every few months? Who will gossip with me and pretend to be undercover agents?"

I back out of his embrace and clench my hands into fists, moving them to rest on my hips. In a power pose, I tell him, "We will find someone. It will be my last mission."

After giving my notice—well, after talking to Mr. T about it—I pick up my phone and text Sally.

> *Hey, any chance you can still get me a job at the law firm?*

Minutes later, she replies.

> *Of course. But what changed your mind?*

> *So much. A lot of different things...I can't be up here with the constant reminder of why I'm hurting.*

Okay. Let me give your father a call. When are you expecting you will want to start?

I gave a month's notice here. So after that.

Not even twenty seconds after pressing send, my phone is ringing.

"Hey, what's up?" I answer.

"You quit your job? Without having another job lined up?" she shouts through the phone.

"Yes," I mutter.

"Vivian, what were you thinking?"

"I was thinking, 'Hey, didn't Sally tell me she could get me a job?'"

"Yes, Vivian, I can..." She pauses, sighing before continuing, "But you should have spoken to me first just in case."

"I realize that. I just couldn't handle it emotionally. That might sound ridiculous, but my heart is broken, and being around someone who played a big part in that is too much for me."

"It doesn't sound ridiculous to me. I understand. I never want you to struggle. Not with finances, not with physical or mental health. Okay?"

"Okay...Thank you."

"You're welcome."

We are quiet for a moment. It's one of the best conversations we have had in years. Even a few months ago, I couldn't have expected this level of honesty or comfort talking with her.

"Vivian?"

"Yeah?"

"It hurts my feelings when you call me Sally instead of Mom." Her voice is soft.

Her confession catches me off guard. I started calling her by her name years ago to annoy her. I assumed it had backfired because she seemed to have liked it. But I never dreamed she'd tell me differently.

"I didn't know," I admit.

"Do you think you might call me Mom again?"

"I'm not there...Yet."

She says nothing for a few moments. "Okay, dear. I understand. I'll call your father. But please, Vivian, for the love of God, don't make any more life-altering decisions without talking to your father and me first."

"Okay, okay. Bye."

"Bye."

I hang up the phone, then realize the easiest part of my non-plan is complete. Now for the rough part, telling Sutton. As human resources and my best friend, I must inform her of my impending resignation.

The wood trembles beneath my knuckles as I knock on her office door. With her job, Sutton has to deal with confidential information all the time, and even her best friend isn't privy to it.

"Come in," she calls from inside.

I peek in to make sure the coast is clear before entering. She looks up from her computer screen, and her face lights up when she sees me.

"What it do, Vivi boo?" she sings at me.

"Nothing much. I got to work. And, oh, I got coffee, was cornered in the elevator and taunted by Hadlee, checked my emails, put in my month's notice, talked to Sally on the phone, and she asked me to call her 'Mom' again. And now I'm here. What about you?"

She gawks at me. "Excuse me?"

"I know. How weird will it be if I start calling her Mom again? It feels weird."

"Stop it!" She points at me. "You know what I'm talking about. Spill."

So I do. I tell her the entire conversation, or maybe exchange is the right word for what happened in the elevator with the pregnant devil. I tell her about my realization of how I can move on. Not just from Nate but with my life. For the first time since the breakup, I feel a little content.

With her elbows leaning on the desk, Sutton rests her chin on her palms. "You realize you don't have to quit, right? I can have Hadlee fired on the grounds of harassment for that stunt she pulled today."

"No, don't. I don't want to be responsible for negatively impacting that baby's life. Even if its mother is a succubus." As I look into her gigantic bright eyes, her sadness seeps through. I give her a small, reassuring smile. "I think this is best for me all around."

"Fine. If that's what you want." She sighs, pushing her chair back to pick through the colorful folders in the cabinet behind her. Reaching inside one, she pulls out a paper and passes it to me. "Fill this out if you are 1,000 percent serious."

"Thank you." I trap her in a tight hug. "You are the best friend a girl could ever ask for."

"Sure, sure." She latches on to me, preventing me from pulling out of the hug.

"Sut, you have to let me go."

"Never." She laughs, squeezing down harder.

The next few weeks fly by. Finding my replacement for Mr. Tillan's assistant was a breeze. We both recognized the moment Melanie walked in that she was perfect. A divorcée with grown children and a background in communications and organization. She was funny and personable without being too gabby. She was perfect. By the third day of her training, she was so efficient and confident that I only seemed to get in the way. For my final week, I focused my attention on the last item of my resignation undertaking.

His partner in crime, though, is proving to be arduous. Melanie might be a good fit for the job, but she is too new. She wouldn't be ready for the level of mischief Mr. T is accustomed to with me. I compiled a list of all the employees, striking out name after name. All were perfect targets, not the perfect accomplice. Sutton would be great for the position, but she was automatically stricken from the list as an HR employee.

On my last day, I still hadn't found the best fit for his partner in pranks. Instead, I left him with the list of potentials that might work. Unfortunately, that list included Hadlee.

Sutton took me out for victory drinks for my last day. After one glass of wine and lots of laughs, the exhaustion of the past few weeks takes over. I say my goodbyes to Sutton and the other coworkers I've grown to love and consider friends, and I head home.

I'm not home for five minutes before a knocking starts at my door. I ignore it since it's 9:00 p.m., and there is no fucking way I'm going to open my door to a stranger. Changing out of my heels and dress, I slip on a tank top and a pair of boxer briefs. I fell in love with sleeping in them years ago after a fling handed me some to wear when we couldn't find my panties. The moment I slipped them on, I was in heaven. Of course, I threw his pair away and bought myself a pack.

The moment I move to climb underneath my blankets, another knock raps against my door. This time, it's harder and louder. A shiver runs up my spine. With light, slow footsteps, I slip into the living room. The pounding on my door continues as I reach the source.

Up on the tips of my toes, I peek out of the small circle. Gasping, I slap my hands over my mouth, my feet moving backward, taking me away from the door. Away from the source of the noise. Away from Nate.

He must've heard me, though, because he talks to me through the door. "Vivian. Please open the door and talk to me. I need to see you. I need to explain. I need you."

My hand trembles over my mouth to keep myself from making a noise.

"Just let me in. It's been over a month. I can't do this anymore. You won't answer my calls or texts."

I don't have the heart to tell him I blocked him. Well, I had Sutton do it for me. I haven't received a word from him because of it.

"How can I fix this?" His words jumble together, followed by a loud *thwack*. "Fuck."

I rush over, peering out of the peephole to see him holding his forehead and swaying as he stands. Did he hit his head? A part of me wants to open the door and pull him inside to take care of him. While the other part is urging me to stay strong.

"You're drunk," I say through the door.

"No. I'm not."

"Nate, please stop lying to me. You're drunk. Call someone to take you home."

"Vivian, please," he pleads through the door. "Please." His voice breaks. "I love you."

It's taking everything inside me not to respond. To not open the door and take him in my arms. To tell him how much I love him and miss him. As I choke back the urge to cry.

Nothing could have prepared me to see the person I love more than anything in this world breaking down, crying and begging me for forgiveness.

The person who I thought was my forever.

My one and only.

Nate pounds away at my door, the hurt in his voice as he pleads with me shredding what's left of my heart. I hate that I'm doing this to him. But I also hate that he did this to us. He broke us by lying from the beginning.

I understand why he did it. I do. But he still should've come out with the truth from the beginning or told me before the whole Hadlee pregnancy nightmare.

My voice is soft as I beg, "Please, Nate. Go away."

With my ear pressed against the door, I hear a sniffle. "Okay. I'll go. I'm sorry."

I tip my head back, wiping tears away as I listen to his footsteps fading away.

As I lie back down in my bed, the fatigue from the past few days disappears as I think of the past. My relationship with men. My relationship with my family. The blame I place on my shoulders for every mistake or misstep.

I don't want to be full of self-loathing and pity anymore. To feel as if I'm not enough. Not pretty enough, not smart enough, not enough to make someone love me...My insecurity causes so many issues. The doubts and jealousies I project onto others.

Could my relationship with Nate still be intact if it weren't for my insecurity and judgment? He wouldn't have lied in the first place if I hadn't let those feelings control me. But I wonder if that would've been enough to save it. A child coming into this world with another woman is too much for most to bear.

My mind races for hours before I fall asleep, thinking about how to repair my way of thinking about myself.

Chapter Twenty-Four

My new job at my father's law firm is exactly as I expected. I smile and answer calls and direct people on where to go. I'm overqualified, but it is a breath of fresh air not to be responsible for anything near the level of what I was handling as Mr. T's assistant.

What I wasn't expecting was how friendly everyone would be. Maybe it's because they already recognized I was Hank Benson's daughter, or perhaps they are nice people. But to say I'm shocked would be an understatement.

Also, I'm stunned by the lack of flirting with me. Not that I want to flirt with lawyers at my dad's firm. But I figured Sally would have tried to set me up instantly like she always said she would. Maybe they're all in relationships, or I'm not anyone's type here. Or perhaps she thought better of it after coming out as a faux bio mom. Whatever the reasoning is, I'm glad about it.

I've even made friends already. Which is surprising because I tend to be quiet and appear standoffish when I am new. But a beautiful blonde lawyer took me under her wing, making me feel included within the first few hours.

During the first few days here, Hank took me out for lunch. Some days it was just us, others, it was his favorite coworkers, and I was his youngest child—the daughter he wanted to show off.

It was fascinating seeing this different side of him. I've always seen my dad as an introvert, but he was outgoing and funny around his colleagues. Which side of him is real? Maybe they both are.

I'm enjoying seeing the whole new side of him. It makes me feel closer to him but also to Sally, weirdly enough. She has sent me a few texts each day. Some were to check up on me and the new job, some to make plans for the two of us, and others were information and links to schools and classes that I might like. Those text messages showed me she was listening when I talked. She is showing she is listening. That she knows me and is trying, and it shows.

I'm not saying it isn't strange.

It is.

But it's a nice strange. Something that I could have never seen coming.

As we leave the building together on Friday, as we have done for the past week, Hank is carrying my lunch bag, insisting I let him since I already have a purse and heels are the worst invention ever for my back. Our phones ring seconds apart. His phone lights up with Bailey's name, and mine with Rian's. We both give each other a sideways glance as we answer.

"Hey, Ri, what's up?"

"It's time, V. Get your ass up here. You are becoming an aunt. Hopefully, today!"

I squeal, "Okay, I'll be there in no time."

Turning to my father, I take in his colorful face. A bright smile reaches up to his eyes. "Can you believe it?"

"Nope," I squeal. "I'm going to be an aunt. And you a grandpa."

"I know. Bailey sounded so excited."

"I mean, yeah, becoming an uncle is a pretty cool thing. Especially when it's your twin's baby, I'm sure."

He stops mid-stride, his arm shooting out to block me. "Wait, is Rian in labor?"

"Yeah, did you hit your head earlier?"

"Amy is in labor too."

"What?" I shout. "Both of the twins are having their kids today?"

"It appears so..." He bends at the waist, letting out a loud cackle. "Well, we don't have to worry about mixing up birthdays now, will we?"

This gets a little giggle out of me. "Or having to endure multiple birthday parties!"

"Or having to worry about forgetting who is older." We both laugh, walking to my car.

His arm drapes over my shoulder as he leans down to kiss my hair. "I love you, kiddo. I hope you know that."

I smile. "I do. I love you too, Dad."

He releases me. "I'll see you at the hospital."

I nod. "See you there, Grandpa."

He beams, shouting, "I'm going to be a grandpa," into the packed parking lot as he retreats with a new pep in his step toward his car.

"Shit," I yelp, almost sideswiping a huge black SUV. "Sorry," I yell back to the very pissed-looking man who is giving me the finger for almost killing him.

Adrenaline rushes through me as I slow my speed a tiny bit to process that close call. I shake off the fear and let the excitement come crashing back in.

My palms are sweaty against my steering wheels as I *carefully* weave in and out of traffic. I know speeding to the hospital is dumb because it will still be hours before I can see the sweet babies, but I can't help it; I'm so excited to meet them. Preferably as soon as possible so I can stake my claim as their favorite cool aunt.

Who will be born first? What gender will the babies be? Who will be cuter? Will the twins even care if I'm there or not? My heart flutters with questions the entire drive.

Once I get to the sixth floor, Amy's and Shep's parents are here, along with his brother. Everyone hugs me the moment they see me, overjoyed by the upcoming births. After an hour, I decide to make a food run, taking everyone's dinner orders. We decide on two different choices of food: Chinese and Italian.

The only person missing from the waiting room is my dad, who went straight home to change out of his suit once he got the call. Well, Hank and the two couples waiting to meet the lives that their genitals created. After getting the okay from the nursing staff, I head back to Rian and Shep's room first.

I knock on the door and wait until I hear Shep say, "Come in."

They're both sitting on the bed with their cheeks high and eyes glowing with excitement.

"Vivian," she cries out, flinging her arms open for a hug.

I'm careful not to touch her IV or the round monitor strapped across her stomach, letting her engulf me with a hug. "Hey, Rian."

"It's happening. We are having a baby." She beams at Shep.

I bob my head as my lips turn upward to match hers. "It's insane. My big sister is about to be a mom. It's happening!"

"It is," she beams, "But not quick enough. I need this kid to come out pronto, Viv. Be glad you aren't me. Earlier, it felt like my insides were being torn apart. But then the sweet gentleman with the large needle came in. And wham bam, here I am. As relaxed as one can be when waiting to have their vagina split from top to bottom."

My jaw drops, and I glance to Shep for help. His face is smiling as Rian stares at him, but the moment her eyes go back in my direction, that all changes. He shoots me a warning glare, telling me to remain calm and not react or poke the bear.

"Okay, well, I'm going to check on Bailey and Amy now. Text me if you guys need anything. Get some rest, Ri, so you can spend all the time in the world staring at your new precious baby once they make its appearance."

I stop at the door. "Oh, hey, Shep, I almost forgot your mom had a question for you and wondered if you would come out there for a minute or two."

"Okay. I'll only be gone a minute. I promise." He leans down, kissing Rian's forehead before joining me. Once in the hall, I tell him the truth.

"Your mom never wanted to talk to you. I wanted to ask if you wanted me to get you something to eat. I know she can't have anything, and I didn't want to upset her by asking in front of her."

He lifts me into a giant bear hug. "Bless you, you smart, considerate angel."

"So, I take it that is a yes?" I squeak out while he squeezes me tighter.

"Yes. God yes. What are we getting?"

After I take Shep's order, I move five rooms down to Amy's room. Knocking again, I wait for approval to enter.

This time I find Amy is asleep, and Bailey is on a chair pushed up against the bed.

"Hey," I whisper, walking over to where he is sitting.

Bailey stands to hug me.

My big brother is going to be a dad. I can't believe it. He and Amy have been together so long that it still boggles my mind that they would choose to have kids after all this time. I assumed they didn't want any. "How are you guys holding up?"

"We're good. Well, I'm good. Amy had to get an epidural earlier and has slept through the contractions ever since. Thank God; those things are some scary shit. It was terrifying seeing her in that much pain."

My heart swells with warmth as he cares so openly about her. It's what I want for myself someday. I want someone to love me like that. I gaze up at him, pulling him closer to my side, tightening my grip around him. "You're going to be a great dad, Bailey. I know it."

He looks from Amy to me. "You think so?"

"Yeah. I do," I reassure him.

His hard features soften. "Thank you for coming. I really needed that."

"You're welcome. Now to the not-as-important issue that I came to discuss with you."

His brow pulls together. "Huh?"

"Food. I know Amy isn't supposed to eat anything, but I'm going on a dinner run for everyone. Do you want anything?"

With a look back at his wife, he sighs, shaking his head from side to side. "I can't. It doesn't seem fair to eat when she can't, when she is doing so much, and I'm doing nothing."

My eyes glisten as tears form. "Bailey, that was the sweetest thing I've ever heard. It's hard to believe you're the same person who gave me pink eye my freshman year of high school by farting on my pillow."

A small laugh escapes from both of us. I smother him in one last big hug before I go, waving as I walk out.

After picking up our orders, I make two trips from my car to the labor and delivery floor—one for the bags of food and another for the drinks. Thank God I wrote all the orders in my notes app. I stop by Rian's room, letting Shep know his food will be in the waiting room whenever he can come eat. Then I stop to give Rian's and Amy's nurse the food we got them. The two are starving and practically cry when I hand it to them. They both wrap me up in enormous hugs to give me thanks.

Once I'm back in the waiting room, I take my place by Sally and Hank before digging into my pasta. Hank was late to arrive because he showered and shaved before coming here because, and I quote, "I have to make a good first impression." The seriousness in his tone had me on the floor crying.

With everyone's bellies full, someone breaks out a pack of cards, and we play a few rounds of poker to pass the time. We all place last-minute bets on the gender of the babies. Occasionally, someone goes to check on the soon-to-be parents, ensuring they are good and don't need anything.

It's a few minutes till midnight when we get word that things are moving along with Amy and Rian, and both should have their babies soon.

At 11:55 p.m., Amy gives birth to a baby boy at a whopping nine pounds.

Not long after, at 12:05 a.m., Rian's baby is born. A little girl weighing in at seven pounds.

We are all exhausted and overjoyed, waiting as patiently as we can to meet the babies. One by one, the grandparents are called in to meet the newest members of our family. Amy's parents go to see her and Bailey's baby boy first, while Sally and Hank are the first ones in the room to meet Rian's baby girl.

They each spend about thirty minutes before leaving. Shep's mom and dad are next to see their new granddaughter. At the same time, Hank and Sally change rooms to see the new little boy in our family. Shep's brother Landon and I sit patiently, waiting for our turns. Well, that's a lie. We both fall asleep waiting on our turn.

The moment his parents return, Landon hits me in the arm, saying, "Let's go." We both wash our hands at the door before going any further. Landon walks ahead of me to pat Shep on the back while gazing down at the baby in the bassinet beside the crib.

I stay next to the curtain, enjoying the new family. I smile at my sister, who is too busy with her husband as they admire their new baby to notice me. After a few minutes, Landon is the first one to acknowledge me. "Vivian, aren't you going to come in and meet our new niece?"

Shaking off my trance-like state, I walk over to see the tiniest pink blanket wrapped around the small body. "Hi," I coo down at her. "I'm Aunt Vivian." I trace the edge of the blanket. My hand shakes as I touch her tiny body.

"You can hold her," Rian says from over on the bed.

Shep lifts her gently from where she is lying and sets her in my arms. I peer down at her, teary-eyed. "She is beautiful, Rian."

"She is, isn't she?" Rian beams.

"Does she have a name yet?" I gently sway in place.

"She does." She beams at me. "It's Ivy Vivian Shepard."

A sob gets stuck in my throat as I stop moving. My head tilts up to see her. "You named her after me?" They both smile at me. "Thank you," I whisper to them.

I don't think I've ever loved someone so much, so fast. It's love at first sight. She is perfect, and visions of me being the cool aunt flash across my mind.

I spend a few more minutes holding little Ivy before Landon begs for his turn. Reluctantly, I hand her off. I hug Rian and Shep before making sure they don't need anything, then make my way to see Amy and Bailey's boy.

Pulling back the curtain after washing my hands again, I gaze at Amy and Bailey sitting in the bed, staring down at the baby wrapped in Bailey's arms.

"Hey, Mommy and Daddy," I say in hushed tones, moving closer to them.

I take in the sight of my new nephew. It's hard to believe this enormous baby came out of Amy's tiny body. Giving them both a big hug, I make my way to the sleeper sofa on the other side of Amy's hospital bed.

Bailey sits down next to me, passing his new son to me. "His name is Remy Bailey Benson."

It's like a whole new ball game holding Remy versus holding Ivy. The two-pound difference feels like twenty. But that doesn't matter. I hold him in my arms until he gets hungry and starts fussing, filling the room with shrill wails. I offer to order the two of them something to eat, but both decline for now, saying morning will be a different story.

I close the door in a slow, silent movement, backing away just as I hit something solid.

I'm mortified when I turn and come face-to-face with a white coat.

"Oh my God, I'm so sorry," I whisper, still trying to be aware of the time and where I'm at.

His blond hair and blue eyes captivate me as a radiant smile stretches across his gorgeous face. "It's fine. It happens at least once a day up here."

A frown takes over my mouth. "Well, that doesn't make me feel any better. Now I'm a part of your daily assault."

This earns me a little laugh and a head shake from him. "I'm Bryan." He extends a hand to me.

With my hand in his, I respond, "Vivian. Nice to meet you, and again, sorry for the assault."

His fingers lightly brush against my hand as he says, "Want to make it up to me by buying me a coffee?"

Is he flirting with me?

He lets go of my hand, flashing a bright smile that emphasizes his high cheekbones.

"Lead the way."

Coffee with Bryan was a breath of fresh air. We chatted the whole time and even flirted a little. I found out that he was indeed a resident. Even though I met him on the labor and delivery floor, he doesn't work in that department. He's an internal medicine resident. But the labor floor has the best lounge and on-call rooms, so that is where he likes to hang out.

When he asks for my number, I feel uneasy. As if I'm betraying Nate by doing so. But I push that feeling down, giving it to him while trying to pass off the queasy feeling filling me as nerves and not Nate.

I fight the itch to pull my phone from my back pocket and call Nate as I walk away from Bryan, heading back to the waiting room. The overwhelming, desperate need to confess my sins and beg for forgiveness fills my heart. As if I've done something wrong for having coffee with an attractive man and giving him my phone number. I know rationally that I'm single and have absolutely nothing to feel guilty about. Still, my stupid heart doesn't seem to feel with logic or understand that Nate and I are over.

Quiet halls surround me as I attempt to find my way back to the labor and delivery waiting room. I just want to grab my leftovers and purse and hightail it the hell out of this place. Rounding yet another corner, I cross my fingers, hoping to find a familiar sight and not to be completely lost.

No such luck, though.

Instead, I am hit with the pungent odor of a cleaning product that manages to burn the hair in my nostrils, make my eyes water, and clear my sinuses simultaneously.

With a sniff and a quick wiping away of tears, I find a janitor bent over as he mops up something I'm sure is better left unidentified by me.

"Excuse me, sir, can you point me toward labor and delivery?" I ask, making damn sure to stay a good ten feet away from his working parameter.

He gestures to a sign on the wall behind me that shows I'm just outside of the unit. I smile and thank him before carefully maneuvering myself around him and down the hall.

I smirk as I find Hank passed out on the uncomfortable vinyl-covered couch. Amy's parents are packing up, and Landon left after seeing baby Ivy, along with his parents, who plan to return as soon as they get some rest. With her back toward me, Sally's blond bob catches my attention as she sits in the chair facing my dad.

I gather my things on the floor beside her chair and turn to leave but stop myself, wrestling with whether I should tell anyone I'm going.

The right thing to do is tell Sally, so in a hushed tone, I call out her name. "Sally."

Nothing.

"Sally," I say, a little louder this time.

Still no response.

Stepping closer, I tap her shoulder. She jerks back, startled by my touch.

"Sorry," I whisper. She must have been asleep in the chair. "I'm going to go. Do you need anything?"

She gives me a half-awake smile. "No, dear, we are fine. I heard Rian and Shep named the baby after you."

I grin. "Yeah, I wasn't expecting that. It's the sweetest thing anyone has ever done for me."

"I'm glad they did if only to see you this happy."

I circle my arms around her, wrapping her in a brief hug. As I back away, I let out a quiet, "Thank you...Mom."

Her cheeks lift in the brightest smile she has ever given me.

With a small wave, I leave. It's almost four in the morning by the time I make it to my apartment. I climb into bed, not bothering to take off my clothes.

This insane day started so ordinary, bland, nothing special. But it ended with two new babies being born into my family. Me becoming an aunt and someone's namesake. My mother and father making me feel loved and appreciated. And me flirting with a cute doctor.

The last part is still making me feel a little weird and queasy. Like I might throw up. But it's natural to be nervous about moving on after being in a caring relationship with someone. Or so I think.

Moving on is challenging.

Hell, right now, it feels damn right impossible. Like I won't ever be able to fill the hole left in my heart by Nate.

It's something that can't be avoided. But at some point, I'll start filling that space bit by bit until it's only a memory.

I fall asleep, replaying the day over and over in my head—the highs and the lows. But the only lows I can think of were the slight feelings of loneliness and the reminders of Nate.

Chapter Twenty-Five

"So?" I ask after filling Sutton in on all the texts exchanged between Bryan and me over the past few days. He asked me for a second date. Apparently, our shared coffee break counts in his book as a full-fledged date. I'm still on the fence but am considering it. "What do you think?"

She peers at me from behind her large coffee mug. "I think if you like him, go for it."

"You do?"

She quirks an eyebrow. "Yes, if that is what you want."

"What the hell, Sutton? How am I ever supposed to decide if you won't tell me what to do?"

Laughing, she leans back in her chair. "Since when are you going to do what I say?"

"Since now," I whine. "Since I wanted help to decide whether the cute hospital man is worth my time."

"Well, I hate to break it to you, but I can't decide that for you."

My bottom lip juts out as I stir the little black stick in my coffee. "When did you get so mature?"

"Babe, I've always been the supes mature one in this friendship."

My jaw drops as I fling my hand onto my chest. "*Lies*. How dare you?"

She reaches across the table, placing her hand over mine. With a light squeeze, she says, "For real, though, Viv. I can't tell you what to do. You are still dealing with the fallout from Nate. Maybe this Bryan guy is just what you need in your life. He could be a pleasant distraction. Or a rebound. Or he could end up being the next love of your life."

A stabbing sensation hits the middle of my chest as she talks. What would this mean if I start dating someone new?

"Or he could be the worst thing for you. Maybe he is a huge asshole who will waste your time. I don't know. And you won't either unless you go out on that date."

With a loud *thwack*, I slap the table with both hands. "You're so right. I'm going to do it because if I don't, I'll drive myself insane with what-ifs."

"Atta girl, going out with a man because if you don't, you will overthink yourself to death," Sutton exclaims, thrusting her fist into the air with triumph.

That went well.

Or at least I think it did.

I step out of the elevator with my high heels in one hand and keys in the other.

My feet hate me. Just over three hours in the damn sky-high heels, and they feel like I've been walking across a Lego minefield.

I knew this would happen, but beauty is pain and all that other bullshit. So I sucked it up and put on the fancy heels to make a damn good impression on Bryan.

Tonight was our first date.

We went to a fancy steakhouse, where I found the perfect mashed potatoes. No lie, I want to be buried beside those mashed potatoes. Just throw a to-go box in the grave with me, and I promise not to haunt anyone.

I was a little shaky with nerves, but with the help of wine and Bryan's ease filling the silence, I loosened up enough to enjoy myself. He told me about his job, his ludicrous hours, and all the insane things that happen in the medical field. We talked briefly about my job and class before the hospital paged him for some urgent matter.

It was honestly a blessing. My social battery is running on empty.

I'm so drained that my brain and body go on autopilot. I'm so oblivious to my surrounding that my foot catches on something in front of my door, causing me to stumble forward, dropping my keys to catch myself on the door.

"What the hell," I mutter, confusion rippling through me as I find what I tripped on—a light square box sitting at my doorstep. My name is on the address label, but no return address or sender is listed anywhere. Picking up the package, I tuck it under my arm and grab my fallen keys to unlock the door. I set everything down on the counter before heading to my bedroom to change out of my boots and dress and into my ratty old lounging clothes.

Once changed and comfortable, I pour myself a glass of Moscato before picking up the box and moving it into the living room to open.

The tape gives way as I tug hard on one end, and I bounce on my toes to see what treasure I must have ordered myself and forgotten. I open the flaps of the box to find an envelope with my name written on it, sitting on top of something delicately wrapped in sparkling rainbow tissue paper. Setting the wrapped item to the side, I tear open the envelope with my thumb, finding a card with a beautiful floral design. It's stunning. My eyes sweep over the flowers with their bright colors of blues, reds, and yellows.

With a deep breath, I open the card, my hands trembling. I don't find the standard factory-printed greeting or saying inside. Instead, I find a handwritten note.

Vivian,

I'm probably the last person you ever want to speak to or hear from, but I needed to give you this. To let you know you are on my mind every day. The only regret I have in life is hurting you. I will never forgive myself for breaking your trust and your heart. You meant everything to me...And still do. I'm sorry if this letter makes you angry or hurts you further. That isn't my intention. I just needed to share this with you. A piece of me that I hope will make you smile.

Yours forever and always,

Nate

I read his words over and over. My breathing turns frantic as my heart pounds so fast I can't hear myself think.

Nate. This is from Nate.

We've been broken up for months. I haven't heard from him since the night he showed up at my door drunk, begging me for a second chance. Why, after all this time, would he do this? Come back into my life with a letter and a gift.

My eyes drift over to the covered item. To the delicate paper covering it. I don't want to open it because that means tearing up something so beautiful. Something that Nate made.

I pick the card back up, examining the flowers. The yellow, blue, and red flowers...Nate made this. He drew this for me. My favorite color, his favorite color, and the bright cherry red all grace the card. My eyes well up with moisture as I smile. The thought and detail put into it are beyond touching.

I take a mental picture of the wrapping before tearing the delicate tissue paper away. Inside lays a children's book. The cover is full of vivid colors. A unicorn is rearing up on its hind legs, attempting to grab a cherry out of a tree with its mouth. My heart stops as I read the title. *The Unicorn and the Cherry.* I'm expecting to see Neil Bloom as the illustrator, but instead, Nathaniel Fisher is listed as the author and illustrator.

As I open the first page, my hands shake, finding a dedication.

To my Cherry,

I could have never done this without you. You inspired me and gave me the courage to be honest about what I wanted. Thank you, from the bottom of my heart. I will never stop chasing you. -N

The tears I've been holding back roll down my face as I read the beautiful story of a unicorn that picked the perfect cherry from the tree, only to drop it and have it roll away. The unicorn chases after the cherry, overcoming multiple obstacles until he catches it.

He wrote about us. About how he didn't cherish me and how he let me down. My chest aches with a combination of pain and love. Nate still loves me and wants to be with me, but the pain of why we aren't together now keeps creeping back in. How am I supposed to get over this? Over him?

I want to. I do.

But I'm not sure I can.

Saturday morning, I'm sitting on my couch with Bryan as he watches medical dramas, shouting out every inconsistency in them. He has ruined *Grey's Anatomy* for me by doing this, so much so that I've already started tuning him out. It's hard to believe I've been seeing this man for a little over two months now.

We've made nothing official, but I'm pretty sure I'm the only person he is seeing. Though if I'm honest with myself, I'm not sure I want this relationship to go any further. I like Bryan. I enjoy hanging out with him, mostly. And I enjoy kissing him because the man knows what he is doing. But I don't experience that spark or passion with him. Hell, we haven't even slept together yet.

As I pick up my home decor magazine from the pile of mail I need to go through, I spot a blue envelope with gold lettering peeking out from the gigantic pile. My chest tightens. Without picking it up, without looking at it, I know who it's from. Him. *Nate*. I sit back and open my magazine, flipping through the glossy pages, attempting to ignore the gnawing need to open it.

But even while reading an article about mixing patterns, I can't stop returning to it. From wondering what could be inside. What else could he have felt the need to say to me? Why does he keep popping back into my life even after I let him go? My blood boils as I think about him and that damn letter. My skin is probably showing my every thought and feeling right now. I shift in my seat beside Bryan, moving my legs underneath me. But what bothers me even more than Nate slipping back into my mind is why I let it affect me so much.

Bryan pauses the TV, angling his body in my direction. "What's wrong?"

I lift my gaze from the magazine. "What do you mean?"

He gives me a pointed look. "Don't play games with me, Vivian. You've shifted back and forth in that spot for the past fifteen minutes."

I can't tell him it's my ex. Mentioning that your ex is on your mind is not a great thing to say to a guy you're seeing. But from the stare he is driving into me, I can tell he won't let this go until I give something up.

With a whine, I admit, "Ugh, okay. I'm just all in my head about the future. Particularly my career. I feel like I should be further along, and I can't stop thinking about it." Technically, it isn't a lie. It's always on my mind, all day, every day. If going back for my interior design degree or opening my home decor store is what will make me feel accomplished. The costs of renting store space, buying products, and start-up fees make me hyperventilate. To say my professional future isn't putting me on edge would be a lie.

He caresses my knee with light strokes. In a quiet voice, he tells me, "You'll figure it out. Sometimes these things take time. But you need to release all the stress." His eyes dart down to my mouth as he leans into me, pressing his lips to mine. He wants more. The way his hand tightens on my leg tells me what he wants. As usual, though, I pull back before it can turn into anything more than a simple gesture, putting a small amount of space between us.

I plaster a fake smile on my face. "Thanks. I needed that right now," I say before glancing back down at my magazine, pretending to be fascinated by the article once more. He slumps beside me as he faces the TV again. He sighs heavily, restarting his show.

What is wrong with me? He is the perfect man.

But I know it wouldn't be right to use his body to take my mind off another man. Or worse, what if while I was getting it on with Bryan, I thought of Nate? The thought alone has my throat burning as my mouth fills with saliva. Bile rises up my throat as a sudden warmth floods my body.

Inhaling through my nose, I try to fight off the nausea. But the urge continues to grow. I rush down to the bathroom, throwing the door open. I barely reach the toilet, slamming down to my knees on the tile. The coolness of the floor helps alleviate some of the sudden sickness. It doesn't stop me from emptying the contents of my stomach, though.

I stay glued to the floor, resting my head on the toilet with my eyes locked shut. I wait, hoping this will pass soon because I cannot take this torture much longer.

I'm unsure how long I have been lying here when a loud knock startles me. Suddenly, I remember Bryan is here, and when I glance up, he's leaning in the doorway. He tilts his head, looking down at me with my face pressed against a toilet seat.

His face wrinkles. "How's it going in there?"

I choke down the taste lingering in my mouth. "Peachy."

"Why didn't you tell me you were sick before I came over? Or before I kissed you? You know I can't get sick. I have too many lives that depend on me."

I stare at him. "I didn't know."

Sighing, he frowns before giving me the universal "just a moment" gesture with his finger before he turns, leaving the bathroom.

I flush the toilet, then move to the sink. Cool water invigorates my skin as I splash water up onto my face.

I don't even stop to see if Bryan is still here before I crawl into my bed, pulling the covers up over me. The wave of sickness has passed, but my body aches from the violent retching moments ago.

Bryan appears in my doorway, reminding me for the second time that he is still here. He sets a glass of water on my nightstand. "Drink this whole cup slowly. Okay?"

I sit up to take a sip of water. I don't know why I don't just tell him I'm better, or that it was a strange fluke. That I'm not sick.

But I just don't.

It's easier this way. "Thank you," I whisper.

"I'm going to head out, okay? I would stay, but I can't be getting sick. I have a shift tonight," he says, fidgeting with his keys.

"You're fine. I'm just going to lie here for a while, anyway," I tell him, giving him a small wave as he leaves. I don't move an inch. I stay still until I hear the door close, counting to sixty before I get up.

I lock my door, scared someone will catch me. That Bryan will return to see me fine. To see me obsessing about Nate and the blue envelope. Moving to the couch, I pull it from the stack. My eyes trace every part. The lettering is elegant with its grand swoops and curls of gold. Never has my name looked so graceful, like a masterpiece, before.

I slide my finger into the small gap in the corner, ripping it open. Inside is a heavy white piece of paper.

Please join us in celebration of

Mr. Nathaniel Fisher

At

The Kensington Hotel

On August the 7th

At 7 p.m.

For the launch of his

Debut book

The Unicorn and The Cherry

My heart drops as I read the invitation.

He invited me to celebrate the book he wrote...

About me.

I place it back under the stack of mail.

Out of sight, out of mind, right?

I crawl back under the blankets into the warmth of my bed and lie there, looking up at the ceiling, unable to sleep. Unable to do anything but let the thoughts of my future pour in. Thoughts of my career, of Bryan, of Nate. I don't know when sleep finally hit me, but it was most welcome.

Chapter Twenty-Six

I 've been a wreck since the moment I opened that damn invitation. Well, if I'm being honest with myself, I've been a wreck since the book came in the mail.

You would think that with the emotional turmoil I'm currently putting myself through, I wouldn't be able to get out of bed. But no, I'm overcompensating like there is no tomorrow.

I've shown up to work thirty minutes early every day and left on time because I planned on working out, and I'm two weeks ahead in my business courses.

All in all, I'm handling everything very well.

I say that, but I've put little effort into communicating with Bryan, pretty much at all. He has tried to call me a few times. Each time I stare at my phone, watching it ring, trying to will it to stop until he gives up.

Later I send him a short apology text, claiming to be swamped with work or school. Honestly, it doesn't matter. He is aware that something is off with me. But I can't bring myself to face him or, hell, even have a simple conversation with him until I figure out this shit in my head.

It's not fair or right to string him along like this without knowing what the hell I want. Bryan is such a great guy; he is an attractive and compassionate man. He is perfect. And once I get my shit together, he will be the first person I tell. Okay, that's a lie. Sutton will be the first person. She's my freaking person.

Sutton thinks I've gone crazy. As the person I've been dragging with me to the gym daily and who sees me avoiding anything deeper than surface-level emotions, she isn't too pleased with me.

"Okay, I can't do this anymore," she pants, hopping off the elliptical next to me to sit on the floor, glaring up at me with her hair stuck to her face with sweat.

"Oh, come on, Sutton, you can do it. It's only, like, fifteen more minutes." My voice is winded as I attempt to appear like I'm not as affected as she is.

She moves over to the sleek metal bench and gulps down her water like a fish. She finishes the bottle so fast that I'm confident she will throw up if she jumps back on the machine. The threat of vomiting doesn't stop me from reaching my arm to her, begging for a drink. She picks up my water, stalking back over and jutting it toward me. "That's not what I'm talking about."

I pause my workout, letting the cool liquid fill my mouth, helping to ease the burning my uncontrolled breathing is causing. My head falls to the right. "What do you mean?" I ask.

Her eyes meet mine with a fierce tenacity that won't back down. "I mean, cut the shit. You are running yourself ragged, trying to avoid a problem."

Shit, she is using eye contact. But I still play dumb. "I don't have a problem unless you count this untoned ass. Which"—I peek over my shoulder at my rounded cheeks—"isn't half bad."

"Is this what you truly want to do? Lie to the person who knows and loves you?" Her body stiffens as she raises her shoulders, snapping her jaw shut.

My ragged breathing fills the air as we stare off, waiting to see who will break first.

I pull the hem of my shirt up to wipe the sweat off my brow. With a huff, I concede. "Okay, fine. You win, Sutton." I hop off the elliptical, snaking past her to the weights we have sitting by the bench. I lift them, curling my biceps as I stare into the mirror. I'm not watching myself, though. I fix my gaze on her.

She doesn't say a word. She waits with her arms crossed over her chest for me to speak again.

"What do you want from me? Do you want me to break down again? To cry? Because I can. I can throw up for you if you want because the thoughts continuously running through my mind whenever I'm not working on a task make me physically ill. So tell me, Sut, what do you want me to do?"

Her mouth forms a sad version of a smile. "That's all I wanted from you. I just wanted you to acknowledge to yourself, at least, that there is an actual issue going on."

"Oh, trust me, Sutton, I am more than aware. But pretending is all that I've got. I can't show what's really going on because I'm not OK, and the moment everyone realizes it, I'm going to break."

"Are you? Because you're acting pretty neurotic, and that's not you. What happened? Please just tell me."

Setting the weights down, I lie down on my back, staring up at the ceiling. I sense her move to lie beside me on her mat. "A few weeks ago, Nate sent me a letter and a gift in the mail." My voice is tight as I press my hands into the mat. "It was a book. A children's book that he wrote and illustrated. I had found out a while before we ended things he had been illustrating for a while and loved it. But he did it under the name Neil Bloom because he didn't want anyone to know, especially not his parents. Anyway, this book wasn't like that. It had his name on it, not the fake Neil Bloom."

"He sent you a children's book?"

"Yes, *The Unicorn and the Cherry*," I say, my voice getting choked up on the title. "He wrote a book about us."

She sighs and puts her hands over her chest. "Oh, Vivi."

"I know."

"So that's what has been on your mind?"

"Yes, but that's not all of it. Last weekend when Bryan and I were hanging out on the couch, I noticed I got a beautiful navy-blue piece of mail...Sutton, I threw up. I knew from the envelope that it was from Nate, and the thoughts that filled my mind made me so guilty that I got sick."

"Shit," she whispers, waiting for me to tell her the rest.

"Well, Bryan left a little after making me take some medicine that I didn't have the heart or guts to tell him I didn't need. The moment he was out my door, I bolted out of bed to get that piece of mail. It was an invitation to Nate's book launch. It's tonight."

Sutton sits straight up. "You're going, right?"

I lift myself, spinning to face her. "I...I don't know. Do you think I should?"

Her eyes grow wide as she looks at me. "Duh! You need to go for one of two reasons." She lifts her hand to count on her fingers. "One, to get some closure, putting an end to everything that is lingering between the two of you. To help you move on. Or two, to get back together with someone who you can't get out of your mind."

"If I go, will you be my plus one?"

She lays her hand over mine, giving me a gentle squeeze. "Of course. I wouldn't miss this for the world. But don't think I'm not mad that you kept this a secret from me this whole time."

I flash her a toothy smile. Opening my arms, I reach around her, pulling her into a hug. "I'm sorry for being so damn crazy and secretive."

"Thank you," she says, breaking free of my sweaty embrace. "But we should probably get out of here because we're both repulsive and will need extra time to get ready."

I glance down at myself, seeing the circles of moisture around my neck and armpits. "Agreed."

In the passenger seat of Sutton's white Volvo, my leg bounces up and down as she maneuvers us throughout the city, weaving in and out of traffic. Sutton is droning on and on about how amazing we both look and how we are goddesses. I appreciate what she's doing— playing her role as hype woman and best friend perfectly.

As we pull into The Kensington, memories of that day and night flood my thoughts. The laughs, the tears, all of it fogs up my mind. We had way too much to drink, forcing Nate and Coop to pick us up and drive us both home. It was also a pivotal day in my relationship with Rian. Her comforting me was the spark that reignited our sisterly bond.

After Sutton pulls into the valet, she turns in her seat. "Are you ready for this, my king?" she asks.

My eyebrows squish together, eyes rapidly blinking at her. "King?"

"Yes, king. Gah, why am I always having to explain things to you? Do you ever read?"

"Explain, because you do things like call me a king, basically saying I'm a man."

She smirks at me with humor in her eyes, shaking her head. "I didn't say you were a man or mannish. I called you a king because kings always hold more power. In the monarchy, if a king marries his wife, she becomes queen. But if a woman is a queen, aka the rightful ruler, and she marries, the man will become a consort, not a king. Why, you ask? Because a king is always higher than a queen. So, to ensure there isn't confusion about who the actual ruler is, they don't allow a queen's husband to be called king. So why limit yourself to being a queen when a king will always hold more power?"

I stare at her in awe. "You are insane but also so freaking amazing, Sut."

With a little shrug of her shoulder, she steps out of the car as the valet opens her door.

I follow my best friend's lead. Taking Sut's words to heart centers me, my nerves, and my fears. I'm a king; I have the power to handle seeing Nate and face my heartache head-on. The heaviness in my chest becomes a little lighter. Sutton gives me one last nod before she strides ahead of me into the swanky hotel lobby.

Our steps match as we stride into a smaller ballroom than the one Ri and Amy's shower was in. Even though it is smaller, it's still large and glamorous. People pack the room. I'm stunned by how big this is. How many people are here for him? The room twinkles with lights that remind me of starlight.

The bar is the first thing on my mind; I need the liquid courage to handle what I'm sure will be a mind fuck. I recognize a few faces right off the bat. Huddled together at the bar, I find Audra and Cooper.

"Well, I'll be damned." Audra shakes her head, her now grown-out pixie cut bouncing all over the place. "If it isn't the heartbreaker, here in the flesh."

I grab the sides of my dress, lunging into a deep curtsy. "It is I."

Her head rolls back in laughter, and her arms fly around me as she gives me the tightest hug. She's still beaming from ear to ear when she lets me go. "You don't know how happy I am to see you."

"I'm thrilled to see you too, Audra. Sorry that I broke up with you by association."

"I won't lie. It stung. But also, I would have done the same." This is why I liked Audra from the beginning. The woman is as honest as she is funny. "But isn't it the worst when the family is as amazing as mine? Why can't you ditch the dick and keep the rest of the fam?"

"I really loved you guys. Speaking of which, where are your parents?"

"They are around here somewhere. Just search for people with big smiles and sad eyes," she says with a closed-mouth smile.

"They aren't taking this whole Nate-following-his-dream thing well?"

"Oh no, they are. They have been nothing but proud...But they're also mourning the death of their dream of him taking over." She shrugs.

As if knowing a change of subject is needed, Sutton squeezes my arm.

"Oh, Audra, this is my best friend and the woman I will marry if we are both still single when we're forty, Sutton. And Sut, this is Audra, the hotter of the Fisher siblings."

A chuckle leaves both of their mouths at my introduction. "You both think I'm funny, so you have tons in common," I announce.

"Ahem." Cooper pretends to clear his throat, driving our attention to him. "Oh, Hi. Vinny and Hutton, is it? Sorry to interrupt your lovely female-bonding session, but I thought I would remind you guys that I do indeed exist."

Audra nods her head in agreement. "Indeed. You do."

At the same time, Sutton scrunches her nose. "Nah."

Cooper's dark eyes flicker with something unreadable. Maybe it's anger, perhaps it's amusement.

Either way, Sutton doesn't flinch or back down. Instead, she stares back with a muted expression on her face. They stand off as both Audra and I glance back and forth between the two.

She wags her eyebrows at me, mouthing, "So much sexual tension."

I mouth back at her, "Right?" I'm in awe that Sut could handle it.

Coop finally breaks eye contact, ending the weird staring contest. "Fuck...Who wants something to drink?"

The four of us grab some cocktails and make our way to a table. A chill runs over my skin, and when I glance over my right shoulder, I find him. Nate's gaze locks on mine as he talks with a few men around him. I give him a small wave before turning my back on him. I clench my fists, trying to still my now-trembling hands.

I try to focus on their conversation, but Cooper, Audra, and Sutton are all engrossed in a topic I can't seem to pay attention to. Just the sight of Nate across the room has my confidence shattered. He looks just how I remember, but different.

His chestnut curls are still as unruly as ever, but something about his eyes was off. He didn't have that same spark I'm used to seeing. Even from across the room, as he smiles and laughs, talking to the surrounding people, I can see the tension in his body. His broad shoulders are stiff as the fitted suit clings to his body like a glove made just for him. He is as stunning as ever. It's almost unfair.

Lost in my thoughts, a loud "tap, tap, tap" coming from the stage before us snaps me from my daze. There is a short, balding man with the most genuine smile. He leans into the microphone. "Good evening, everyone. I'm David Davidson, and yes, I know. To answer the question now burning in all your minds, my parents were indeed high when they named me... They have admitted it." A chuckle ripples around the room. "I'm sure we all know why we are here—to celebrate Nate and his lovely new book." He pauses as most of the heads in the room turn to find Nate in the crowd. "But what most of you don't realize is this is not Nate's first book." He raises his eyebrows. "Nate has been a part of many other children's books and graphic novels. All under the pseudonym Neil Bloom. Imagine my surprise when the kid came to me and pitched—well, not pitched. That would imply it was merely an idea. No, Nate came to me in early May with a written and illustrated book ready for publishing, with his name front and center."

My head pounds with the sound of my heart beating. My clammy hands wring together in my lap. I force a neutral expression on my face as I listen to David Davidson tell me all about the man who can't escape my thoughts.

"Nate, come up here and tell us all why you decided now was the time to publish under your name." With a wave, he beckons Nate onto the stage.

With one hand in the pocket of his charcoal slacks and the other holding his drink, Nate bends to get a little closer to the mic. "Well, I'm not sure. But I think it can all be summed up by saying I was going through something personal and felt I needed to be the best version of myself. And the best version of me is one who doesn't hide his passion and what he loves." He gives David a lopsided smile, letting one of his dimples show. The same dimple that makes my heart flutter with love every time it appears. "Does that cover it?"

I sense Sutton's attention on me. She knows this must add to my already massive amount of confusion with Nate. But my expression gives nothing away. I keep my gaze trained on the stage as David lifts his glass. "To Nate and *The Unicorn and The Cherry*."

I raise my glass along with the entire room. I cheer to Nate, then down every drop of one of the many sweet alcoholic drinks Coop picked for our table.

Heat fills me from the alcohol and from being near him again. *Air.* I need air.

I excuse myself from the group and escape to the garden patio outside the ballroom. Sutton, being the best friend ever, immediately jumps to go with me, but I insist I'm okay and talk her into staying with Cooper and Audra.

Once outside, I'm met with the succulent scent of jasmine. The smell makes me smile as I walk through the maze of flowers and shrubs to find a bench. It's simplistic and beautiful. The soft sound of water trickling in a fountain and the cool breeze brings a sense of peace and serenity.

Lost in thoughts of my future home having a little slice of heaven like this, I don't notice him as he approaches me.

"Vivian," Nate says, his voice low and shaky.

My stomach drops.

A yard away, he stands, waiting for me to make the next move.

My teeth gnaw on my bottom lip, and my eyes widen in shock. I didn't expect to be alone with him. My lids snap shut as I swallow back any tears threatening to form before looking at him again. "Hey."

"You came." His voice is disbelieving, like he didn't think I would show.

"You invited me, didn't you?"

"Yeah—yes, I mean, of course. I just wasn't sure if you would show."

"To be honest, I wasn't sure if I would either."

His throat wobbles as he looks down. "Why did you?"

"I don't know," I admit.

He steps closer, saying, "Vivian, there is so much I need—" He cuts off when someone walks up to us. Not someone...*Bryan.*

Before I realize what's happening, Bryan has stepped between us. My body tenses as my heart pounds so fast it's almost visible through my clothes.

"Vivian, you're here! How did you know?" Bryan asks, pressing a kiss to my cheek.

"I-I." I blink back my shock. "What are you talking about?" I glance over his shoulder at the pain and confusion etched on Nate's face.

"My resident mixer...You didn't know?" He steps back. "Wait, if you didn't know, why are you here?"

Still focused on Nate, I glance back at Bryan for a moment. My mouth opens, searching for the right words. Fuck, for any words. "I..."

With his head hung low, Nate turns, walking away. The sight is enough to break my heart for the second time. "Nate," I call out, my voice cracking. "Nate, stop." Bryan rears back, glancing over his shoulder where Nate had been standing before looking me up and down with a questioning stare. I wince, whispering, "I'm sorry."

I run after Nate, trying to catch up with him as he walks deeper into the gardens.

"Nate," I beg, grabbing his arm. I force him to turn and face me. "Stop."

"Why, Vivian?"

"Because I need to talk to you."

"That's not what I meant," he grits through his teeth. "Why did you even come?"

"I told you; I don't know. For closure?"

He lifts his head to the sky. With a huff, he asks, "Closure? You brought your new boyfriend for closure?"

My vision blurs as the tears build up. "Stop it. I didn't invite him. I had no idea he would be here."

"Sure you didn't."

"How can you even be upset with me? We haven't been together in months, and in case you forgot, you lied to me about being with a girl who enjoyed tearing me down daily and are having a child with her," I say, gritting my teeth together.

"I'm sorry, Vivian. How many times have I had to tell you it isn't my baby?"

My heart stops, the air around me stilling as I process what he said. The baby isn't his? "How would I know that?"

"For fuck's sake, Vivian." He grips his hair at the roots. "I texted you and left you multiple messages about it all. Hadlee's baby isn't mine."

A stabbing pain shoots through my chest as I try to control my quivering chin.

"You never read or listened to them, did you?" His voice falls quiet.

A tear rolls down my cheek to my neck. "No. I had Sutton block you."

He walks a little further before sitting on a bench and cradling his head in his hands. "This hurts so much. I love you more than anything. All I've done since you ended it was work on myself. Work to become the man you deserve." His voice cracks. "But you found someone else."

His words destroy any bit of composure I had left in me. I sit down beside him, pressing my face into his back. "Nate, I don't know if I can move on from this."

His body shifts under my touch, under me. My cheeks flame as I move to not touch him anymore.

He stands, and a wave of rejection slams into me. Now it's my turn to cover my face, burying it in the crook of my elbow.

"Vivian," Nate whispers, "Look at me."

He pulls my arm away, kneeling in front of me on the ground. "Please forgive me. I can't live with myself any longer, knowing you hate me." He blinks back the unshed tears threatening to fall.

Needing to reassure him, I reach for his hand, and it's like home. The warmth of his touch is everything I've been missing. "I could never. Never once did I hate you, Nate. Never. I promise you that."

A small smile forms on his lips. "You don't know what that means to me."

I rest my head on his shoulder. "I'm sorry Bryan showed up."

His breathing hitches. I bring my hands to his face, forcing him to look me in the eye. "You need to hear this. I'm sorry he showed up and kissed me in front of you. I hate that I made you feel like I moved on." My thumb strokes his cheek as his eyes flutter closed.

He turns his head to press a kiss into my palm, and shivers dance down my skin as his lips connect with my skin. "Did you read the book?"

"Of course. It is so beautiful, Nate. It's the sweetest, most romantic thing anyone has ever done for me." The lump in my throat grows thicker. "I'm so proud of you."

His arms engulf me, pulling me close to him. We stand together, arms tightly clinging around each other like we never want to let go.

Chapter Twenty-Seven

After a few minutes of agonizing bliss, I break the tender and somewhat painful embrace with Nate and bolt. Leaving him standing there, probably more confused than ever.

Curious stares burn into my profile as I pull Sutton to the exit. She doesn't ask why we are leaving or why I'm rushing. She just lets me drag her in silence.

Once in the car, Sutton waits until we are out of The Kensington's circle drive before laying her questions on.

"So?" she asks.

"I don't even know where to begin," I tell her.

"Begin with everything that happened after you went outside. I know Nate followed you because Cooper and I were spying."

"One, you're all creeps. Two, yes. He did."

"Based on how we Irish goodbye'd it back there after being gone for a good thirty minutes, I'd guess you did not get closure."

"You have no fucking idea. He bared his heart and soul to me, and then suddenly, Bryan was there."

"Wait, what?" she shouts, pulling the car over onto the side of the road. After unbuckling her seat belt, she turns to face me. "So, Bryan showed up? When you were with Nate?"

Groaning, I nod.

"Fuck. Then what?"

"Then Bryan kissed me. Nate left, and I ran after him."

Sutton grimaces, motioning for me to continue with the story.

My eyes pool with tears once again tonight. "You should have seen his face. It was like I had drained the life force from his body...He was so upset, Sut. It gutted me."

She lets out a long sigh, her hand over her heart.

"Then we both yelled about how we are still hurting, and I ended up letting him hold me for, like, fifteen minutes..."

"By letting him hold you, do you mean you both clung to each other for dear life, in what some might call a hug?" she questions.

I cover my face with my hands. "Yes. I also smelled him, like, a lot."

"What are you going to do?"

"I don't know. Both Nate and Bryan hate me."

"Nate doesn't. That man's obsessed with you." Sutton pulls back onto the road. "Bryan, though..."

"Ugh." I throw my head back. "Why am I such a mess?

She doesn't answer me, focusing on driving instead. She offers to stay the night. But I need time by myself to think—to reevaluate everything. To pick apart every minute of the night and every bit of my conversation with Nate. To analyze it in extreme detail.

I make a beeline for the fridge the moment I get home. The glass wine bottles clink against each other as I throw the door open. I grab the Cupcake Moscato and take a swig straight from the bottle as I head toward the living room.

Sinking into the deep cushions of the couch, I kick off my shoes and cross my legs like a child, caging the wine between my thighs and clutching my phone in my hands.

Taking a deep breath to calm my nerves, I unblock Nate.

My phone lights up with notification after notification and message after message from him.

Day of breakup:

> *Vivian, please don't do this. Let me explain.*

> *You know I have zero feelings for her. It was one time before we had met, and it wasn't anything like what you and I have.*

> *Please, Vivian. I love you.*

My chest aches.

I might shatter into a million pieces at any moment, so I bring the bottle back to my lips to help dull the ache.

The day after the breakup:

So that's it. You won't even talk to me? Or try? I get that you're hurt. I get that I lied. And I understand. I do. I understand what this could mean for me…for us, but you won't even wait to see…Do you not love me?

If the situation were reversed, I would be hurt, but I would stay with you. 'Cause being without you is like a world without color or laughter. Like a world without art.

His words hit me straight in the chest. They are so beautiful that it hurts.

Two days postbreakup:

I'm sorry. My last texts were out of line, though I meant every word.

Just talk to me.

Please.

Three days postbreakup:

I miss you.

The week after the breakup:

Vivian, the baby isn't mine. I spoke to Hadlee, and she is too far along for it to even be questionable if it is my baby.

> *Will you please talk to me now?*

> *I don't know what else to say, but I'm sorry.*

One and a half weeks postbreakup:

> *Hey, Viv, it's Coop. Nate's passed out on the floor of his bathroom. He doesn't know I'm doing this, and I plan to delete this message immediately after sending it, but I had to try.*

> *The man is miserable. Can't sleep, can't eat. He is a shell of himself. I made the mistake of thinking a little alcohol might help. A little did, but he didn't stop drinking once his pain of losing you resurfaced.*

> *I'm honestly concerned. He is my best friend. My favorite person. And seeing him cry straight up terrifies me. I don't know what to do to help him. Please, Vivian, talk to him. He loves you more than anything.*

Three weeks postbreakup:

> *This silence is killing me. Please, Viv, just answer me.*

Three and a half weeks postbreakup:

> *The baby isn't mine. And you still don't want me. It feels like my heart is being ripped out of my chest. That's what you ignoring me—you not being in my life—is like. It feels like I can't breathe.*

Four weeks postbreakup:

> *Okay, I understand you need space. I wish that weren't the case, but it is. So I'll give it to you.*

> *I will be here when you are ready to talk. I will wait for you.*

Five weeks postbreakup—the night he showed up drunk at my door:

> *Viv...You are it for me.*

> *Please give me—us another chance.*

After he showed up drunk:

> *I'm sorry. For everything.*

Seven weeks postbreakup:

> *You quit your job? Why?*

> *It feels like the last tether I had to you has been cut. Please tell me what's going on with you. I need to know you are okay.*

Twelve weeks postbreakup:

> *I heard "Toxic" on the radio today, and it reminded me of you. And that time on our third date.*

Sixteen weeks postbreakup:

> *I just finished the second season of The Vampire Diaries, and I still don't under-stand how anyone could ever want Damon and Elena together.*

Sixteen weeks and three days postbreakup:

> *Update: I get it. I see it. I ship it. Delana for life.*

Today:

> *I don't know if you got the invitation or are planning on coming tonight, but I hope you are.*

Tonight:

> *I'm not sure if you'll get this or if I'm still blocked, but I'm so confused. Did I do something wrong?*

> *I thought...Well, I thought that hug meant something.*

> *Was I wrong?*

My heart aches reading his pleas. This man tried so hard for me, but I blocked him. Cut him out of my life at the first actual sign of trouble.

That it crossed his mind that I might not love him back makes me feel like the air has been sucked out of the room. My breathing snowballs with every thought. Clutching my chest, I try to stop it. But I can't. Nothing is helping to prevent the full-blown panic attack from taking over.

I press call. "Vivian?" Nate's voice saying my name makes my heart skip a beat. He must hear my breathing because his voice soon changes from hopeful to scared. "Vivian, what's wrong?"

My voice shakes as I choke out, "I can't...I-I can't breathe."

"Viv, are you having a panic attack? Or is this a hang-up-and-call-911 situation?"

"P-Panic attack."

"It's going to be okay. Just close your eyes. Can you do that for me?"

I nod, doing what he asks, even though he can't see me.

"Okay, baby, now focus on my voice. You are going to be okay; you know that, right?" He pauses, waiting for my response, but again, I nod into the phone. "Cherry, I need you to answer me."

"Yeah," I mutter, my breathing still rapid. "Talk to me about something else, please. I need a distraction."

"Okay, how about how pissed I am that Elena had Alaric compel her to forget Damon? I mean, seriously. What the fuck. My heart crumbled into a million little pieces when he returned, and she didn't remember she loved him."

I let out a small laugh. "You really watched it?"

"Of course. You loved it so much that I had no choice but to give it a real chance. And now I'm addicted."

"I told you," I gloat, my breathing slowing down.

"Yeah, you did. And I'm glad."

Neither of us says anything for a minute. We simply listen to each other's breathing. His gentle, even breaths help soothe me.

"Nate?"

"Yeah?"

"Sorry I blocked you. I just now read all your messages."

"I'm sorry t—wait, is that what caused your panic attack? Shit, Viv, I'm so sorry. I never wanted to cause you any more hurt."

"This isn't your fault. It's mine."

"Still."

"Nate, thank you. For caring about me, even when you don't have to."

"I'll never not care about you."

"Goodnight, Nate."

"Goodnight, Viv," he whispers, clear disappointment ringing through his voice. "Please call me if you feel another attack coming on. Or if you just want to talk. Any hour. It doesn't matter."

Unable to say anything else, I nod and silently hang up.

After seeing Nate tonight, reading his texts, and having him talk me down from my self-induced hysteria, I recognize what I have to do. I text Bryan, asking to meet up in the morning to talk. Thankfully, he agrees.

My stomach churns with unease as I sit at a bistro-style table outside the small café Bryan insisted we meet at. With my hair skillfully tamed into being straight, I appear confident. At least, I hope that's what I'm projecting outward. Inside, I'm a fucking mess.

Not because I'm unsure.

But more because I know exactly what I need to do, and it scares the living shit out of me.

I twist my finger in my copper locks as I wait for Bryan. Still dressed in his baby-blue scrubs from his shift, he gives me a sleepy grin before sitting across from me.

"Did you order anything yet?" he asks, looking inside the menu.

Nodding, I answer, "Yeah, I ordered us both a coffee. Is that cool?"

The dark circles under his eyes beg for sleep. "God, yes. I got called in at 3:00 a.m., so that makes coffee as necessary as oxygen."

Our server arrives a second later, placing the cups in front of us. I stir my mocha goodness around while Bryan pours, I shit you not, five packs of sugar into his.

He lifts his gaze from his cup. "Don't judge me. I'm exhausted and about to be dumped. I may have as much sugar as I want."

My body tenses as I shift my gaze back to my coffee, swallowing the lump in my throat. "How did you know?"

"How did I know?" He laughs. "Viv, you ran after another guy last night, then a few hours later, you texted me asking to talk...It's pretty obvious."

I cringe. "I'm sorry for that. And for this."

"Don't be. We both knew this was coming."

"We did?"

He places his hand over mine. "Vivian, yeah, we did. You never cared when I got paged away during a date or when I couldn't talk for hours, hell, sometimes even days."

I frown, my forehead wrinkling. "I assumed that was a good thing, seeing as your job is so important."

"At first, I did too, but then it hit me. It wasn't because you understood. It was because you didn't care. I didn't care that much either."

"Oh."

He pulls away, taking a sip of the steaming cup before him. "Don't take that the wrong way. I liked you, and I still do, but I figure we were both just placeholders in each other's lives."

"Yeah. I'm sorry, though. I didn't even realize I did that to you until about a week ago." I stare him in the eye, hoping he believes me. And can forgive me.

"Honestly, Viv, I don't think I did either. But once I put it all together, it made sense." He leans over and whispers, "I mean, we never got further than kissing and the occasional under-the-shirt action."

My head falls back as laughter falls from my mouth. "Shit. You are so right."

He frowns, looking at his watch. "Duty calls." He smiles down at me, draining his coffee cup. "Even though it didn't work out with us, I am glad to have met you."

"Me too," I say, knowing he will find someone else quickly. Hard not to with his perfect hair and smile.

With a small wave, he leaves.

"Whew," I let out.

Behind me, I hear, "Right? I didn't expect it to go that well for you."

I glance over my shoulder, finding a man with a ball cap, oversized sunglasses, and a thick brown mustache two tables behind me. There's something off about him, but I can't tell without staring. Bringing my eyes back to my coffee, I can't help but want to take another glance.

As I go inside to use the restroom, I have to walk by the man, but when I move past his table, he turns his head away from me. I gaze back at him, and a long strand of warm blond hair peeks out of the back of the hat, along with a tattoo that I recognize.

I knock the hat off her head. "Sutton, what the hell?"

Still giving me her back, she says in a deep voice, "No Sutton here. The name is Saul. Saul Pale."

I move around the table to meet her face, crossing my arms. "What are you doing?"

She pretends to have just spotted me as she lifts her sunglasses. "Oh, hey, Viv. What are you doing here?"

She picks up her coffee, avoiding meeting my gaze as she takes a long sip. "Ugh, fine." She flails her arms out. "You caught me. I came to spy on you."

My jaw drops. "You're spying on me? Why?"

"Because I love you, that's why."

I sit across from her. She toys with one edge of her mustache before attempting to rip it off.

"*Motherfucker*," she shouts, stopping in the middle of her lip.

Tears form in both of our eyes as I double over, laughing at the stupidity that is my best friend. Sutton is gasping for air between laughs as the tears fall down her face.

"I'm not sure if I'm crying because of how dumb I am. Or because of how much this hurts."

"My money is on both." I clutch my sides in pain.

She shakes her head frantically. "I can't do it. I can't." She points to the mustache still dangling from her face.

I wipe away the moisture under my eyes. "Here, let me see how bad it is."

I reach up to examine the damage, or so she thinks. Quickly grabbing the dangling piece of fake facial hair, I yank.

She screams, "Jesus, fuck!"

At this point, I'm beyond able to stop my hysterical laughter. I snort, causing Sutton to spew saliva over my face. I don't know how long we sat there misty-eyed and giggling. But it was just what I needed.

Most people want to forget their breakups. I usually do too. But today, thanks to my goofy best friend, it was a day I'll never forget. A day I never *want* to forget.

Chapter Twenty-Eight

After a lot of crying and laughing with Sutton, we eventually talked about what I planned to do about the whole Nate situation.

I took a page from Sutton's playbook; I drove by his favorite places. You know, just wondering what he might be up to, without letting him know, of course.

Okay, yes. I am subtly stalking him.

Is it creepy? I don't know, maybe.

Okay, it absolutely is. But I don't know what else to do.

How do you tell the person you're in love with that you made a mistake and want them back? Calling him or texting him seems wrong; it's too impersonal. But asking to meet is awkward.

What I want is to run into him organically. But I can't figure out how to do that without staging the whole situation. Which is where I'm at.

Creepy but hopefully a little romantic. Hell, that's probably what all the stalkers tell themselves. That it's romantic, and they won't mind once we are together. Ugh, yep. It's official. I'm a legitimately crazy person.

You would think being this self-aware might make me stop driving past his home, parents' business, favorite bar, and gym. But no, it doesn't. I can't spot him anywhere, making my heart drop slightly.

I pull into the nearest ice cream shop, giving up on my light stalking. Holding a cone with two scoops of mint chip, I walk to the park across the street. The sun is shining through the trees, and a light breeze cools my skin. I sit on a yellow wooden bench, watching kids play and dogs chase after their owners.

A smile dances on my lips as I take in my surroundings while enjoying my first lick of ice cream. My shoulders wiggle back and forth as I let the sweet taste fill me with happiness.

"Vivian?"

I freeze. My shoulders stop their dance as I pivot to see who is behind me. Stunned, I take in Nate's warm eyes, sparkling with joy as his eyebrows lift in question. With his ball cap turned backward and sweat dripping down his body, my breathing hitches as I take him in.

His breathing is labored, and his golden skin is flushed. It's clear now why I couldn't find him anywhere. He was on a run.

I hurry to clean my mouth with the napkin in my free hand. "Nate. What are you doing here?"

He sits down beside me. "I was just about to ask you the same thing."

I lift the ice cream. "Isn't it obvious? I'm enjoying a delicious cold treat on this hot day."

He chuckles. "I meant, what are you doing in this area? You don't live anywhere near here."

"Oh, yeah. I was driving around and ended up here."

"Really?" He rests his forearms on his legs.

Mumbling under my breath, I add, "And maybe I was looking for you."

His body straightens. "What was that?"

With a deep breath and all the cojones I can muster, I admit, "I said I was looking for you." Covering my face with one hand, I bring my ice cream cone to my lips. I take another lick of it before I prep to run away in humiliation.

"You were looking for me?" he asks as I try to hide from his gaze. "Why?"

Nerves eat away at me. So instead of answering him, I shrug.

"You ran away the other night, so why are you looking for me today? And why are you trying to hide from me and eat your ice cream simultaneously? Which isn't working, by the way. It's ending up all over your face."

I search for my napkin.

"*Ahem.*" Nate draws my attention to him and the napkin he is holding in his left hand.

I reach out for it, but he pulls it away and behind him. "I'll give it back if you answer my questions."

I wish my eyes could shoot literal daggers and not metaphorical ones. "Seriously?"

"Yes. Answer my questions or have mint chip smeared across your face."

I take a deep, calming breath, but it isn't working. I can't get my pounding pulse to slow down. The words rise up my throat, and I can't stop them from blurting out of my mouth. "I'm embarrassed. About today and that night."

I glance at him and find he's studying me. Uncomfortable, I stare back at the ground. "The other night, you bared your heart and soul to me, and I wanted nothing more than to do the same, but I couldn't. Not when I knew I needed to end things with Bryan. It wouldn't have been fair to him. Or you...And today, well. I've been trying to stalk you. This is the most humiliating thing to admit, especially to your prey—but here I am, telling it to you because I want a damn napkin and you. I want you."

He reaches over, handing me the napkin.

As I frantically clean my face, I drop what remains of my melting ice cream into the trashcan beside the bench.

I just told him all of that, and all he did was hand me the damn piece of paper to clean myself with.

On the verge of crying yet again, I squeeze my eyes shut as hard as possible, hoping to control my emotional state.

"Viv, look at me." His rough fingertips brush along my jawline and down to where my hand is sitting in my lap, clasped together. He encases my hands with his. "Please, Vivian, look at me."

I peel my eyes open to find him squatting in front of me. The sun bounces off the shiny curls peeking out from under his hat.

His voice becomes uneven as he asks, "Is that all true? What you said?"

My mouth goes dry, suffering like I haven't drank anything in days. I nod, wetting my lips.

His throat bobs, and taking a deep breath, he asks, "Do you love me?"

I can sense his vulnerability peeking through him like he might shatter. Like I could tear him apart with my answer.

Bringing my hand to his face to cup his jaw, I force him to lift his head and look at me as my voice cracks. "Of course I love you." I press my lips to his lightly before inching back. "I love you more than life itself."

Relief flicks across his face.

"I love you so much, I would donate a vital organ to you." Letting go of his jaw, I lean in again, grazing my lips against his. "I love you like Damon loves Elena."

With those last words, his stillness ends. He reaches behind me, one hand holding my lower back while the other tangles in the hair at the nape of my neck. His lips claim mine, his tongue sliding along my lower lip, teasing and begging for more. My body tingles as I open for him, allowing his tongue to slip into my mouth and gently stroke mine.

I move my hand back to his face, pulling him into me as much as possible. His lips are everything I remember and somehow more. They are pure sin as I taste his familiar desire.

A low moan vibrates from his throat just as someone walking by shouts, "This is a public park. Go somewhere else, God damn it!"

He pulls back, his eyes meeting mine. A fluttering fills my chest as he leans in to place another kiss on my lips. This time, it isn't hungry or full of raw passion. This kiss is tender and sweet.

Nate beams down at me. "I love you." He pulls me up, wrapping me in his arms. Breathing him in, I savor every moment.

After leaving the park, we head back to Nate's. We hold hands as he walks me to my car, his thumb caressing my skin the whole time. My cheeks ache from the wide grin that's been fixed on my face since that first kiss.

Once back at his house, he interlaces our fingers again, leading me back to his bedroom. Lying in his bed, we kiss and talk and kiss some more until we're caught up on each other's lives. I tell him about the DNA bombshell and starting back at school, and he tells me how his parents reacted when he told them he wouldn't be taking over the family business.

That night, even though my body craves him, his touch, we just lie together, holding one another. Not wanting to fall asleep out of fear, as if we will wake up and this would all be a dream.

I can tell how much he wants me. Wants to feel my touch, to feel my body again, to be inside me. But we both know what we need tonight is more than the physical.

Falling asleep beside Nate, touching him, feels right. Like my soul is calm and at home with him. But even then, my mind won't find peace until we discuss why we were torn apart.

Even though I wake before Nate, I stay snuggled up to him, studying his breathing, trying to memorize every freckle and curl as I bask in his body's warmth. I hope this—our love—will never end.

After a while of being the creep I am, I drift back asleep, only to be woken by the sweet aroma of coffee wafting through the air. I follow the smell, finding Nate with his back toward me, pouring two cups of coffee.

Wrapping my arms around his middle, I press my face into his muscular back. "Good morning."

He spins in my arms to face me, stooping to place a quick kiss on my lips. "God, I've missed seeing that mess of hair every morning."

I gawk at him before shouting, "What?" I fling my hands into my hair, finding a gigantic rat's nest of a tangle near the top of my head. "Ugh, why do you even love me? I'm a troll."

"You are beautiful, rat's nest and all." He grins.

I push him aside, trying to hide the smile tugging on my lips as I grab a coffee cup before walking out to the patio to sit in the sunshine. Nate trails behind me, grazing my lower back as we walk to the table. It feels so right when he touches me like this—like he wants to be touching me at all times and wants me to feel him too.

When Bryan's hand was on my lower back, I felt uneasy, wishing for space. But with Nate, it's comfortable and natural.

My head tilts back, letting the warmth fill me. It reminds me of last night and being in Nate's arms this morning. I look across from me, finding him staring at me. His face is stiff and flat as he swallows. "Viv, can we talk about it?"

I wrap my arms around my legs, hugging them to my chest. "I know we should and need to, but I'm scared." That's an understatement. I'm terrified. Terrified to hear if he was hoping the baby was his if she made him think it was. Scared shitless to have that pain come rushing back.

His face falls at my words. "I understand. I am too."

I scoot my chair closer to him, grabbing his hand. Before placing it on my lap, I kiss the top of it. "Just hold my hand, and I can do it."

"Are you sure?"

"Yeah. I know it's something we need to do. So we can move on together."

"Okay, first let me say I never intended to hurt or lie to you. I rationalized it as a white lie. Something that wouldn't hurt you or me in the end. But I was wrong." Pausing, he turns a little more to face me. "When we met on New Year's, yes, I had slept with her a week before when I was lonely and drunk. And yes, I was at that party with her, but she knew what had happened was a one-time thing, and that I was just there so Coop and Sarah could have some alone time."

He swallows before continuing, "When I saw how she treated you and how you reacted when you thought I was with her, I panicked. I wanted you to give me a chance so badly. So I said nothing had ever gone anywhere near that far. And I told myself I wasn't lying to you because I was so drunk, I barely even remember it. I know it's wrong, but that's what I was thinking."

He stares down at our clasped hands, squeezing tight. "Are you okay?"

With a deep sigh, I look up. "Yeah, I guess I understand. It still hurts, though, knowing that she ever had any part of you. It made me feel like you might compare me to her. And how could I ever live up to that expectation?"

"What are you talking about?"

"I'm talking about that. I'm this"—I gesture up and down my body from my tangled hair to my chipped toenail polish—"and Hadlee is every man's dream girl. How could I not get insecure?"

"Viv, I would never compare you to her. You are the most amazing, funny, gorgeous woman in the world. She has nothing on you."

I gnaw on my lip, letting his words sink in.

"I'm serious. I hate that I could ever make you feel like that. You are my everything, Cherry."

My head moves up and down, and he lets out a loud breath before adding, "Good, because there is more. After you...ended things. I called Hadlee to talk about everything I had learned. I needed confirmation either way. I needed to figure out how I was going to fight for you. If I thought there was still hope or not."

I listen as he tells me about learning who the father of her baby is. My heart is trying not to break with every word.

"So she agreed to meet at this bistro near her apartment. It terrified me, Viv. I was terrified of what it could mean for you and me. But the moment she told me how far along she was, it was like holding the winning ticket to the lottery. I've always wanted to have kids, but that moment solidified my desire to have a family with the right person. With you."

As he talks, I blink away the tears, gnawing at my bottom lip.

"She told me the father was an ex-boyfriend and that she had been seeing him on and off for a while. She appeared apologetic for not clarifying it immediately with me on the phone. I hate that my lie caused you so much pain. I hate that you dated Bryan because of it. Honestly, even though you broke up with him, I'm still jealous, and I hate it."

"You should know it never went further than kissing."

"Really?" His voice sounds hopeful as his face lights up.

"Yes. It always felt like cheating when I was with him."

A huge grin takes over his face, showing every tooth in his mouth. "That makes me so fucking happy."

"Well, good. Now that that's all out of the way. Let's circle back to how you want to have babies with me."

A blush rises from his neck to his cheeks as I climb out of my chair and into his lap. "Tell me more about how we would start this family," I say, pressing myself into his lap.

A moan slips from his lips as he slides his hands up my legs to my hips. His fingers dig into me as he moves me on top of him, creating a friction-filled frenzy of lust between us.

I arch into him when his lips find my neck. My body throbs with desire with every tease he brushes against my skin. Moisture pools between my legs, and I can't get enough of him as I rake my hands along his chest.

His teeth scrape my neck, moving upward until he finds my bottom lip. He lightly nibbles on it, coaxing a breathy moan from me before he pulls my lip between his. I deepen the kiss, causing every roll of my hip against his growing erection to be filled with increasing tingles and shudders of pleasure.

My hand moves down his body, and I grab the bottom of his shirt, pulling it off and placing a kiss over his heart. I climb out of his lap, kissing a trail down his chest to his tight stomach until I get to the waistband of his sweatpants. His muscular thighs twitch beneath my tight grasp before I press a fervent kiss onto the growing bulge beneath the gray fabric.

His breath becomes labored, and his gaze darkens as desire flickers through him. With the lift of his hips, he helps me pull off his pants and underwear. I peer into his eyes, palming his dick as I bring my tongue up his length.

He hisses through his teeth as I pull him into my mouth, taking him all the way. His head rolls back as he lets me bring him closer to the edge. He wraps his fingers around the edge of the chair in a death grip as his hips move on their own. Desperate to take control, to find his release.

"No," he growls, pulling out of my mouth. He grabs my waist, tugging me to stand. Quickly, he pulls off his T-shirt that I slept in, followed by my cheeky panties. As he leans back, his gaze drifts over my body, inspecting every inch of my bare skin. I reach out, palming him again as his dick twitches. His tongue sweeps across his lips, licking them in a purely sinful manner. Calloused hands find my waist as he drags me to straddle him again. I align myself with his hard length, moaning as I slowly lower onto him until every inch is inside me.

His hands find my breasts as his mouth devours mine, and my hips move in a frenzy as I ride him like I'm making up for lost time. With my hands on his shoulders, I increase the fury of my movements, circling up and down on him as the pleasure builds inside me.

As if sensing how close I am, Nate stands with his arms wrapped around me, lifting me with him. He takes a few steps before laying me down on the table in front of us, taking control. He slams into me as one hand holds my hips in place and the other presses into my clit.

My back arches as I shudder around him, pussy clenching down on him as my orgasm bursts through me. That was all it took for him to find his release. Both of us panting as we come undone together. He continues to move as he spills every drop of himself inside me.

With his head laying on my chest, he brushes his lips over my heart. "God, I love you," he pants.

"I love you," I say, running my fingers through his hair. "My
magical unicorn of a man."

Epilogue

Once again, I am stretched out on the floor of my dark closet with a bottle of wine in my hand. The sound of babies crying floats up the stairs through the crack in my door. The door opens just as I take another sip, causing me to choke. Nate smiles down at me, holding glasses in one hand and another bottle of wine in the other.

He sits on the floor beside me and presses his lips to mine. "Hey, babe."

I can't get enough of his intoxicating scent. I pull his mouth back to mine. "I." *Kiss.* "Need." *Kiss.* "More."

He reaches around my waist and pulls me into his lap. I lace my fingers behind his head. Even in the dark, I can see the warmth radiating off his face as he gives me one of his dimpled smiles. I move my mouth over his jaw, pressing light kisses into his skin, my hips circling of their own accord.

He lets out a groan. "Cherry, I need you to stop that." His fingers dig into my hips.

My lips find his ear as I whisper, "Stop what?"

"Stop squirming, or we will need to leave before dinner has even started."

"I'm okay with that."

Laughter vibrates through his chest as he forces my hips to still on him. He stands, pulling me up with him. "As much as I love having you alone and sitting on me like that, I think we've hidden here long enough."

My nose scrunches as I shake my head. "Nope, not long enough."

"Come on." He hauls me out of the closet, leading me down the stairs to where my family is.

We sit together on one of the oversized chairs in the living room, my fingers intertwined with his. I can't help the grin that forms on my face. Just having him with me at my parents' means the world to me.

I'm no longer alone.

With Nate here, I feel content, like I belong. With him by my side, I know I can do anything.

As my siblings bounce their babies in their arms, I lean back into Nate, asking, "How many do you want?"

"At least two. I want a little you and me running around, driving us crazy. But I'm willing to make as many as you want."

My heart swells at what our future holds. "I think two sounds good. One for me and one for you."

We stay like that. Holding on to each other for the rest of the evening, Nate squeezing tight when he senses my irritation or anxiety building. I know that whatever happens, he'll be here for me. And I'll be there for him.

Acknowledgements

We did it!

This might be a surprise since this isn't my first book published, but Vivian and Nate's love story was the first story I wrote. For years I had dreamt of writing, telling the stories my mind would weave, but didn't. I always found something more important to do. Or I lost motivation. That was until covid and the blessing in disguise that was social distancing. It gave me the time and opportunity to explore my creative side and accomplish things I never thought I would.

It doesn't matter if no one reads this book, *even though I would appreciate it if they did*, or if people end up hating it; I *really hope people love it*. The fact that it is the first manuscript I finished is a huge accomplishment. It's something I am beyond proud of myself for.

Cherry was like a catalyst. Almost immediately after I finished writing it, I jumped into the next story my mind was dying to tell.

Soon I was putting my all into *Anger Management,* and *Cherry* fell onto the back burner while I chased that rush of completing another novel.

To Jeanine, my development editor, you are a savior. You weeded through the mess that was this manuscript and helped ensure Vivian and Nate's story came to life. Thank you!

Brooklyn, once again, you are the real MVP. Thank you so much for not only caring about this book but me as well. Your live reaction texts while reading it for the first time are something that I can never thank you enough for. It was just what my nervous heart needed. As you might have guessed, my first instinct upon getting your notes and corrections back was to crawl under the covers and never come out. But you made me laugh as you helped to improve my writing. I never thought I could have so much fun while editing. Seriously you made editing this book an experience I will always treasure. Also, thank you for bearing with me as I channeled my inner Megan thee Stallion to take on the longest note that ever noted. And I'm sorry to inform you that I have used the word spunk at least once a week in conversation. It is the worst, yet I now love it.

To my spawn, thanks for being supportive and understanding of my love of writing and reading. I love you more.

Loren, you are such an amazing friend and person. Thank you for always being so kind and encouraging. It means so much to me that you used your precious free time as a new mother to read my book. I am so beyond thankful to have you in my life.

Tori, thank you for helping me procrastinate every damn day. Whether it be sending reels back and forth, laughing over our super romantic co-star horoscope, or having unhinged talks over our latest reads. I love and adore every moment of our friendship.

Ashely, thank you for being the first one to take a chance on me. Your willingness to read those first rough drafts was everything to me.

Thank you to everyone who took a chance on Vivian and Nate. Hopefully, you got swept up in their story and enjoyed their journey to find their HEA. As a writer, I hope I did their story justice and that you love their story. Words cannot express how much it means that you took a chance on me as an author. Thank you, thank you, thank you!

About Author

Registered Nurse by day romance writer by night. Bretta dreamed of becoming a writer since she was a little girl but finally wrote her first novel during the pandemic-imposed social isolation.

A self-proclaimed triple threat, Bretta loves to read smutty books and has an unabashed addiction to Coca-Cola. When she's not writing or caring for patients, you can find her daydreaming about her next book, making sarcastic comments, or being a mediocre crafter. She lives in Oklahoma with her hot mess son and a few furry babies.

9 789898 877203